T0365925

ALWAYS OUR LOVE

————The Always Love Trilogy————
Book 3

TAWDRA KANDLE

Always Our Love

Jenna Sutton celebrated her twenty-first birthday by persuading Trent Wagoner, the guy she'd been crushing on for months, to sleep with her. When he broke her heart and crushed her dreams by rejecting her afterward, a devastated Jenna tried to end her life.

Trent has told his side of the story. So has Jenna's mom, and her cousin, and just about everyone else in the small Georgia town of Burton.

Now it's Jenna's turn.

Over two years later, Jenna's finally figuring out her life. Her job at the county historical society is steady and predictable, two elements she appreciates right now. She's living on her own, and her world is peaceful, if lonely.

That is, until Lincoln Turner comes to town.

When Linc's wife was killed in a car accident, she left him with two small children and a bleak future. Six years later, he's a recovering alcoholic who's just gotten his kids back and is ready to tackle a new position as co-owner of a building restoration company . . . in Burton.

Jenna isn't looking for love, and Linc definitely doesn't want any attachments. And neither of them is ready for the sparks that fly when a huge project brings them together. Still, the road to true love has more bumps than they could imagine. Making their way to a happy ending won't be easy.

But this is Burton, and happily-ever-afters are a specialty of the house.

OTHER BOOKS BY THE AUTHOR

The King Series
Fearless
Breathless
Restless
Endless

Crystal Cove Books
The Posse
The Plan
The Path

The Perfect Dish Series
Best Served Cold
Just Desserts
I Choose You

The One Trilogy
The Last One
The First One
The Only One

DEDICATION

To my Temptresses: all the wonderful, wild and wacky women who love the voices in my head as much as I do. You are my cheerleaders, my sounding boards and my favorite readers.

My friends.

This book is dedicated to you all with love.

PROLOGUE

Jenna

"HOW DO I LOOK?"

I turned away from the mirror and struck a pose, full-on model stance with my chin thrust up and my lips pouted out. From her spot on the bed, where she was idly scrolling through her phone, my friend Lucie rolled her eyes and grinned.

"Oh, please. Like you don't know you look totally adorable."

I shot her a mock-glare. "I do *not* look adorable. I've been doing adorable my whole life, and today it's over. I'm twenty-one years old, and I'm not going to be the baby of the Sutton girls anymore." I looked back into the full-length mirror, critically eyeing up my short and flouncy little skirt that was paired with the tight lace-edged tank that made my boobs look amazing. The high-heeled sandals were going to be murder on the dance floor, but they made my legs look incredibly long. "Tonight, I look hot. And sexy. And completely grown up."

"Okay, okay, hot mama. Yes, you look good." Lucie's smile faded a little. "But you're going to freeze off that cute little ass. It's fucking winter outside, baby cakes."

I shrugged. "I'll wear a coat to the Road Block. Once we get inside, it'll be hot anyway." I licked my lips and leaned in to check my eye makeup one more time. "Plus if everything goes like I hope it does, I won't have to worry about getting cold. I'm going to have someone to keep me real warm."

Lucie blew out a sigh. "Jenna, are you sure about this? I mean . . . I get it. It's your birthday, you're finally legal, and you want to blow off some steam. Have some fun. We can do that. But this obsession with Trent Wagoner—"

"It's *not* an obsession." I pointed one perfectly manicured finger at her. "I'm not, like, stalking him or anything weird like that. We're friends." One side of my mouth curled up a little. "Friends who are going to become much closer tonight."

That was the plan, anyway. When I thought of Trent's tall, rangy body, the way his eyes warmed when he talked with me . . . I knew I wasn't misreading the situation. He felt the same way about me that I did about him. He just had to.

For most of my life, I'd known Trent in the same way I'd known everyone else in my tiny hometown. If we'd passed on the street and someone had asked me his name, I'd have been able to give it, along with a few salient details about him. And maybe even just a few more, because people liked to talk about Trent, so I'd heard some extra stuff about his background, his family and his general reputation. He'd been born here, but no one knew whom his dad was. His mom was an alcoholic, and worse, she'd been known to turn to solicitation when times got tough. She'd been in and out of jail during Trent's childhood, which meant he'd been in and out of foster homes.

I vaguely remembered him from school, although he was several years ahead of me. He'd been a loner, although he did party, too. He was a little too wild for most of Burton, but while he was young, much of the town tended to shake their heads and tsk about his awful family life.

Once he'd graduated, Trent had begun doing seasonal work at the local farms, living on site while they rushed to bring in the crops. But during the winter months, he'd had to find some other kind of employment.

And that was how we'd met. My uncle had hired Trent to work at his hardware store in town, and I'd already signed on for a part-time job there. I was in my third year of community college—and yes, it was a two-year school, but I hadn't been able to settle on a major, so I was still meandering my way through classes. Uncle Larry had given me the job that fall as a favor to my mom, his sister, and to my surprise, I found I enjoyed the work. Even more, I enjoyed my co-workers.

Trent and I had become friends right away. He was easy, with his teasing ways, and I was surprised at how smart and serious he could be. He was always respectful of me, never making me feel uncomfortable even when we worked alone together. He didn't seem very much like the guy I'd heard of from others in town.

"Kid's got a good head." I'd overheard my uncle talking

to my dad one night after a family dinner. "Works damn hard, doesn't mess around. Doesn't much like customer service, but I get that. I'm thinking about bringing him on permanently, if he'd be willing to forego the farm work this year."

I liked that idea, because in my head, it was only a matter of time before Trent and I were a couple, and having him in town all the time would be so much easier on both of us. I had it all planned out: Trent sometimes teased me about how young I was, so I figured he was just waiting for me to turn twenty-one before he made his move. Once that happened, we'd date for a while . . . say, maybe six months or a year. And then we'd get engaged, and my mom would plan the wedding . . . we'd live somewhere in town, and I'd stay home and raise our babies—there were going to be lots of those, I was sure—while Trent worked. Where he was working was still murky in my mind, but he'd find something. These things always worked out.

It would be totally perfect, and all I needed to make it reality was for Trent to give me a sign. Ask me out. Tell me how he felt about me. And tonight, that was going to happen. I knew that Trent hung out at the Road Block every Friday and Saturday night. The bar was owned by my cousin Rilla's husband, Mason, and it was the most rocking spot in Burton. Of course, it was also the only place that stayed open past ten o'clock and served alcohol, so the competition wasn't very stiff. Mason brought in the crowds like crazy, with the hot bands that played and the huge dance floor he'd been smart enough to include. I'd been there a few times to dance, but I'd never had a drink, since Mason was all too aware of my underage status. He was protective of me, probably because Rilla was, too. And he might've been just a little scared of my dad.

Tonight, though, giving me a drink—or more than one—would be perfectly legal, since I was finally twenty-one. No more baby sister, no more jailbait, no more boring little girl. Jenna Sutton was finally going to try out her wings.

Lucie sighed. "Jenna, I'm not going to try to talk you out of it anymore. You're right. You're old enough to know your own mind and make your own decisions. But darlin', this guy's got heartache written all over him. And we know it. We've seen the chicks he picks up. Do you really want to be one of Trent's one-night wonders?"

"It's going to be different with us. What he feels toward me isn't just lust. We're friends, and now we're taking it to another level. I'm going to be the woman who changes him from a man-whore to my man. Just you watch."

"And you don't think a lot of the girls who've let him fuck them seven ways to Sunday didn't think the same things you're saying now? You don't think they thought they'd be the ones to change him?"

A niggling doubt shot through my heart, but I ignored it. "Maybe they did, but they were wrong. I mean, Lucie, come on. He's got to change and settle down at some point, right? Why not now? Why not with me?"

Lucie threw up her hands. "Sure. Why not?" She stood up, reaching for her jacket. "Are you ready? Let's get this show on the road." She sounded resigned, with not a trace of excitement in her voice.

"Hey there, party pooper." I poked her side as I slid my arms into the sleeves of my own coat. "It's my birthday, remember? So how about at least pretending you're happy to be going out with me? You know, fake a smile. Try a squeal. It won't hurt you."

"Beg to differ. I am not a squealer, and if I try to fake it, I might end up pulling something essential." She jerked her head toward my bedroom door. "After you, Miss Birthday Girl."

The crowd at the Road Block was just as insane as I'd expected. After all, it was winter in Burton, so the farmers didn't have as much to do as they did the rest of the year, and everyone got a little bit stir-crazy from being inside. They were standing three-deep around the bar, and the dance floor was filled with people—mostly women, for sure—rocking out to an older song I vaguely recognized.

"We're never going to get a table." Lucie yelled the words into my ear, but I shook my head. She forgot sometimes that I had connections.

Pushing through the group near the end of the bar, I managed to brace my foot against the bottom of a barstool and hoist myself up a little, so I could be seen above the other heads. Cupping my hands around my mouth, I bellowed, "Mason!"

The huge hunky guy pulling beers glanced over his shoulder. Spotting me, he smiled and inclined his head, acknowledging that he'd heard me. I watched as he finished filling the mugs, building the beers with a finesse I knew I'd

6

never have. Turning, he set the drinks onto small squares of paper napkins and slid them across the polished oak bar to the guys waiting.

Only then did my favorite cousin-in-law meander down my way. He reached across, gripped my shoulders and pulled me close to kiss my face with a smack of his lips. "Happy birthday, little girl."

If anyone else had referred to me that way, I would've been annoyed, but I knew this was just Mason's way. Besides, the truth was that I *was* little compared to him. Just about everyone was.

"Thanks, Mase. Do you have our table ready?" I pointed behind me, to where Lucie stood, lips pursed and arms folded as she struggled to maintain her footing in the jostling crowd.

"Sure do, baby doll." His eyes scanned the room, and when he saw who he was looking for, he cocked his head and gestured for her to come over. The waitress who responded was pretty, with dark blonde hair and a ready smile.

"Andrea, can you show my cousin here to the table I reserved for her?"

She smirked. "Would that be the one with the balloons and the big sign that says *Happy Birthday, Jenna?*"

I groaned. "You didn't. Tell me you didn't. This is supposed to be an adult thing, Mason. Not a kiddie party."

He had the audacity to laugh at me. "The balloons were Rilla's idea, and don't you go getting mad at me for doing what my beautiful wife asked me to do." He winked at me. "Now the sign, that was all me. But you got to roll with it, kid—after all, I did save you a table on my busiest night of

7

the week."

That was true, and I wasn't really mad, anyway. I leaned up again and kissed his cheek. "Thank you, Mason. Now, before I go to our table, what's going to be my very first legal drink?"

"How about a Shirley Temple?"

I ignored him and pretended I hadn't already been thinking about this for weeks. "Give me a Cuba Libre, please." I glanced over at Lucie, who'd turned twenty-one back in the fall. "What'll it be, Luce?"

She shrugged. "Just a soda water, please." She hooked her thumb to her chest. "Designated driver, remember?"

I nodded, all the while thinking that if my plans went off as I hoped, I wouldn't need her to drive me home. Speaking of which . . .

I took advantage of my position looming over the rest of the patrons to scan the room for the one person I desperately needed to see tonight. But there wasn't any sign of Trent, at least not on this side of the restaurant. I couldn't see all the way to the dance floor or to the other tables, of course, so there was a good chance he was over there.

I waved to Mason as Andrea put our drinks on a tray and began to lead us to our table. Before I got out of earshot, though, he called to me once more.

"Jenna Sutton, you behave yourself, you hear? I don't want to have to carry you home so Boomer can rant about me letting you get drunk on your first night of being legal. Got it?"

I waved again and blew him a kiss, offering my most beatific and innocent smile. Mason only shook his head. I'd

8

never been able to get much over on him.

Just as Andrea had said, our table had a big sign, and a bunch of balloons were tied to one of the chairs. I rolled my eyes at Lucie. "Whatever. At least we won't lose our table, right?"

"Sure." She pulled out the chair without balloons and sat down. "Not that I'm planning to leave it much anyway."

"God, Luce. Can you maybe just try a little bit of a smile? For me? As a gift for my birthday?"

"I can't help if I think this whole night is a stupid-ass idea. If you really wanted some fun, we could've driven into Savannah. We could have celebrated there. You might've met some fun guys who aren't jerks. Maybe ended up having a happy birthday."

"Oh, I plan on that. The happy birthday, I mean. And it looks like the present I've been wishing for just walked in."

The doors had swung open on the bar side, and a group of guys who looked a little familiar moseyed in. At the back, not quite part of them, was Trent.

He was wearing the same old beat-up leather jacket he wore to the hardware store every day. His light brown hair looked messy, probably because there was a decent wind blowing around out there. Even as I watched, he smoothed it back, raking his fingers through the long strands. His eyes scanned the room, and my heart skipped a beat: I'd casually mentioned, three or four times, that I planned to be at the Road Block tonight. Could he be looking for me?

But even though I was pretty certain his gaze swept over my table, complete with balloons, it didn't stop. He didn't so much as pause when I was sure he'd seen me. Instead, he wandered over to the bar, stopping along the way to greet people as he went. Girls grabbed at his arms, trying to get his attention. A few other men slapped him on the back, and I noticed that most of those were other seasonal farmhands. Guys from town, the ones I'd known and sometimes dated in the past, ignored Trent.

It made me furious, the way people in Burton treated him. Trent was one of the kindest, smartest and hardest-working people in town, and he deserved better from all of them. Once we were married, they'd all see. I had a sudden image of the future, of the two of us standing outside the Baptist church on Front Street, while one of the elders patted my arm, saying, "We sure misjudged this young man before he married you. You're the only one who saw his true potential."

"Why're you grinning like that?" Lucie cocked her head at me, brows drawn together. "You look like you know something no one else does."

"Maybe I do." I shot her a saucy wink. "Hey, don't you think we need more drinks?"

"You haven't finished the one you have." She pointed at my half-empty glass. "Pace yourself, sweetie. And I know you don't want to listen to my advice, but throwing yourself at Trent isn't a good idea. If you're so sure he feels the same way, let him come to you."

"I'm more than sure. But I don't need to play hard to get, Luce. That's high school shit. I'm not a kid who has to play games. I'm a woman who knows what she wants and isn't afraid to go for it."

"Jenna. Honestly. I applaud your female empowerment

speech, but chasing after a dude who's pretty much the un-disputed man-whore of the town isn't exactly enlightened thinking."

Since I'd been a little girl, my temper had been legend-ary in my family. I thought I'd learned to control it in the last few years, but just now, I was ready to explode, which was why I spoke without thinking.

"Jealous, Luce?"

Hurt and betrayal flashed over her face. "No, Jenna. No, I'm not." She pushed herself to stand up, grabbed her jacket from the back of the chair and looped her pocketbook over her head. "But I'm also not going to sit here and watch you make an ass out of yourself over a man who barely knows that you exist—or if he does, looks at you like a kid sister. I don't need this shit, and I definitely don't need it from the person who's supposed to be my *best friend*."

She spit out the last words, yelling them over the music, and then turned and pushed her way through the crowd. I watched in shock as she stalked out the door and into the night.

Damn. One good thing about my temper was that it was short-lived. I felt instant guilt for what I'd said to Lucie. We'd been friends since grade school, but ours was a relationship of contrast, not similarity. When I'd begun experimenting with makeup, Lucie had been deep in learning about music, playing the guitar and listening to the same dark songs over and over. She'd never cared about how she looked, what she wore or how others saw her—or at least that was what she wanted the world to think. I knew that her hard shell pro-tected a girl who'd been hurt by the taunting words of bullies from elementary school on and whose parents had never paid enough attention to help her cope with that.

In high school, where I was popular and gone out with boys from our freshman year through graduation, Lucie had never had a single date. She'd never gone to a dance, never participated in anything extracurricular and barely scraped by with passing grades. We were complete opposites: the head cheerleader and the emo chick.

Still, we'd remained friends. Actually, we'd grown even closer after graduation, when we both chose to attend the local community college instead of going off to a distant school. Lucie was pursuing a business degree, which she hoped would help with her eventual career in music. She played gigs on weekends in Savannah or at small bars in nearby towns. If I were being honest with myself—and I almost always was—Luce was more together and driven about her future than I was. She had plans, and I had . . . well, I had a vague outline of how I wanted my life to be. Once Trent had entered the picture, some of that vagueness had morphed to include him in the role of husband and love-of-my-life. But I still didn't have anything concrete to count on, not like Lucie did.

I knew she remained insecure about her looks and her total lack of experience with boys. Or with men. Hell, I didn't know that much about the opposite sex—I was still a virgin, the result of having dated often but never seriously— but I knew more than Lucie, who had trouble just talking to guys, unless it was about music. Even then, she shut down the minute they expressed any interest in her as a person, beyond her guitar and songwriting.

Once, about a year before, I'd finally gotten up my courage and asked Lucie a question that I'd been curious about for a long time.

"Luce, are you . . . you know. Is it boys you're interested in? Attracted to, I mean?"

When she'd frowned at me, puzzled, I'd rushed to add, "It's okay if you're . . . you know, not. You're my best friend, and I love you no matter what. I just wondered, because if the guys aren't doing it for you, there's no need to pretend about it around me. I accept you for who you are."

Realization dawned in her eyes. "Oh . . . you think." With a half-laugh, Lucie shook her head. "I wish that were it. No, I'm hetero. It's the dudes for me. Not that any of them ever see me, of course, or would want anything to do with me if they did."

"That's crazy, Lucie. Any man would be lucky to go out with you. You just need to try a little bit harder. You know, maybe smile every once in a while. Flirt. Act like you care."

To my utter amazement, Lucie had begun to cry. She didn't burst into tears the way I did when I was upset; rather, her eyes welled up, her shoulders shook in silent sobs, and she covered her face with two hands.

Once I'd gotten her to calm down, she'd admitted that she had a massive crush on the drummer in the group she played with sometimes on weekends. He treated her like one of the guys, and she almost never spoke to him, but it was slowly killing her to watch him pick up a different girl every week, knowing that she could never be like the women he was banging so casually.

I'd tried to encourage her to talk to him, explain her

feelings, but it had never happened. As far as I knew, Shane the drummer was still trolling band groupies for his weekend sex fix, and Lucie was still pining away, wishing he'd notice her and terrified that he would.

So what I'd said to her tonight? Yeah, that went beyond the boundaries of a gentle jab. It was a sucker punch, and one no decent girl would ever use against her friend. I'd taken information Lucie had never shared with another living soul and used it to hurt her. I was a bitch.

Part of me knew at that moment that I should've run after my best friend, caught her before she left the parking lot and beg her to forgive me. I should've told her that we could go back to my house and binge-watch *Veronica Mars* while we ate my mom's amazing brownies. I should've groveled.

But I didn't, because just as I was deciding, Trent came back into my view, emerging from the crowd around the bar. I spotted a woman wearing a tight, low-cut dress approaching him. She tilted her head and twirled a lock of her bleach-blonde hair around one finger, and I wanted to pull every strand out of her stupid head.

I didn't have time to wait. And I couldn't go after Lucie, because if I did, there was no doubt in my mind that Trent would go home with this bimbo, and I'd lose my shot with him. Maybe forever.

Before I knew what I was doing, I stood up and pushed my way across the dance floor. With a confidence I wasn't quite feeling, I walked right up to Trent and smiled, ignoring the trashy ho whose fingers were teasing his bicep.

Cocking my head, I raised one eyebrow. "So what's a girl got to do to get a happy birthday kiss?"

Trent looked down at me. I'd expected—hoped—to see in his eyes a flare of happy surprise, maybe even banked desire. But even I had to admit to myself that there was nothing but a friendly smile on his face, the same expression I'd seen at work.

"Hey there, Jenna. Happy birthday." He bent to kiss my cheek. "How's the celebration going?"

"I think it's looking up now that you're here." I offered my hand. "Come dance with me."

He laughed. "Sorry, darlin'. I don't do this kind of dancing. Why don't you go find your girlfriends? This is a chick song."

I looked back over my shoulder and realized that he was right; the majority of people on the dance floor just now were female, which probably had something to do with the fact that Carrie Underwood was belting out the lyrics. My face heated, but I wasn't going to let a little embarrassment get in the way of my plans for the night.

"I'd rather stay here with you." I flicked a glance to the blonde who was still hanging on Trent's arm. "You could buy me a drink. You know, to help me celebrate. Now that I'm legal and all."

The bitch next to him giggled, and not in a nice, sisterhood solidarity way. I wanted to claw her face.

"Honey, you may be legal now, but you're still on the hands-off list." Trent lifted his beer up and cast a wary glance over to the bar, where Mason was still working hard. "If you think I'm going to risk getting your cousin up in my face, you're wrong."

"Cousin-in-law." I made the correction automatically,

as if it mattered. "Mason doesn't care. Besides, he can't tell me what to do."

"Maybe not, but I have too much respect for the guy to risk it. But hey, I'd be happy to buy you a soda and some nachos."

It wasn't what I wanted, not by a long shot, but it was a start. "Okay." I jerked my head backwards. "Mason set up a table for me. Let's take the party over there."

Trent hesitated. I could see something battling in his eyes, something sober with something hard. But after a moment, he nodded and followed me.

"Nice balloons." He smirked as I dragged out the decorated chair and sat down.

"Yeah. Rilla's idea, I guess. Well, you know family."

I could've bitten off my tongue. Bitterness flickered across his face, because, of course, he *didn't* know family. Not the kind I did, at least. All he had was a mother who'd abandoned him time after time and a town who talked about him behind his back.

Before I could say anything, apologize for my words or try to take them back, Andrea the waitress was at our table. "Y'all okay here? Need to order food? Refresh drinks?"

"Nachos." Trent lifted his bottle. "Another of these." He glanced at me. "Jenna?"

I smiled at Andrea and tapped the rim of my glass. "More of this, please." The ice in my Cuba Libre had melted, leaving it looking like plain soda. Trent didn't even blink, but Andrea's eyes narrowed ever so slightly. I raised my eyebrow just a little, and she shrugged.

"Coming right up." And then she was gone, melding

back into the melee of bodies surrounding us.

Trent leaned back in his seat, assessing me. "So . . . it's your twenty-first birthday and you're out at a bar alone?"

I sighed. "I wasn't alone. I came with my friend Lucie. But she . . . uh, she had to leave. Earlier than she expected. And I wasn't ready to go yet."

"Uh huh." He tipped the beer against his mouth, finishing it off. "Well, you don't want to hang around here too long on your own. I mean, I know your cousin is the owner and all, but still—some of the guys can be a little rough, the later it gets. And Mason can't be everywhere."

"Hmmm." I rested my elbow on the table and pressed my chin into my hand. "Then I guess I need a bodyguard. Can you think of anyone who might be up for the job?"

"Jenna—" He began to speak, the vaguest trace of a frown creasing his forehead, but somebody pushed against his chair, distracting us both. Just as he was turning back to me, another waitress—not Andrea—dropped off our drinks.

"Food's coming." She flashed a smile and then was gone, heading to another table.

I raised my glass. "Here's to . . . friends."

Trent tapped the neck of his new bottle to my drink. "Happy birthday, Jenna. I hope tonight is everything you want it to be."

There was no way to hide the grin that spread over my face. "Me, too."

Trent took a healthy swig of his beer and then pushed back his chair to stand. "Be right back. Need to hit the men's."

Watching him stride away from me toward the hallway in the back that led to the restrooms, my resolve strengthened. His jeans hugged that perfect backside to perfection, and lust rose in my chest.

Oh, yeah. I wanted a piece of that.

"Jenna." A voice at my shoulder caught my attention, and I glanced back. Mason stood behind me, his jaw tense and his eyes clouded as he set the plate of nachos on the table. I stiffened, waiting for him to yell at me for hanging out with Trent.

"Rilla just called. The baby's picked up some stomach bug, and he's puking all over. She's starting to feel sick, too, and I need to get home to give her a hand." He seemed to notice the empty chair across from me for the first time. "Where's Lucie?"

Relief flooded through me. He hadn't seen her leave. "She, uh . . ." My gaze strayed in the direction of the bathrooms, mentally willing Trent to stay in there until my protective cousin-in-law was safely away.

Mason misread my meaning, though, and his expression cleared. "Oh, gotcha. Okay, well—listen, you take it easy, all right? Don't stay here too late, and you and Lucie stick together. Rocky's at the bar if you need anything."

"Sure, Mase." I patted his arm. "Go on now, and tell Rilla I hope she feels better. Oh, and if you guys want me to come over tomorrow to sit with the kids so you can get some rest, just call."

"That's sweet, honey. I'll keep it in mind." He bent to kiss my cheek. "Be safe, darlin'. Happy birthday."

I exhaled, closing my eyes. It was as though the gods of hook-ups and good times were smiling on me: the last huge obstacle between Trent and me getting together had just swung out the door.

"Hey." Trent reappeared, picking up his chair and turning it in one hand so that the back hit the edge of the table. He straddled it, folding his arms over the table. "Great, food. I'm starved." He scooped up a chip with a pile of cheese and peppers and slid the whole mess into his mouth.

Picking up my glass, I tossed back the contents, feeling the welcome burn of the rum down my throat, warming my stomach. The rocking song that had been luring crowds to the dance floor segued into a slower, more seductive beat, and imbued with new courage, I stood up' and snagged Trent's hand.

"This one's not a chick song. It's most definitely not something I want to dance to with my girlfriends. Come on. Give me just one dance tonight."

He paused. I would remember that long after the song ended, after the night ended, that Trent had hesitated. That he didn't pursue me, but that it was me who tugged him to his feet and led him onto the dance floor. It was me who wrapped my arms around him, pressed my boobs into the hard planes of his chest and tucked my head beneath his chin as we swayed to the music. And before the song ended, it was me who threaded her fingers into the hair at the back of his neck and coaxed his mouth to mine for a searing, no-holds-barred kiss.

That moment, slow-dancing with Trent Wagoner on the dance floor of the Road Block, was the last purely happy moment of my first twenty-one years. It would be a long time before I found another reason to smile . . . or another way to be happy again.

CHAPTER ONE

Two Years Later

Lincoln

"THE WATER FEELS AMAZING."

I turned my head toward the glare of the ocean as Abby Donavan—uh, Abby Kent now, I had to remember that she was married—dashed up the beach to where I sat next to her husband Ryland. I had to smile; I still wasn't used to this more spontaneous, impulsive version of the contained Miss Abigail Donavan. When I'd met her a few years back, she had been our boss on the restoration of an old hotel, and I'd described her as steely. Maybe even a little bit icy. The lady had definitely melted, and I knew for sure it was more than the heat of the Florida sun that had done the trick.

In the beach chair next to me, the man who was responsible for most of Abby's melting grinned. "Looking good there, Mrs. Kent."

She shot him a saucy smile before dropping to the beach blanket in front of me, where my daughter sat with her arms around her knees. "Becca, come out with us! It's so much fun. You can body surf with Ollie and me."

Becca's jaw tensed as she shook her head. "No, thanks. I'm fine here."

"Bec." I nudged her rear end with my foot. "Why don't you go enjoy the water? This is your first beach trip. Don't you want to play in the ocean? Have some fun, darlin'."

My daughter replied without turning her head to look at me. "No, thanks. I don't want to go into the ocean." She paused a beat before adding, "It's not safe. See that flag? It means there's a rip current. People get carried away, and they can't swim back."

"We're not going that far out, sweetie." Abby pulled a towel out of her bag and dried off her legs. "I'm keeping my eye on your brother, too. We won't go any further than just our hips, okay?"

"No, thanks." Becca hugged her legs a little tighter as she repeated the words. "There could probably be jellyfish, too. And there can be bacteria in the water. Sometimes people die just from putting their feet in."

I fought the strong desire to roll my eyes. "Becca, don't be—"

Ryland jabbed an elbow into my ribs. "Hey, Becs, how long have I known you?"

She glanced back at us, frowning. "Ummm . . . I don't know. All my life?"

"Yeah, just about. Did you know you were the first baby

I ever held? Your mom didn't give me a choice about it. She just plopped you into my arms. Now, would your mom have done that if she didn't trust me?"

She gave a tiny headshake.

"Okay. And you know how much I love both you and your dweeby little bro?"

For the first time all day, my daughter's mouth curved into a slight smile. "Yeah."

"So you also know I would never, ever let you do anything where you might get hurt, right? Never. I'd throw myself in front of a speeding train to push you out of its path. Take on a grizzly bear if it were chasing you. You got that?"

Becca nodded.

"Then do you think, really think, that I'd let Aunt Abby take you down to the ocean if there were anything the least bit dangerous there?"

She pursed her lips and lifted one shoulder. "I don't know."

Ryland cocked an eyebrow at her. "We got to stick to logic here, tootsie roll. And logic tells you the truth."

"But Uncle Ry—"

"Hey." He pointed to her. "Not finished yet. Because I want you to think of something else. Do you know how much I love Aunt Abby?"

Becca sighed. "Yeah."

"So you know I'd never want her to do anything where she might get hurt either." Ry glanced at his wife. "I'm going to tell you something I haven't even told your dad. Aunt Abby and I are going to have a baby." He paused, letting that news sink in. "As much as I love you and Ollie, as much as

I love Aunt Abby and this little peanut in her belly, would I sit back and let all of you do anything where you might get hurt?"

Becca's head swiveled in Abby's direction. I could almost feel her struggling to accept what Ryland was saying, to let it begin to overcome the fear. Finally, she gave a tiny shake of her head.

"Okay. I'll go down." She stood up, brushing sand from her legs. "But only a little bit in, right? Not deep."

Abby rose, too, and extended her hand. "I promise, baby girl. No further than you want." Over my daughter's head, Abby smiled at me and winked. "We'll just play around by the surf."

Hands linked, the two tripped across the sand. I watched them go, grinning when Ab body-checked Becca and pretended to be sorry. It gave me a sense of relief to see my little girl finally relaxing a little bit. She might've been going on twelve, but she was always going to be my baby.

Which reminded me . . .

"So." I tilted down my sunglasses and folded my arms across my chest, fastening Ry with a glare that was more bark than bite. "Something you needed to tell me?"

His smirk was huge and not at all repentant. "Hey, the situation called for something big, so I gave it to her."

"Yeah, jackass, telling my daughter before me that you're going to be a dad. What the hell, man?" I couldn't hold the faux-mad any longer. Reaching across between the chairs, I punched his arm. "Congratulations, bro. 'Bout time."

The expression on Ryland's face could've lit up NRG Stadium. "Yeah, right, about time. More like a miracle. Between Abby working so hard to get the hotel up and running and me being on the road all the time, trying to move the business down here, what's more amazing is that we were in the same state long enough to make it happen."

"So is this the reason you've decided to stop traveling altogether?" I pushed my glasses back into place and leaned against the webbed chair.

Ry shrugged. "Well, it was in the works anyway, you know. It was always the plan, for me to move all the operations down here, so we could start a real life together. We figured that we'd talk babies after that, but it turned out someone had other plans."

"Babies are like that." I stared out into the blinding blue of the ocean. "I don't think I ever told you this, but Becca wasn't exactly planned. Sylvia and I had only been married about seven months, and we were living in this cramped apartment, barely more than a room. Working for Leo Groff back then, remember, but still pretty far down the food chain. Syl and I had plans—we had that crappy little apartment so that when I had to travel for a job, she could come with me. I came home one night, absolutely dead on my feet. Filthy from a project we'd just started. I remember I was pissed because I could tell she hadn't started dinner yet, and I was starved. Syl was curled up in the corner of this ratty old sofa we'd inherited from her aunt, and she'd been crying. I finally got it out of her that she'd taken a pregnancy test."

"Oh, man." Ry's voice was filled with empathy. "What did you say?"

"What could I say?" I lifted one shoulder. "I mean, it

was a done deal. And she hadn't exactly gotten knocked up by herself. Takes two to tango, and let's just say, I always liked a good tango. So I hugged her tight, told her she'd just made me the happiest man on the planet, and we started picking out baby names. After Becs came along seven months later, neither of us could imagine our lives without that kid." I sighed a little, remembering. "All this stuff works out for the best."

"Yeah." Ry fidgeted, his chair creaking as he settled again. "You know, Linc, I'm pretty sure that's the first time I've heard you talk about Sylvia without . . . I don't know. The deep pain. Like maybe you were about to lose it. It's good to hear you say her name again with a smile."

"We had good times. We had a great marriage, and I've never regretted one minute of our life together." I hesitated, waiting for the usual boulder of grief to roll over me. But this time, as it has been lately, the feeling was not as devastating. I still missed Syl every day. I still sometimes talked to her when no one else was around. But the pain didn't feel like it was going to consume me anymore. It was sadness, but it was no longer despair. "It's not that common to find the love of your life when you're seventeen. I was one of the lucky ones, and I'm never going to forget it."

"So you believe that?" Ryland regarded me with curiosity. "That we all get only one great love?"

I dug trenches in the sand with my heels until I hit the cooler damp layer. "Don't you? Isn't Abby your one and only love?"

"Of course." He didn't miss a beat in replying. "And I'm counting on us having at least a hundred years together."

When I raised one eyebrow, he lifted his hands. "What? My family is very long-lived. But if something wacky happened and I bought the farm after five years, I'd like to think Abby might find someone else. Someone not quite as attractive as me, of course, because hey, you can't expect to hit the jackpot twice."

"Don't forget humble," I added dryly.

"Never would. I'm just saying, maybe sometimes second chances come along. Look at Jude and Logan."

Jude and Logan Holt owned the hotel whose restoration had brought Ryland and me to Crystal Cove two years before. They'd been married as long as I'd known them, but Ry had told me their story: Jude had been married to Logan's best friend and business partner, Daniel, for over twenty years before he passed away from cancer, leaving her with two nearly-adult kids, her own beach-front restaurant and their company's unfinished projects. Apparently, although he'd never let it be known, Logan had secretly loved Jude all those years. It was only well over a year after Daniel's death that he'd begun to court his friend's widow.

Knowing them now, as I did, I couldn't imagine any other ending for those two. Logan clearly worshipped the ground Jude occupied, and she was head-over-heels for him. They shared not only their businesses—which had only expanded in the past years—but also her grown children and her two grandchildren.

"Yeah, that's true." I gave Ryland a brief nod of agreement. "But I think that's the exception, not the rule. Most of the people I know who end up married again, or in another relationship after they lose a spouse, don't find the same fire.

They're together for comfort and companionship. And that's great, but it's not an epic love. I don't think anything can ever touch that first time you fall."

"Maybe. Maybe not." Ryland fisted sand and let it sift through his fingers. "So, you ready for this change? Ready to become a man who stays in one place again?"

"I think so." I stretched out my legs, letting the sun bake them. "It's going to be good, I'm pretty sure. Burton seems like a nice town, and it'll be a fresh start. For all of us."

"And you need it." My friend stared out ahead of us. "How's it going, anyway? The transition with the kids, I mean. They seem to be doing okay."

"It's hard to tell yet." I rubbed my fingers over my forehead. "We haven't settled down to real life yet, you know? I picked them up from their grandparents' house just about a month ago, and since then, we've been on vacation, more or less, down in Orlando and then up here visiting with you and Abby. That's nothing different than what we've done other summers. The real adjustment will come when we're alone in our new house, just the three of us, and I have to enforce the rules all the time. I'll have to come up with a routine, and they'll be getting used to new schools. That's going to be the test."

"Still." Ryland cast me a sideways glance. "They seem happy."

"Mostly." I wanted to be optimistic, but the truth was, realism served me better. "But you see Becca. She's scared of everything. Afraid to move and afraid to stay still. We were at a theme park last week, down in Orlando, and she got a little ahead of me in the crowd. I didn't worry, because I had my eye on her the whole time, but when she looked around and couldn't spot me, she freaked out. Took me nearly an hour to calm her down."

"Hmmm." Ry frowned. "That seems a little extreme."

"It is. Maybe not for a five-year old, but Bec's almost twelve." I lowered my voice, although there was no way either of the kids could hear me down in the waves. "That's Doris. She's always been a little bit of a worrywart, but since Sylvia's accident, she sees disaster and tragedy around every corner. Becca's picked that up, and it's going to be a tough habit to break."

"Maybe once you three are settled in Burton, she'll relax a little. Have you thought about therapy?"

I nodded. "Both kids have had some counseling over the last six years. We might have to step it up a little in Becca's case, though."

"Ollie seems pretty happy." Ryland watched my son as he splashed the females and made them squeal.

"Yeah, but he worries me, too. I don't think the kid has quite wrapped his mind around the idea that they're living with me now, for good. The other day, he said something about when he goes back to Texas. You know, he was only three when Sylvia died. He doesn't remember her at all, and Doris and Hank are the only parental figures he knows. I was more like a visiting uncle than a dad to him."

Ry gripped my shoulder briefly and then released me. "It'll come together, man. Don't stress it too hard. Kids are resilient, right? Isn't that what everyone says?"

"I guess." I sighed. "We needed this week in the Cove. I appreciate you and Abby letting us stay."

"Hey, our hotel is your hotel." He laughed. "Or something like that. And don't worry. When we find a house, we're going to make sure it has plenty of room for you guys to come down whenever you want."

"You're seriously going to move out of the Riverside?" Since before their marriage, Abby and Ryland had lived at the hotel that our company had restored. Abby was the manager, so it was easier for her to be on property. They had a roomy, comfortable apartment, and I'd never heard either of them complain.

"We are. We thought about trying to make it work there for a while longer, but the truth of the matter is that no hotel guests want to hear a crying baby in the middle of the night, and I'm given to understand that sometimes babies do that. Cry at night."

It was my turn to smirk. "Now and then."

"Yeah, well, anyway, Ab wants to do up a nursery, and I want a place where I can put in my own workshop. I've talked Cooper into partnering with me on some local projects, and it would be nice to have a place to do some of the work at home."

"You're becoming domesticated, Ry." I ignored the twinge of envy I felt. "It looks good on you."

"I never could've gotten here without you, buddy." Ryland cleared his throat. "If you hadn't come on as my partner and agreed to head up the new headquarters of Kent and Turner, I'd still have to be on the road. I'd still have too much responsibility to handle the local stuff, the artisan work. So . . . thanks, Linc. I can't tell you how much Abby and I appreciate it. How much we owe you."

I coughed away the lump in my own throat. "You don't owe me anything. You . . . Ryland, you stuck by me when everyone else was ready to give up. When I was an ugly mess from the booze, when I cried my way through every day after Sylvia, you're the only one who stayed. If it weren't for that, I'd probably be dead in a ditch somewhere, and my kids would be orphans, raised by their grandparents. And you gave me the courage and the wherewithal to take them back, too. If you hadn't believed in me, I'd have let Hank and Doris keep them. I'd still be miserable, alone. So don't think I'm doing you some big favor. You're giving the kids and me a way to start over. To make a new life."

"Guess we're both good for each other." Ryland didn't look my way, which was fine by me. After all, we were men, and gazing fondly into each other's eyes wasn't our thing.

After a few minutes, I felt like it was safe to speak again. "Really appreciate you hooking me up with Meghan Reynolds, too. She found us a house that looks to be perfect for the kids and me. I'm looking forward to getting up there and settling in."

"I think the location will be just what we need business-wise, too." Ry took a swig of his water bottle. "There's still a lot of historical restoration work going on in the greater Savannah area, and you'll be central to jobs in Atlanta, too. Alex Nelson gave me some contacts from when he used to live there." Alex and his partner Cal now ran the Hawthorne House, a bed and breakfast that was also owned by Jude and Logan Holt. Before he'd moved down here to the Cove, Alex had worked in corporate event planning in the Georgia state capital.

"I can't believe I forgot to tell you." I smacked the arm of the chair. "I had an email this morning from the Baker Foundation. The approval came down from the state on restoring that old plantation house, and we got the contract. So my first big job is going to be local to Burton."

"Dude." Ry lifted his hand for a high five. "That is huge. How'd you forget to tell me?"

I shrugged. "I don't know. I saw it on my phone right as we were leaving for the beach, and then Ollie couldn't find his other shoe, and with one thing and another, I guess it just slipped my mind. Oh, and keep it quiet for now, okay? The local historical society hasn't been informed yet. This was just a heads' up from one of the Baker Foundation board members."

"Will do. But hey, this is awesome. I'm jealous, though. A plantation? I've always wanted to take on that kind of project."

"You're welcome to come up and put in some hours whenever you want. Bring Abby, so she can see our new house and hang out with the kids."

"We'll plan on it. Don't worry, I won't be able to keep her away from checking out your new digs. Plus, I'm pretty sure she's gotten attached to your kiddos."

We both looked down to the ocean. Becca had ventured far enough in that the water hit her knees, and she was giggling as she watched her brother pretend to be a dolphin. My breath caught for a moment; I couldn't remember when I'd last heard my daughter laugh with that kind of abandon.

"I think the feeling's mutual." The edges of my mouth curled. "Makes me wonder if we should've settled here instead. The kids would have you and Ab, and there'd be a sense of familiarity, at least."

"Maybe. But at the same time I'd love to have all of you right here in town, I think it's like you said. You need a fresh start, and in Burton, you'll get that. You won't be that far away from us, and we can visit."

"Yeah." A lump rose in my throat. "I guess there's part of me that's scared shitless I'm going to screw this up. The kids, I mean. Becca's growing up. She's going to hit those teen years before I know it, and how do I talk to her about all the 'your changing body' shit? That was supposed to be Syl's job."

Ryland blanched. "Dude, don't look at me. I guess you'll have to find some female up in Georgia who can help you out. Ask Meghan. She's a chick."

"But that's just the beginning. There's always going to be stuff I need to handle, not just as a dad, but as a mom, too. It's terrifying, Ry. You think this baby part is going to be a tough gig? Just you wait, buddy."

"Thanks, Linc. Appreciate all the encouragement." He shook his head and gnawed at his thumbnail. "You know what, though? It's going to be okay, for both of us. We'll make it through, 'cause we're both strong manly men. We got this."

Scooping up a handful of powdery sand, I let it sift through my fingers. "I hope so, Ry. I really hope so."

CHAPTER TWO

Jenna

"**S**O HOW MUCH DO YOU love me?"

I turned my head as Cora, my de facto boss, sailed into the reception area where my desk was pushed into a small niche in the wall. Desk might have been a generous description for the narrow table where my ancient computer monitor sat, but since it was all I had, there'd be no complaints from my direction.

"Umm . . ." I frowned. "I love you the appropriate amount, I guess? You know, I'm fond of you in the way a lowly, grateful employee should be of her wonderful boss."

"Well, get ready to amp that up a little, because I have good news." She waved a single sheet of white paper in one hand as she tucked her gray curls behind her ear with the other. "Guess what I have here?"

I was still preoccupied with the letter I was trying to compose. "A memo from the county, saying I should get a raise for my exemplary work doing everything no one else in this office wants to do? Or maybe a requisition for a real workspace for me?"

Cora laughed. "Sorry, none of the above. But it *is* something you've been waiting for. Something you put a lot of your heart and soul into, not to mention blood, sweat and tears."

"You're piling on the clichés pretty thick there, Cora. Must be something—" Suddenly, the most improbable possibility began to dawn in my mind. "No. It's not, is it? It can't be. It hasn't been long enough. These things take time, you told me that, and so did Ray and Molly . . . months, you said. Maybe even longer."

Cora didn't say anything, but her smile became broader.

"Oh my God." I slumped back against the chair. "Did they—is that the approval? Did the state give us the green light?"

"Green light and full speed ahead!" Cora tossed the paper into my lap. "I've never seen this kind of proposal get approved so quickly."

I scanned the letter, but only two words jumped out at me. "Fully funded. They not only gave us a yes, they're paying for it?"

"Well, not the state." Cora leaned against wall across from me. "And that may explain why this is happening the way it is. The entire project—the restoration and the initial operation expenses—is being covered by the Baker Foundation."

"That's kind of unusual, isn't it?" I'd been working at the Bryan County Historical Society for just over a year, first as a volunteer and only more recently as a (lowly) paid member of the staff. "It seems like we're always scrambling for funding."

"You're not wrong. But every once in a while, someone has a connection to or a passion for a certain project, and then it's easier to find the money. Really, it's all in who you know. In this case, Oak Grove Plantation is not too far from the Reynolds' farm, and the scuttlebutt I hear is that Meghan Reynolds has the ear of someone connected to the Baker Foundation. I don't know for sure, but I imagine Mrs. Reynolds said something to the Foundation about our proposal, which is what put us on the fast-track."

"Hmm. I know Meghan a little." Even though she'd been married to Sam for over two years, it still sounded odd to hear her called *Mrs. Reynolds.* "She's a good friend of my cousin Rilla, and my dad's been close to Sam as long as I can remember."

"Did you say anything to her about submitting the proposal?" Cora quirked an eyebrow at me.

I shook my head. "No. I haven't seen Meghan or Sam in . . . a while." I didn't socialize if I could help it, and I hadn't even visited my cousin Rilla for months.

"Then it must have been something else. Maybe just the fact that the plantation is near their farm, or . . . well, who knows. The important thing is that we've got the go-ahead. It's time for you to run with it."

"Me?" I was pretty sure my mouth dropped open. "Why me?"

"This is your baby, Jenna. You brought us the idea, you spearheaded the county's decision to take on the project, and you wrote the proposal to the state. I'm not taking it away from you at this point."

"Seriously?" My mind was spinning. "You're going to let me handle it? Really?"

"Seriously and really. Now, there are a few aspects of this project you need to be aware of. Because the Baker Foundation is footing the bill, you'll have to be in close contact with them—I imagine they'll appoint a liaison to work with you. Also, it seems they've laid out a few stipulations."

"Like what?" I hadn't ever been in charge of one of our jobs; I'd only worked on a few, never as a project manager. I assumed this foundation just wanted some input on some of our design and execution decisions.

"They're requiring us to use a contractor they've selected. That seems to be the main condition. The rest have to do with operations after the restoration is complete, consultations with their historians and hiring practices. But for your purposes, it's just the contractor."

There wasn't exactly a large pool of potential experts located near Burton; I supposed Savannah probably had more. I myself only knew of a few, and one in particular I was aware of had a bad rep. "Tell me they're not insisting on Randall Cranks."

Cora laughed. "No, not good old Randall. They want us to use a restoration specialist firm, actually. It's called Kent and Turner. The company is new to our area, but they've done some work around the country and made a name for themselves. I've heard good things. Apparently, their first permanent office just opened here in Burton."

"I hadn't heard." Truth was, I didn't hear much nowadays, and even if I did, I seldom remembered anything that didn't directly pertain to me. My mother tended to chatter away when we were together, and I automatically filtered out the information I didn't need.

"You can start by setting up a meeting with them next week, and then I'll help you put together a calendar for the project, based on what they say. We'll need to factor in some promotional events along the way, so I'll get Joanna in on the conversation, too." Joanna Phelps handled our press and promotional services, and I knew she was always keeping her eye out for an opportunity to bring more exposure to the historical society.

"All right." My stomach had begun to churn as nerves hit me. "But Cora, are you sure I'm up to this? There are so many other people who could do it. I know this is an important project for us. For the whole county. I don't mind if you'd rather have someone else be in charge. I'm not sure *I* trust me to do it right."

"Jenna." She laid a hand on my shoulder and held my eyes. "You can do this. You're intelligent, competent and capable. I have no doubt that you will make sure everything runs smoothly. If you need any help, of course we'll all be here for you. But there's not a single reason you shouldn't be in charge."

I let those words roll around in my head for the rest of the afternoon, as I went about my regular office chores, answering email, routing calls and talking with my co-workers. Everything was fairly casual and laid-back at the historical society. I remembered when I'd first started volunteering here, right after I'd come back to Burton. I'd expected to find a group of elderly ladies, fussing about genealogies and planning ceremonies at the local cemeteries. But that couldn't have been farther from the truth. Although there were assigned positions within the small organization, everyone worked together, and I'd never been told that something wasn't my job. Quite the contrary. I'd been encouraged to try new tasks and take on bigger responsibilities, especially once I'd been officially hired.

We closed at four every afternoon, mostly because a high percentage of our staff were senior citizens and preferred to eat their dinners earlier. I locked up the back door of the small cottage that served as our office and made my way down the sidewalk, across the street and around the block on autopilot, turning in at the propped-open entry to Sweetness and Bites.

The bakery had been my favorite refuge since I was a kid. I'd found it completely by accident when I was in fourth grade and mad at my sister Christy. My mom had insisted she take me along to the library—where Christy had secret plans to meet the boy she'd been crushing on for months. My sister wasn't stupid enough to deliberately disobey our mother, who could be kind of scary sometimes, but she hadn't hesitated to grump at me all the way from our house as we walked through town.

Finally, a few blocks from the library, I'd stomped my foot and refused to go any further with her. Christy had thrown up her hands and turned to me.

"Fine. Fine! If you're going to be such a huge crybaby, you can just stay right here." Her gaze had lifted to the sign behind me. "Right here at this bakery."

Before I could respond, she'd steered me into the small shop, where the most delicious aromas I'd ever smelled surrounded me. Standing just behind the glass counter, a woman with long black hair and wire-rimmed glasses regarded me with a warm smile.

"You look like you need a chocolate chip cookie and a big glass of milk," she'd said, and that was how I met Kiki Payton, owner of Sweetness and Bites. She'd let me hang out at one of the small tables in her shop until Christy came back for me, flushed and apologetic, and in a very good mood. Since Kiki had talked with me about sisters and young love, I was ready to make up, too, and after that day, Kiki's bakery became my go-to spot when I needed a break from being the baby of the Sutton girls.

Of course, on the worst day of my life, when hope had been extinct and despair had gripped me with vicious talons, I hadn't turned to Kiki. Facing her had felt impossible, and I knew that we'd both struggled with my failure there. For several months, I hadn't seen my friend, and by the time I'd worked up the courage to go back, she'd been away, gone on tour with her hot new boyfriend, who just happened to be country music's newest star, Troy Beck. Since her return a few months ago, we'd fallen back into our old routines, even though neither of us ever mentioned what had happened on that horrible day in March two years ago.

"Jenna Sutton." Kiki greeted me the way she always did. "What's shakin', bacon? How're you doing?"

I dropped onto one of the ridiculously narrow chairs that flanked the café tables. "Oh, you know me. Peachy with a side of keen."

"Now isn't it peculiar that you'd use that particular phrase?" Kiki's mouth curved into a half-smile. "Look what I put aside for you about ten minutes ago." She bent to reach into the back of the display case and handed me a small white plate.

I laughed when I took the pastry out of her hand and got a whiff of it. "Peach. Of course." Picking up a fork, I scooped a bite toward my mouth. "Mmmmm. Delicious, as always."

"Coffee today or tea? Or would you rather have something cold? Sure is hot out there."

"Whatever you have is fine." I never hesitated to put my choices wholly in Kiki's hands, since she usually knew what I wanted before I did.

She cocked her head, studying me. "Iced green tea, I think. It'll go down nicely with that pastry."

"That works." I watched Kiki pour the tea over ice in a tall glass and then added a sprig of mint from the plant on the windowsill.

"So something good happened today." She came around the counter to set down my drink and took the chair across from mine. "Tell me about it."

"How do you do that?" I sipped the tea and smiled. "And this is amazing. Thank you."

"Of course." She waved her hand. "And you know me. I'm just a little extra perceptive, particularly when it comes to my favorite people. Now spill."

Popping a bite of peachy yumminess into my mouth, I chewed and swallowed quickly. "I wrote up a proposal last month for the historical society to take over and restore Oak Grove Plantation. Usually, these things take a long time to

40

be approved, if they ever are. I mean, we write these kind of proposals all the time, and just a small percentage get the go ahead. But we got word today that this one was already approved. And Cora is putting me in charge of it."

"No shit?" Kiki's eyes sparkled as she grinned. "Jenna, that's wonderful! You must be so excited."

I shrugged. "I guess."

"Oak Grove Plantation. That place has been a dilapidated mess as long as I've known it. I used to go parking out there."

"Yeah, I've heard—" I paused, narrowing my eyes. "Wait a minute. You didn't live here when you were a teenager. You moved to Burton when you were in your twenties."

Kiki tilted her head, mischief dancing on her face. "And your point is?"

I rolled my eyes. "Not a thing. I'm just thinking maybe you had a better adolescence than I did, even if it was when you were closer to thirty."

"Sweetie pie, adolescence had nothing to do with it. The idea that only the young can have fun is idiotic, and I'm living proof."

"Yeah, I know. If you and Troy were having any more fun, it might be illegal."

"It's true. I've never been happier in my life. The other night, when I went upstairs after I'd closed the shop down here, Troy had made me dinner. He had the table all set, and the main course was . . . ah, well, let's just say he was holding the serving platter just about here—"

"Whoa, whoa, whoa! Enough." I clapped my hands over my ears. "Seriously, Kiki. I know I'm supposed to be all grown up now, but I still see you as the adult in this friendship."

She laughed. "What I was about to describe was most definitely adult."

I pushed away my plate. "Aaaand that's it for my appetite."

"Oh, don't be silly." Kiki nudged the pastry back toward me. "Eat up. You need those calories, honey, you've looked a little skinny lately."

"Thanks for that confidence builder." Still, I took another bite and savored the flaky dough as well as the mix of tart and sweet on my tongue. Say what I might about Kiki's judgement, but the woman had a gift when it came to baking.

"You don't need any confidence building. You are a strong and fabulous woman. Now tell me more about this project of yours. Are you excited?"

I hesitated. "A little. Well, at first, I was really pumped. But then I started thinking of all the things that could go wrong. I don't have any experience with heading up a job this size. I don't have any experience with heading up anything bigger than a tea party."

"Bull." Kiki crossed her arms over her chest and stared me down. "You've got this, Jenna. Stop second-guessing yourself and just go for it. I know Cora wouldn't give you the chance if she didn't have complete faith in you. And I'm sure everyone at the society will be there to help you out, if you need them."

"I guess." I drew in a deep breath. "It just feels overwhelming. I'm going to be working with a contractor who's new to this area, and that makes me nervous. Everyone in town is going to know about this restoration, and if I screw it up, it won't be any secret that Jenna Sutton fucked up. Again."

"Are you finished?" She pursed her lips. "Because you're wrong, okay? No one is waiting for you to mess up, Jenna. Anyone in Burton who knows you is going to be rooting for you."

I blinked back the unexpected moisture that sprung to my eyes. "Once I would've believed that. Now . . . it doesn't feel that way."

Kiki leaned toward me, her forehead drawn in worry as she laid a hand on my arm. "Jenna, what happened with—"

The bell over the door rang, and we both turned. A girl stood in the entrance to the bakery, one foot inside and one out, as though she was ready to make a run for it if the interior of the store didn't live up to the sign. She was probably about ten or eleven, I thought, not quite a pre-teen. Brown hair hung in a single braid down her back, and big brown eyes widened in near-panic when she spotted Kiki and me sitting at the table.

"I'm sorry." She held out one hand. "I didn't mean to interrupt. I thought this was—" She craned her neck back to look at the door again, checking the sign which was turned to OPEN. "I didn't know you were, um, having a meeting."

"Darling girl, come right in." Kiki jumped to her feet and walked toward the girl, arms outstretched. "Don't be silly. You didn't interrupt anything. Please, come in."

The girl took one tentative step, glancing at me. "Are you sure?"

"Of course I am. I'm Kiki, and I own this lovely establishment. And you are so very welcome here." In one smooth move, Kiki folded the new arrival into a quick hug and then stood back, beaming. "You're new to town, aren't you?"

"Yeah—yes, ma'am. We just moved here last week." Her gaze darted around the shop, and I couldn't miss the spark of delight when she spied the goodies in the glass-fronted case.

Apparently Kiki hadn't missed either. She steered her young customer inside and pointed to the chair she herself had just vacated. "Sit down. I'm going to bring you something delicious and perfect." As she passed me on her way to the back, she patted my shoulder and added, "Jenna, introduce yourself and get to know our new friend."

Before, which was how I termed my life prior to March two years ago, I used to babysit regularly. I spent hours entertaining little kids, playing with my cousin Rilla's children and keeping my charges safe and happy. But it had been a long time since I'd had any real interaction with kids, and I couldn't quite remember how to talk to a girl who was this age.

"I'm Jenna. Jenna Sutton." I held out a hand, because it seemed like the right thing to do.

She stared at my outstretched fingers for a minute before she took them, gingerly, and she gave me a little squeeze. "Becca Turner."

"Hello, Becca Turner." I tried on a smile. "Where did you move here from?"

"Uh, Texas. Canton, Texas."

I nodded. "I've never been to Texas. I guess it's a lot

different from here, though."

"Yeah. I think it is. But I don't know. I haven't seen too much, since we've only been here a little while. We drove up here from Florida, so I mostly saw highways and trees."

"I was born here, and I've lived here all my life. I've been to Florida and to South Carolina, but never as far away as Texas. You're lucky that you've gotten to travel." I took a swig of tea. "Do you have family around here?"

She shook her head. "No. My dad's job is here, so that's why we moved."

"Really? What does he . . ." Suddenly something clicked in my brain. "Did you say your last name is Turner?"

Becca nodded. "Uh-huh. He works with old houses. My father does, I mean. He and Uncle Ryland have a company, and they make old broken-down buildings look like new."

"Yeah, I thought so." Coincidence was a crazy thing. "I actually just heard of their company today."

"Well, isn't that funny?" Kiki emerged from the back, carrying a large rectangular plate, piled high with cookies. "That's the beauty of a small town, isn't it, Jenna? You just never know who you're going to end up connected to." She set down the plate. "Here you go, darling. I made you up an assortment plate." She pulled over another chair and flipped it around so that she was leaning her chin in her hands on the twisted metal of the chair back. "I'm especially anxious for you to try the chocolate coconut almond cookie. That's a new recipe."

Becca lifted the small round brown cookie. "Almonds? And coconut?"

"Yes." Kiki cocked her head. "You're not allergic, are

you? I wouldn't want to give you anything that puts you at risk."

"No." The girl shook her head. "No, it's just that . . . my mom used to make this kind of cookie. She, um . . . she died when I was only six. These are one of the only things I remember really well, that she cooked, I mean." Her thin lips pinched together, and I saw her throat work as she swallowed. "Gramma tried to make them, but she could never get them right. Her cookies never tasted like my mom's did."

Kiki reached across and brushed a strand of hair away from Becca's face. "Well, at least she tried, right? And you should taste this one. Maybe it's not the same either."

Becca took a bite, and I felt like I was holding my breath along with Kiki until the girl nodded. A single tear rolled down her cheek. "That's it. That's exactly it. How did you do it? How did you know?"

"I didn't." Kiki covered Becca's hand with her own. "Sometimes things just happen that way. This morning I had a nudge to bake this particular cookie—I'd seen the recipe in an old cookbook, months ago. And when you came in, I had a hunch it was for you. I'm glad it worked out."

I forced a laugh, even though chills were running down my spine. No matter how often I'd experienced Kiki's odd sense of knowing, it never failed to freak me out just a little. "Kiki's nudges and hunches are old news to those of us who've known her forever. Don't worry, kiddo. She only uses her powers for the positive, never evil." I grinned, hoping to lighten the moment.

"It's so good." Becca swiped her fingers over her cheek and sniffled a little. "Thank you."

"You're very welcome." Kiki sat back, studying both Becca and me, her eyes narrowing a little. "So, Becca. Tell me a little about yourself. How old are you? And do you have any brothers or sisters?"

"Twelve, and one brother. His name is Oliver, but we all call him Ollie. He's a dweeb."

Kiki laughed. "I've been given to understand that all little brothers are. I only had a little sister, so I can't speak from experience, and Jenna here's the youngest of four girls, so she doesn't know, either."

"He likes bugs and snakes and the twelfth Doctor. I hate anything creepy-crawly and snakes freak me out."

"And which Doctor?" Kiki leaned forward, expectant.

"The tenth one. Of course."

"Whew!" The older woman clapped a hand over her heart. "That's a relief. We can be friends now that we know we agree on the important things in life." She lowered her voice. "Jenna here—she's not a Doctor Who fan. Can you imagine? Sydney and I—Sydney's my niece, she runs the catering place next door—we tried to get Jenna to watch the show with us, and she didn't get past two episodes."

I shook my head. "True story. I'm not much for crazy screwdrivers and alien invasions, I guess."

"What *do* you like?" Becca rested her cheek in one small palm.

"Oh . . ." It had been a long time since I'd had to think about the answer to that question. "Um, I like to read. And I love superhero movies. You know, like *The Avengers* and *Thor*?"

"Yeah, my Aunt Abby likes Thor, too. I don't know why,

though. He seems big and stupid to me."

I smirked a little. "Give it a year or two, kiddo, and I bet you'll start to see it."

"Jenna likes to dance, too," Kiki put in. "She took lessons growing up."

"I took ballet for a year in Canton, but I didn't like it that much. But I like to watch people dance. One time my grandparents took us to see *Sleeping Beauty,* and it was so cool."

"We went to *The Nutcracker* in Savannah when I was ten." I sighed, remembering. "I thought it was the most beautiful thing I'd ever seen. But I knew I didn't have that kind of discipline. I liked modern dance more, for myself."

"You could've done anything you wanted, Jenna. Don't sell yourself short." Kiki helped herself to a sugar cookie from the plate. "Becca, believe it or not, I've known this chick here since she was about your age. I'm sure you find it hard to accept that I could be that old, but it's the truth. She came in here one day when she was fighting with her sister, and I fed her a chocolate chip cookie."

"And I was hooked." I finished my peach Danish and took a final drink of tea. "She couldn't get rid of me after that."

"Never wanted to." Kiki's tone held more meaning than her words did. "Not once, in all those years."

There was an awkward moment of silence, and then I stood up, pushing back my chair. "Well, I should go. I have a lot to do tonight." The lie tasted bitter on my tongue, and I wondered if Kiki suspected how empty my evenings really were. "Kiki, thanks for the pastry and the tea. I'll probably be in later this week. Becca, it was nice to meet you. Good luck in Burton." I paused before adding, "I'm sure we'll run into each other again soon. Small town, you know."

"Don't worry, Becca's going to be a regular here. I'm sure of it." Kiki beamed at the younger girl.

"There are worse places she could hang out." I hoped my friend understood what I was saying, even though I couldn't quite muster up the words. "Bye, y'all."

I stepped outside into the June heat and turned back toward the Bryan County Historical Society where my car was still parked. Somehow, despite my visit with Kiki and meeting Becca, I felt more alone and isolated than ever.

For the last year or so, being alone had been a relief. I felt safe and in control; moving to my own small apartment from my parents' house hadn't been easy, but I'd quickly realized how much I liked being able to relax. With my mom and dad, my every move made them anxious. They'd greeted me each night with questions designed to sound casual, although if I answered the wrong way, I'd catch them glancing at each other over my head, telegraphing questions or worry. It made me want to scream.

I knew that having me living on my own caused them stress, but it allowed me to let down my guard every evening. It gave me the freedom to stop putting on a happy face. I did my daughterly duty and called or texted to reassure them that I was alive and well. I ate dinner with them once a week. I commented on my sisters' posts on social media and responded when they sent cute pictures of their kids or cats.

For the last year, maintaining status quo had been enough. It had been all I'd been capable of doing. But as the bright midday sun began to give way to the dimming light of dusk, I somehow felt a twinge of regret and the unsettled feeling of missing something vital.

What that was, however, I couldn't—or wouldn't—have said.

With a sigh, I climbed into my car and drove home, by myself.

CHAPTER THREE

Lincoln

"OLLIE, GET A MOVE ON." I stood just inside the front door of our house, my arms crossed over my chest. "I don't want to be late for this meeting."

"Daddy, I can't find my other sneaker!" Frustration filled my son's voice. "I think Becca hid it."

"I did not. You never put anything away. You leave your stuff out all over the house, which is why we're always looking for it at the last minute." Becca stomped down the steps, a scowl on her face. She wore a pair of denim shorts that came nearly to her knees and a sleeveless cotton blouse with its tail knotted at her waist. Pristine white Keds completed her outfit, and her hair was in its perpetual neat braid. I thought briefly of other girls her age I'd seen around town, dressed in cut-offs and T-shirts with dirty sneakers or flip-flops, and hair escaping from sloppy ponytails. I knew I should've been grateful, and maybe a little smug, that my daughter resembled a throwback to the 1950's, but instead, I wished she might've veered a little more toward her own decade.

Summers were meant to be carefree months of running wild, of playing in sprinklers or pools or creeks, coming home with mud-caked feet and filthy hands. At least, that had been my own experience, and it was what I wanted for my kids. Ollie was cheerfully embracing that life, but Becca clung stubbornly to the standards her grandmother had instilled over the past six years. Even now, she stood in front of me, twisting her fingers as we waited for her brother.

"He hasn't unpacked his room yet, you know." She spoke to me in a furious whisper. "I told him I'd help. I offered to even *do* it for him. But he said he didn't want me touching his stuff, and then he tried to slam the door in my face, only he couldn't, because there was too much of that precious stuff on the floor."

I sighed and rubbed my forehead. The reality was that the whole house was still in a state of chaos. I'd had great intentions of getting all the boxes unpacked and put away before I launched into this project, but . . . yeah, that hadn't exactly happened. It shouldn't have been that difficult. After all, I'd sold just about everything after Sylvia's death; the kids' stuff had gone with them to my in-laws' house, and I'd traveled the last six years with just clothes and personal effects. I'd kept a few boxes in Sylvia's parents' basement, things from Becca and Oliver's babyhoods that Syl had saved. But everything else, I'd sold or given away.

When I'd taken the kids back and bought this house,

Abby had insisted on putting together what she called essentials. She'd called Sylvia's mom and talked to the kids, determining what kind of furniture they needed, and then she'd used her contacts in the hospitality industry, the same people who helped her furnish hotels, to set us up with beds, dressers and assorted other sundry bedroom items. She'd also furnished my bedroom from afar, promising me that she'd keep it all simple and manly. And of course, Abby had also convinced me that the kids and I needed a couch and chairs for our living room and a table for the kitchen.

Her housewarming gift to us was everything else for the kitchen: pots and pans and plates and glasses, silverware and tea towels. When I'd protested to Ryland, he'd simply shaken his head.

"Linc, buddy, I learned a long time ago that when my wife makes up her mind, it's best for me to just get out of her way or lend a hand." He'd laid a hand on my shoulder, squeezing. "Abby's so happy for you and the kids, being back together and starting a new life. She wants to celebrate that, and this is how she wants to do it. So do me a favor, and just say thank you."

I was truly grateful. I couldn't imagine trying to make a home out of empty rooms, now that we were here. But I was also overwhelmed. I'd never had to do this part of a move before; Sylvia had always handled unpacking and setting up while I went on with the business of my job. She'd made it look easy, and now I wondered how she'd done that, particularly after the kids had been born.

The only room that was already set up and perfect was, of course, Becca's. She'd worked long and hard to put her books on the shelves, her clothes in the dresser drawers and every little knick-knack she'd brought from her grandparents' house placed in just the right spot. The boxes from her room were broken down and stacked on the back porch.

I'd managed to set up my bed and put sheets on it, but the comforter Abby had sent was still in its plastic bag. My clothes were in the duffel bag on the floor. I had a path that led from the door to the bed, but that was about it. I'd worked a little in the kitchen, a little in the living room and a little more in the garage, where my tools were set up. But I hadn't spent enough time in any one room, clearly, and today I was starting work again. Or at least I was having a meeting, which was going to lead to the start of work.

Which reminded me . . . "Oliver! Get your butt in gear. We need to leave five minutes ago. Just grab whatever shoes you can find."

"Okay, okay." My son appeared at the top of the steps and stumbled down, holding one sneaker and one . . . was that a soccer cleat? I rolled my eyes, but before I could send him back to his room, his expression brightened.

"I see my other sneaker. It was right behind you the whole time, Dad." Ollie jumped the last few steps and landed at my feet, where he stretched to grab the lost shoe where it had been hidden under some brown wrapping paper. Opening the door, I pointed outside, shaking my head as both kids meandered to the truck.

"Where are we going again?" Ollie's voice was muffled as he bent over to tie his sneakers.

"I'm going to a meeting at the site of my new project. You and Bec are going to hang out with a couple of friends of mine, at their farm."

"You know people here? I thought you'd never been to Burton until we moved." Becca sounded vaguely accusatory. Sometimes it felt as though she was always trying to catch me in telling her a lie, in misleading her on purpose. I tried not to believe that my mother-in-law might have said things to my kids . . . things they didn't need to know . . . but sometimes I wondered.

"I don't know them well," I admitted. "Do you remember The Rip Tide, that restaurant on the beach in Crystal Cove, where you guys had hamburgers?"

"Yeah, those were awesome." Ollie wasn't a boy to ever forget food.

"We met the owner that day—Jude. Her daughter Meghan lives here in Burton, on a farm. Meghan helped me find our house here."

"Did you ever meet her in person?" Becca frowned.

"Ah, once, when she and her husband were visiting the Cove, and I was there to see Uncle Ry."

"Oh. She has a husband?" Becca perked up a little. "Does she have any kids?"

"Yep, she has a husband. His name's Sam, and he's a farmer. The place they live has been in his family for generations. No kids for them, but they own a farm stand, too, and Sam's sister helps run that. She has two kids."

"Do they have, like, animals on the farm? Horses and cows and stuff?" Ollie leaned forward from the backseat.

"Sit back, please." I glanced at him in the rearview mirror. "No animals, I don't think. But probably a lot of fun stuff to run around and climb on, if they say you can. Maybe you can go up in the loft of the barn and jump down into the hay." I had memories of doing that at my great-uncle's place when I was growing up. "Oh, and I think there's a lake or a river nearby, so maybe you could go down and play there. Go fishing or something like that. Catch frogs."

"Are there snakes?" Becca's tone sharpened with worry. "Because we shouldn't go near the water if there might be snakes. There are six different poisonous snakes in Georgia. There're three types of rattlesnakes: the Eastern Diamondback, the Timber and the Pigmy. And then there's the Eastern Coral Snake, the water moccasin and the Southern Copperhead."

"Good God, Becca. How in the world do you know that?" I tried not to be irritated that she'd made it a point to be familiar with six ways to die from snakes in Georgia.

"I looked it up. You're going to be out at that old house, and there could be snakes everywhere." She sounded slightly hysterical. "If there's a creek, there're probably water moccasins. And Aunt Abby told me they're worse than alligators. When we were in Florida, she told me gators mostly want to leave people alone, but moccasins are vicious and will actually try to bite you."

"I want to catch one." Ollie, being the consummate little brother, knew exactly what to say to get the biggest rise out of his sister. "Dad, if I catch one, can we put it in a terrarium at home? I'd keep it in my room, and I'd feed it mice and stuff."

"Daddy!" Becca's shriek nearly deafened me. "Daddy, tell Ollie he can't go down to the water while you're not there. He can't catch a snake, and if he brings one into the house, I'm moving out."

I counted to ten under my breath. "Oliver, don't torture your sister, okay? You know snakes scare her."

"Yeah, just like everything else in the world." Ollie mumbled the words, but I knew by the way her back stiffened that Becca had heard him.

"I'm not scared of everything. I'm cautious about stuff that I know is dangerous. Stuff that could make you sick or kill you." She sniffed. "Like snakes. If you get bit, Ollie, I swear I'm not going to cut open the bite marks and suck out the venom. And so you'll just swell right up and die. And I'll take all your Pokemon cards and sell them on the Internet and get lots of money."

"Dad wouldn't ever let you do that. Would you, Dad?"

"It's a moot point, buddy, because you're not going to get bitten by a snake and die, okay? I have no time for that. Plus, I need your help setting up the rest of the house. You can't leave me to Becca's mercy. She'll make me stay up until it's all done, and then I'll sleep through work and lose my job."

Becca giggled. "I would, too. I wouldn't let you go to bed until everything was unpacked and all the boxes were gone."

"See that? So if you get near any body of water, just stay away from the snakes. No picking them up to tease Becca— or anyone else." I was a little out of practice being a full-time dad, but some things didn't change, and I knew that my kids took things literally. Ollie might not have disobeyed me to torment his sister, but if someone else was there, I could see him taking advantage of that loophole in my words.

"Daaaad." Oliver groaned, pulling the single syllable out at least three extra beats. "It'll be so boring."

"Hey. I don't want to hear that. When I was growing up, my mom would've washed out my mouth with soap if I'd used the B word. She always told me being bored was the sign of a weak mind." I looked into the mirror again just in time to catch him in something that sent a shot of pure irritation up my spine. "And don't you ever roll your eyes at me, dude. I'm your father, and I deserve your respect. That's just rude."

"*You* do it." He mumbled the talk-back, but I heard it anyway.

"Yeah, well, there're a lot of things I do that you shouldn't. I'm the adult, remember? When you're grown up and on your own, you can roll your eyes, catch snakes and be bored to your heart's content. Until then, it's my way. Got it?"

"Yeah." I felt rather than heard his heavy sigh. It settled deep in my heart, making me second-guess taking the tough-dad stance. Some days I just couldn't figure out which was the right way to be a parent.

I felt the warmth of Becca's hand on my arm. She was reaching across the console to offer me some measure of comfort. "It's okay, Daddy. He gets all grumpy sometimes. Gramma says it's a boy thing."

Chuckling, I patted her hand. "I think you and your gramma may both be right, honey. It's okay. I was a boy, too, a long, long time ago."

We made a turn off the paved road and down a dirt driveway. I slowed the truck as we bumped along, and Becca grabbed for the door handle, her face going pale.

"It's okay, baby girl." I flashed her a smile. "This is just their driveway. See? That's Sam and Meghan's house up ahead."

We slowed to a stop in front of the large white farmhouse just as the front screen door opened. A beautiful tall redhead stepped out with a toddler on her hip and a girl who looked to be about Becca's age following in her wake.

"Hey, there!" Meghan came down the steps to greet us. "Welcome to Burton. Welcome to the Reynolds farm." She gave me a quick one-armed hug.

"Thanks. We're happy to be here." I pointed to my children. "Meghan, this is my daughter Becca and my son Oliver. Kids, this is Mrs. Reynolds."

"Oh, God, no." She looked horrified. "Please. I'm too young to be Mrs. Reynolds. Call me Meghan, or Meg or Meggie, or even hey, you."

Ollie laughed. "My gramma says hey is for horses, and you don't call people that."

"Well, she's probably right, but I'd rather be hey than missus." Meghan smacked a kiss on the cheek of the child in her arms. "So this little gremlin is my niece Colleen, and this . . ." She nodded to the girl standing alongside her. "This is my oldest niece, Bridget. Bridge, I think you and Becca are going to be in the same grade this year."

If Bridget and Becca had been boys, at that point they would've socked each other on the arm and run off to play ball or something. But since they were both female, they stood where they were, nodding and looking uncomfortable.

"Thanks for letting them hang out here today. I haven't quite worked out the logistics of working and parenting here yet."

Meghan waved her hand. "Don't even mention it. I'm happy to help out whenever I can. I work at the elementary school in town, so if you ever need a hand in getting the kids home, I don't mind dropping them off on my way."

Part of a weight lifted from my shoulders. "Really? Aw, you don't know how much that means to me. Thanks."

"Burton's all about community and helping each other out." She hesitated before going on. "It's not perfect, for sure. And living in a small town takes some getting used to. Growing up in the Cove, it felt almost like coming home to me when I moved here. But people are going to be nosy, and you're going to get to a point where you wish they'd butt out. Just try to remember most of them mean well."

"I'll try to keep that in mind." I swatted Oliver on the backside and leaned in to kiss Becca's cheek. "You two be good, you hear? Listen to Meghan. Don't give her any trouble."

"They won't. Go on and do what you need to, and don't hurry back."

Bridget took one step toward my kids. "If you want, we can cut through by my house and go see the horses over at Mr. Nelson's farm. There's a little stream we need to cross, but it's fun."

"Okay." Ollie was ready to follow her anywhere at the mention of horses. Becca hung back, no big surprise; she glanced first at Meghan and then at me.

"Maybe I should stay here and help with the baby."

I started to speak up, but Meghan cut me a quelling look. "Well, sure, Becca, you're welcome to stay here with Colleen and me, but I'm actually just about to put her down for a nap. So you might get bored, just sitting around while I do that. And I can tell you, it would be a lot more fun to explore the farm and check out the horses."

"But isn't it kind of . . . dangerous to go off on our own? Without a grown up, I mean?" Becca twisted a strand of her hair around one finger, her face troubled.

Meghan laughed. "No, honey, there's nothing danger-ous out there, I promise. The worst that might happen is you'd fall into the stream and get wet, but it's shallow all the way across, especially this time of year. And Fred's horses are so gentle and kind . . . they wouldn't harm a fly. You should go and have fun."

Becca still wasn't convinced. Then Bridget spoke again. "We could stop in at the farm stand, too, and see my mom. She'll probably give us something to eat."

I saw the way my daughter's eyes lit up. Horses, streams, farms . . . they all might be fun, but moms trumped every-thing. I felt that same sense of heaviness that I had just a little earlier. There was a lot I could do for my daughter, but bringing back the mother she still missed so desperately wasn't one of them.

"It's okay, Daddy?" Becca needed just one more push of reassurance.

"Of course it is. Go. I want a full report when I get back."

"All right!" She turned, and as kids did, the three of them sprinted across the driveway, heading for the back of the house. I stood still until they were out of my view, with nothing left but a cloud of dust and the echoes of their laughter.

Next to me, Meghan sighed and shifted the baby. "She's struggling, isn't she?"

I nodded. "Yeah, seems like. I keep thinking it's just going to take time, but I wonder if there's something else I should be doing. Should I push her, or let this just run its course? Do I get mad, or try to stay patient? I wish there were an easy answer somewhere."

"I think you just sang the anthem of parents everywhere." Meghan grinned wryly. "I don't have any experience to speak from, but I hear what my friends say. And Ali and Rilla are always second-guessing themselves. My brother and his wife Lindsay are the same way. I'm pretty sure you just have to play it by ear and ride it out."

"Those are mixed-up metaphors there." I ran one hand through my hair. "Thanks for the thought, though. And again, for keeping the kids."

"No problem. Good luck this afternoon." Meghan tugged down the baby's shirt over the tot's round stomach, smiling when the little one rubbed at her eyes. "You're meeting with Jenna, right?"

"Yeah. Guess it would be silly of me to ask if you know her."

She raised one eyebrow. "Of course I know her. Actually, Jenna's dad was one of the first people I got to know here in Burton. He's the town mechanic, and he fixed my car when it broke down." Her smile grew bigger, and her eyes twinkled. "When I left his shop the day I met him, I swore I'd never set foot back in this backwater town again. And now look at me."

"Town got to you, huh?"

"More like Sam got to me. I love Burton, don't get me wrong, but I'd live wherever Sam wanted, just to be with him."

I remembered that feeling. I knew what it was like to love someone so much that where we lived didn't matter. But sometimes remembering was too painful, when all I had left was that memory. Pushing away the hurt, I changed the subject back to my meeting.

"So this Jenna—what's she like? Tough? Does she know what she's doing, with this job?"

Meghan tilted her head to one side. "Tough? Ummm . . . in a way, yes. Jenna's the youngest of Boomer and Millie's four girls, and where some kids in that position would be spoiled, I get the feeling Jenna had to up her game so she wasn't left behind. When I first knew her, she was just a kid, really spunky, but kind of scattered." She paused. "She's had sort of a rough couple of years since, though, and she's done a lot of growing up. Now she's very serious. Focused. I hear she's doing good things at the historical society, and I'm sure they wouldn't have put her in charge of this project if there was any doubt about that. Just . . . I don't know. Give her a chance, okay?"

I held up both hands. "Hey, I'm not planning to go in there and mow the girl down. I don't know what you've heard about me, but I'm basically a teddy bear."

"Ha!" Meghan shot me a skeptical smirk. "That's not what I hear. You might be surprised to know that the lines between Crystal Cove and Burton buzz pretty frequently.

Between my mom talking to me, and now that Alex and Cal are living down there, I get word from them, too. Alex is pretty close friends with Abby and Ryland. I know this job is important to you, being the first one for your company in its new format. I'm just saying, remember this is Jenna's first time in charge, too."

I decided it wasn't worth it to argue the point anymore, so I only nodded and opened the door to my truck. "I'll keep that in mind. I have my phone if you need anything, and I hope I won't be more than a couple of hours. Text me or call if anything comes up."

Oak Grove Planation was only about a ten-minute drive from Sam and Meghan Reynolds' farm. I found the turn-off without any difficulty, thanks to the GPS feature on my phone, but if I'd thought that the Reynolds' driveway was a little bumpy, this one threatened to give me whiplash and a concussion. My head hit the roof of the cab more than once.

The damn poor excuse for a road twisted through overgrown trees and bushes, making me wonder what the original approach had been like. Back in the day, when Oak Grove was a showpiece in the neighborhood, it was likely that this had all been open, with a driveway wide enough for carriages and horses to use. Nature had been attempting to reclaim the land for close to sixty years, I knew. Left unchecked, it wouldn't be long before this road would be completely engulfed, indistinguishable from the rest of the forest.

But I was here to make sure that didn't happen. Not

that nature didn't have its place; I respected native flora and fauna, and I'd actually been part of a few side-jobs to reintroduce plant life that had been threatened with extinction. In this case, however, human history took precedence over everything else.

I was just beginning to wonder if I'd missed a turn when a sudden curve opened up the road, and within seconds, a huge white house rose out of the tall weeds. I came to an abrupt halt, just staring at it, taking in the ruined splendor that had once upon a time been a home.

Oak Grove had been built in 1839, with the owners embracing the popular Greek Revival-style of architecture so well-loved in this part of the world in those days. The first thing that struck me as I looked at the house for the first time was the absolute symmetry of it: the windows were perfectly spaced, and the double glass door was in dead center, between the middle two Doric columns. A balcony nestled between the wide lower porch and the gabled roof, and two smaller matching wings flanked the main body.

I thought for a moment that if I blinked, I might catch the house flickering between its current dilapidation and past glory. I could almost see it, the gleaming carriages pulling up to the porch, where women in wide-skirted gowns were handed out by waiting gentlemen. I could hear the music, the voices and smell the cooking food . . .

Caught up in something that was half-vision, half-daydream, I jerked in surprise when a slim, dark-haired figure walked across the porch. I knew almost immediately that she must be Jenna Sutton, here to meet with me, but her sudden appearance was so unexpected that my heart pounded.

I coughed a little to cover my discomfort and then eased the truck a bit closer to the house before I turned it off and climbed out.

"Mr. Turner?" Her voice was clear and calm, carrying across the space between us. There was no mistaking the Georgia in those words, the softening of the vowels that always cried South to me. I took a few steps closer and lifted my hand to wave.

"Yes, I'm Lincoln Turner. You must be Ms. Sutton." I risked standing on the bottom step and extended my hand. "Pleasure to meet you. I'm looking forward to us working together."

Jenna slid off the dark sunglasses that shaded her eyes and regarded me for a minute, as though making up her mind whether or not I was safe to touch. For a flash of time, she reminded me uncannily of Becca; her face wore the same expression of uncertainty and trepidation.

And then she slid her hand into mine, holding it firmly as we shook. Now that we stood nearer to each other, I could see how young this chick really seemed to be. Her dark hair was drawn away from her face and caught in a low ponytail at the nape of her neck. Wide hazel eyes were checking me out, surreptitiously, of course.

She was shorter than me, but not tiny. Jeans that were still a pretty vivid blue covered long legs, topped by a simple gray shirt with a V-neck. Being that I was a guy, I automatically took note of her rack—hard to tell, as the shirt was kind of loose, but it looked to be decent—and the way her jeans hugged the curve of her ass, which wasn't bad at all. She wore cowboy boots with a low stacked heel, and I could tell by their wear that they weren't just for show.

Releasing my hand, she took a step back, replaced her glasses and stood with her hands on her hips. "I'm looking forward to it, too. I know I should be cool and keep it business-like, but I have to tell you, I'm really excited about this project." She turned her head to glance up at the house. "She's a beauty, isn't she?"

I had to laugh, which made Jenna swing her gaze back to me. I couldn't tell for sure since she had her eyes covered with the sunglasses, but by the stiffening of her body and set of her mouth, I realized she probably thought I was laughing at *her*, at her enthusiasm. Nothing could've been further from the truth.

"Sorry. I'm actually pretty amped about it, too. I only laughed because my partner Ryland—he's the Kent in Kent and Turner—that's how he starts every new job, by saying exactly what you just did. At least, that's what he does with the good ones. He goes to see them before I do, usually, and by the time I get there, he's fallen half-way in love. I've always had to be the one to come along and point out the issues in his beloved—you know, like cracked foundations and bad roofs. I'm the guy who jerks the needle off the record in the middle of the romantic song, you know? I pour a bucket of cold water over his candlelight dinner."

Her mouth had relaxed as I spoke, and now it curved into a small half-smile. "That's quite a few metaphors there, Mr. Turner. And you don't come off very well in any of them. I'm sure it's not that bad."

I rubbed my jaw. "Oh, you should talk with Ry. Pretty sure it's that bad and worse. But it's always been okay, because that's what you need in any partnership: one person who's a misty-eyed romantic, and one who's a stone-cold realist. I've been happy to play the voice of reason up to now."

She cocked her head. "Only up to now? So are you warning me that I should expect raptures of poetry to spout out of your mouth on this project? That might actually work, because if the new partnership is between you and me, I can assure you that I won't be the dewy-eyed romantic. I'm perfectly happy to be that bucket of frigid water. What did you call it? The stone-cold voice of reason. I'm all over that."

Laughing, I shifted my weight, testing the strength of the porch railing before leaning against it carefully. "Oh, sugar, I don't know. You already ruined that image when you told me this house is a beauty."

Jenna straightened, drawing herself up to full height, and I knew I'd stepped onto a landmine. "First of all, calling something what it is doesn't mean I'm caught up in a fantasy. This house *is* a beauty. There's nothing that's up for debate about that. I could go piece by piece, architectural point by point, and prove that without issue. Second, please don't call me 'sugar.'" She spit out the word as though it were full of venom. "I'm not some kid who doesn't know what she's doing. And I'm not just a clueless woman you can push around, either. I've done my research, I've run the numbers, and I know what we can and cannot do here. I'm perfectly capable—"

"Whoa there." I held up one hand to cut her off. "Whoa there, Ms. Sutton. I'll apologize for calling you sugar—this time. I can't promise it won't happen again, because I do it a lot. It doesn't mean anything. It doesn't mean I think less of you or your abilities or your position in this job. It's just how I am. Calling a woman by a term of endearment isn't a sign of disrespect in my book. Sorry if it came across like that. And second—" I raised my voice a little to stave off the interruption I could see was coming. "Second, I didn't say you were caught up in a fantasy. I didn't mean to imply that about Ryland when he calls a building beautiful either. I was trying to say that we complement each other, because if you don't have the love of the structures, the vision to see what they were and what they could be again? You're just going through the motions. You're not going to do anyone any favors by taking a job where you don't feel the passion. It's a balance. Some passion, some realism, and a good healthy dose of hope—you need all that before you take the leap into a project like this."

Jenna nodded slowly. "Okay. I get that. And I'm sorry for flying off the handle. I guess I have a knee-jerk reaction to not being taken seriously by a certain type of man. I apologize if I let my bias show."

"Apology accepted." I craned my neck to look up toward the top of the house. "And just so you know we're both on the same page, I was sitting out there in my truck, right when I turned the curve and saw her for the first time, and to tell you the truth, I was tumbling head over heels in love, just like Ryland does. I've never seen anything like this. I did some finishing work on a couple of planation houses in Alabama and Tennessee, back when I was with my first company, but I've never seen it from the start. Kind of blows my mind that this is sitting out here, about to be absorbed by the trees, and no one's done anything about it for so long."

"Yes." This time, Jenna's intensity was more passion than pissiness. "I know. I mean, I've lived in Burton my whole life. I knew Oak Grove was out here, but it was kind of like the church or the school or something else that was just there. I'm sure you've read the history, but the owners wouldn't do anything to bring her back and wouldn't sell so someone else could. I didn't think about it at the time, but it's kind of maddening now. Why would you let this precious piece of history go to ruin, when there are other people willing to take it off your hands?"

I shrugged. "People are funny about some things. What's important is that we can put a stop to the ruin now. I looked at the structural reports you had done, and they seem promising. A lot of weather-related wear and tear, sure, and just typical aging of a house that hasn't been touched for over seventy years. But it doesn't sound like anyone came in and did intentional damage, and the good news is that there were no previous attempts at renovation. We don't have to undo someone else's mistakes."

"Exactly. Cora—she's my boss at the historical society— she's told me horror stories about owners who didn't realize they were living in a historical house, who took down walls and tore up flooring, all in the name of modernization. Then we have to go in and try to recreate something that was, instead of just saving it."

"I've been there, too. It's a sad thing." I let my eyes wander over the side of the house, caught sight of something I hadn't noticed before and straightened to stand again. "But here—hey, is that the original stone on the fireplace chimney? Fuck me." I glanced behind me. "Sorry. On the job, I kind of tend to have a gutter mouth. This is going to sound sexist, but we don't have too many women on projects, and so I let the man thing take over. It can get bad."

"You don't have to apologize, Mr. Turner. I've heard the word fuck before." She sounded slightly amused.

"Well, then, I take back my sorry. And one more thing. I'm Lincoln, or even better, Linc. Mr. Turner makes me feel like I'm about to be called down to the principal's office."

"Duly noted." She hesitated, and I sensed she was wrestling with something. "And I'm Jenna. If we're going to be working closely together, it doesn't make sense to stand on formality, does it?"

"Nope." I hooked my thumbs in my belt loops. "So Jenna. According to the report, the lower level of the house is safe enough for us to walk through. I have a couple of hardhats in my truck, just in case and because this is now an active job site. Care to give me the tour?"

She grinned broadly, and for the first time, I thought I might be getting a glimpse of the real Jenna Sutton. "Definitely. Let's grab the hats, and I'll lead the way."

CHAPTER FOUR

Jenna

"SO, WHAT DO YOU THINK?" I stopped just inside the front door, which Linc had propped open with a stick from the yard. It was sweltering in the house, even just on the first floor; I could feel waves of even hotter air rolling down the stairway from the second level.

Linc must've felt them, too. He ran one large hand over his face, wiping off the sweat that had beaded there. I'd been watching him sideways all along our short tour, taking in his broad shoulders, smooth movements and even the easy way he had of talking. I was trying *not* to see how snugly his jeans fit what looked to be a killer ass or how the muscles flexed in his huge arms. At the same time, I kept waiting for panic to set in; I'd been jittery for days before this meeting, nervous about having to interact with a stranger. To my surprise, I'd felt relaxed almost from the minute he'd grasped my hand in greeting. It turned out that Lincoln Turner wasn't the intimidating contractor I'd expected.

"Well, the first thing I think is how much Ryland is going to hate that I'm doing this job and he isn't." A wicked grin spread over his mouth. "Matter of fact, I just might have to call him on the way home and rub it in."

I couldn't help laughing at his obvious glee. "That doesn't seem very nice. Won't he be coming up here, too? Or does he have another building he's working on right now?"

"Oh, I'm sure he'll wander up, maybe a little later in the summer. Right now, he and his wife are moving into a new house, so they've got their hands full. Plus, I think he wants to give me the space to handle this one on my own. It's kind of our new paradigm. Used to be, he started the jobs and then I came in with my team to do the finishing. This is the first one I'm overseeing from beginning to end on my own. Ry's working on some smaller jobs down around his area, and he's handling all the administrative shit that comes with transitioning a new company."

"Ah." I nodded. "I'm glad you said that, about this being your first solo job. It's the first project I'm running, too. I guess we can make our mistakes together."

Something I didn't quite recognize gleamed in Linc's eyes. "When it comes to first times, I'm not sure whether it's better that both parties are virgins, or if one of them should have some experience." He waited a beat before adding, "Building virgins, I mean, of course. In this case, I think we'll be okay, since even though I've never run the whole show, at least I've handled the last phase myself."

My face grew even warmer than it had been, and I was

positive my cheeks had gone red. *Nice.* Way to look sophisticated and worldly. I should've ignored his innuendo—if in fact that was what it was—and gone on with our discussion as though he hadn't mentioned virgins and first times. But instead, I heard myself speaking, an unfamiliar tone in my voice and no clear idea of what I was about to say.

"Is that the best part, do you think? The end? I mean, you get to miss out on most of the grunge work, right? The dirty stuff? By the time you'd take over, it would just be making it all pretty and shiny, I'd think. Bringing it to a happy ending." I mimicked his pause for effect. "You know, the fun stuff."

Linc narrowed his eyes at me. "I'm not sure whether you were teasing me or shooting me down just now. I'm going to assume you wouldn't question my ability to handle a job from beginning to end and just say . . . yeah. You're right, most of the nasty work was finished before my team got there, but don't think just because something's pretty that it isn't hard." He seemed to hear his own words as they were coming out of his mouth. "Difficult, I mean. Time-consuming. Requiring attention to the smallest detail . . . aww, shit. There's nothing I'm going to say now that'll redeem me, is there?"

I was laughing so hard that I couldn't speak, and as I held my sides, it occurred to me that I hadn't laughed like this—real, genuine laughter—in so long that I couldn't remember doing it. "Seriously . . . just stop. I can't breathe."

Linc chuckled, too. "Okay, well, the point is that what my team did was just as important as the early work that Ry and his crew accomplished. We put the polish on their efforts."

"I'll concede. You're both wonderful, and you can both go to the prom."

He frowned quizzically. "What's that supposed to mean?"

I flipped over my hand. "Oh, you know. It's just something my mom used to say when my sisters were fussing at each other. 'You're both pretty, and you can both go to the prom.' I must've picked it up from her." I took a deep breath. "So back to business here. I know you probably need some time to write up a report and lay out your plans, but what's your gut reaction, seeing it? What problems do you foresee us running into on this restoration?"

"Our biggest challenge, as it always is in a job like this, is figuring out how to make it functional and up to code without losing the historical integrity." Linc rubbed the rounded top of the newel post that flanked the stairs. "For instance, just standing in here now, we know this place needs climate control. Air conditioning and heating both. But the fact that it's so stinking hot also tells us that it's probably pretty air-tight, which is unusual for a house this old. That's good news—means that it was probably well-built from the beginning."

I turned in a slow circle, letting my eyes wander over the cobweb-covered, dusty walls and windows. "Can you even imagine what it must've been like back then? When it was new? Or even when it was just a little old, in the heyday of the plantations?"

"Yeah. The rooms full of people . . . women in those big dresses, men smoking cigars and talking politics or crops

. . ." His eyes were soft and unfocused, as though he were actually seeing it. He gave his head a little shake and glanced down at me, embarrassed. "I guess I've watched a few too many old movies late at night."

"In our line of work, I can only see that as being a benefit." I hugged my arms around myself. "I can't wait to see it brought back. Knowing I'm going to have a part in that is very gratifying. I can't imagine how you must feel, with all the houses and buildings you've restored."

"Sometimes it's just like that. Other times, when we've had to make concessions to the owners' wants or likes, it can be bittersweet. Like I can see the possibilities, but I couldn't realize them."

"I can see how that would be tough." I touched the decorative molding on the long window next to me. "You won't have to worry about that here, though. We're committed to as high a degree of historical accuracy as possible, just as you are."

"That makes everything much easier," Linc agreed. "It also takes a lot off my plate, because I won't have to handle the heavy-duty research. I already took a look at your preliminary timeline on the house's history, and it's helping me put together our plan."

"I'm glad. I thought once we got a little further along, we could do a room-by-room inventory for things like knobs, handles and built-in furniture. One of our interns is doing research into curtains, rugs and other home furnishings of the period."

"Awesome. Well, I'll get working on my end, and once we have a firm starting date, I'll be in touch. It won't be long." He stepped through the door and out onto the porch.

"Thanks. I appreciate you meeting me out here, too. I thought it was important for us to be on site at the very beginning." Following him outside, I broached the topic I'd been considering since his arrival. "I met your daughter the other day. At the bakery? She's lovely."

"You met Becca?" He cocked his head. "She told her brother and me that she'd found what she called a 'really cool bakery'. She said something about the owner being um, different, but she didn't mention anyone else."

"Oh." I felt a little deflated. "Well, I guess I didn't make a very big impression. Doesn't really surprise me—Kiki's pretty amazing. I don't blame Becca for liking her."

"Hey, just because she didn't tell me about you doesn't me she didn't like you. My daughter . . ." Linc sighed and raked his fingers through his light brown hair. "She's going through a rough patch just now. I made her leave the house that day and go explore the town. I figured she'd end up hiding in the library, so I was pretty psyched when she told me about finding the bakery."

"She was very polite." I tried to think of what to say about Becca's visit to Kiki's without making it sound weird. I had a hunch the little girl hadn't told her father about the cookie incident.

"Yeah, she's polite. She's quiet. She's generally well-behaved. I don't have any complaints about her. But sometimes . . ." Linc's voice trailed off. "Well. You don't want to hear about my family problems."

I wanted to argue with him that I did, in fact, want to hear about his family. It dawned on me that for the first time in ages, I was with someone who didn't know anything about Poor Jenna. He didn't know how I was Before, and although it was likely that he'd eventually hear whispers in town about *what that poor Jenna Sutton's been through*, for now I could tell he was clueless. His manner around me had been too laid-back and easy for him to have known. And it was a relief to think about someone else's problems or worries for once. Not being the center of attention was freeing.

"I don't mind listening. I bet moving to a new town, especially such a small community as Burton, would be tough on a kid her age. And if you ever need to work meetings or anything around your children's schedule, just let me know. I'm pretty flexible."

"Ah." Linc bobbed his head. "I see Becca told you about her mom. So you know I'm a single dad."

My face flamed again. "I'm sorry. I didn't mean to be—to sound intrusive. Or like I was pitying you. Believe me, I wasn't. I just wanted you to know that if something comes up, I'll understand. I can't imagine being a father on your own is easy."

"Not hardly." He stared off into the tangled trees. "And I'm still getting my sea legs, so to speak. I don't know if Becca told you, but she and my son lived with my late wife's parents for the last six years. I've only had them for a few months, so we're still figuring out how that works."

"No, she didn't mention that." I had a sudden and overwhelming compunction to share with this man, this virtual stranger, that I too was still getting used to a new situation. But I knew deep down that it wouldn't sound the same. The kinship I felt with him, the hurting part of me that reached out to the same pain in him, wouldn't be easily translated. And I was so accustomed to being misunderstood that I swallowed back the words . . . again. "Well . . . like I said, just let me know if you need any, uh, help. Or if you need to set up our meetings at a certain time, I can do that."

"Thank you." Linc pulled out his phone and checked the screen. "I better get going now. The kids are over at Meghan and Sam's farm, and God only knows what they've gotten up to."

"Oh, Meghan can handle anything. She's got a way with kids. They have big parties out at the farm now, and it seems like she's always surrounded by the children. She's the art teacher at the elementary school, you know, and she gives private art lessons during the summer."

"Something for me to keep in mind. Might be good for Becca." He moved to the next-lower step and paused. "Well, I'll be in touch once I have everything set up on my end for the initial structure work. Oh, and we're going to have to talk about widening the access road, too. Some of the equipment coming in might not make it through there as it is."

"Hmm. I hadn't thought about that. I'll mention it to Cora and see how they usually handle this kind of thing. I'd figured we'd put off working on the landscaping and grounds until most of the work was finished on the house itself."

"And that makes sense, definitely. Anything you planted now would be at risk for being trampled or crushed. But the driveway's got to be a priority—both cutting back some of that foliage and maybe smoothing out the dirt."

"But not paving it? That wouldn't be historically accurate."

Linc smiled. "No, not paving. Might think about some gravel on it, though. That could be a good compromise."

"I think I can work with that." I stayed where I was, the higher step keeping me closer to being eye-to-eye with Linc. "Can I ask you something real fast? Before you go, I mean."

His forehead creased as his smile faded. "Sure. Lay it on me."

"I told you this is my first time being in charge of a project this big. But I do know that normally, once we've gotten approval from the state, we accept bids on the job from contractors. This time, though, the foundation funding the restoration stipulated to your company being hired. How did that happen?"

"Ah." Linc slid his hands into the back pockets of his jeans, stretching his T-shirt over his chest and making me wonder idly if I could read those muscles with my fingertips, like I used to examine the relief map in grade school.

I gave my head a little shake. *What the hell was wrong with me?* I decided to blame it on the heat and the atmosphere of this old plantation house. With more than a little difficulty, I focused on what Linc was saying.

"Well, it wasn't anything we set up, if that's what you're wondering. Ryland and I didn't ask for special consideration." He stretched his neck, as though tension had knotted it. "But we do know one of the board members at the Baker Foundation. Cal Rhodes was a friend of Lucinda Baker. He lives in Crystal Cove now—he and his boyfriend Alex run the bed and breakfast there. Ryland knows them both pretty well, since Abby was the manager at the B&B before, and she was friends with both of them. As I heard the story, Cal got your proposal, and Alex knew about Oak Grove since he grew up here in Burton. They were both enthusiastic about it, and about that time, Ry and I had decided to base the company here. We didn't ask them to make our doing the job a condition of the funding—that was Cal's idea—we planned to bid on the job, though. I hoped it wasn't going to be a problem."

Slowly I shook my head. "It isn't. I was just curious. I didn't know about the connection between Alex's boyfriend and the Baker Foundation. It makes more sense now."

"Do you know Alex?"

I lifted one shoulder. "Small town, so the answer to that question is pretty much always yes. I know of him, at least— he and my sister Carla were in the same high school class. And I'd heard that he had moved to Crystal Cove."

A tic jumped in Linc's cheek. "If you—if the historical society would feel more comfortable, you can go ahead and post for bids for this job. I don't want anyone thinking that we called in favors to do it. Ryland and I don't play games like that." He'd stiffened, I noticed, and his jaw was tight.

"That's not even in question here. Oh, trust me, we did some research into y'all when we saw which company was stipulated, but we were all overwhelmingly impressed. I don't have any doubts at all that Kent and Turner is the best fit for this project. I was just curious about how it all came about."

Linc regarded me for one long moment, and then he nodded, his face relaxing again. "Sorry. I can be a little defensive when it comes to anything related to this company. Our reputation and integrity are important to me, especially. Ryland's built this business, and he's taken me on, let me add my name to it. That's not something I take lightly."

I raised one eyebrow. "From what I saw in my investigation on line, you're every bit as responsible for the success of the company as Mr. Kent is. You've worked as many, if not more, jobs, and in one interview I read, he even said he wouldn't be where he is today without your guidance and help. And isn't it true that *you* took *him* under your wing when he started out?"

He smirked. "Damn. That's some detailed research you did."

I refused to let myself flush again. Okay, well, I refused to *acknowledge* that my face was probably pinking up for a third time. It was damn hot out here; who could help such things?

"I'm always thorough, no matter what I do." I sounded prim and proper, but that was all right. I didn't mind that.

"Hmm. I'll be sure to keep that in mind." Linc winked at me—*he winked at me*—and sketched a salute of sorts. "Gotta run. I'll talk to you soon."

I stayed in place as he stalked to the pickup truck, swung in and turned it around in the space in front of the house. I didn't move until the red taillights disappeared into the brush. Only then did I let myself wilt.

I felt as exhausted as if I'd run ten miles. Well, I told myself, it was no wonder; this was a new experience, and I'd handled my very first contractor meeting without too many missteps. I was glad to realize how comfortable I already was with Linc Turner. That would only make this job easier for both of us.

The house was silent as I checked the rear doors and then pulled out the stick keeping the front door open. It was a little silly to secure the property at this point, but it made me feel better to at least make the gesture. Once everything was closed, I climbed gratefully into my little car and blasted the a/c, adjusting the vents to blow icy air right into my face.

I was just navigating the huge potholes and bumps of the driveway when I heard my phone ring. My car audio system picked up the call automatically, and I saw my mother's name on the read-out. With a sigh, I hit the button on the steering wheel that let me answer the call.

"Hey, Mom. What's up?"

"Hi, there, baby girl!" she chirped in what I privately called her be-cheerful-for-Jenna voice. "Whatcha up to?"

Sarcasm threatened. I often wanted to answer her flippantly: *Oh, just lying around, juggling razor blades.* But that would be cruel, and I'd already put my parents through too much. I choked back the words and answered her honestly.

"On my way back to the office. I met with the contractor out at Oak Groves—ouch." I hit a particularly deep bump and my teeth rattled.

"Really? How did it go?" The ever-present worry hid just behind her bright tone.

"Fine. His name's Lincoln Turner, and he seems like he'll do a good job on the restoration. And I think working with him should be pretty easy, too."

"Is he . . . how old is he?"

I frowned, not sure where she was going with this. "Uh, I don't know. He has an almost twelve-year-old daughter, so I guess . . . early thirties?"

"Oh, he has kids. Well, that's nice."

"Yeah, they just moved to town." I sighed a little in relief as I pulled out onto the paved road. "Anyway, I'm excited to get going on this. Can you even imagine how great it'll be to have Oak Grove restored?"

"I can't wait to see what you do with it, honey. You always did have an eye for making things pretty."

I rolled my eyes, confident in the knowledge that she couldn't see me from her desk at the veterinarian clinic. "It's not a dollhouse I'm decorating, Mom. It's going to be hard work. I have hours, if not days, of research ahead of me, and months of construction."

"I know it's more than just decorating, Jenna." My mother came closer to snapping at me than she had in a long time, and I winced in surprise. "I'm just saying that you have a knack, that's all. And don't roll your eyes at me."

"I didn't." The denial was automatic and instantaneous.

"Hmm." She was silent for a moment. When she spoke again, she sounded calmer, and I hated it. Those few seconds of annoyance were the most genuine emotion I'd gotten from either of my parents in two years. "It's going to be wonderful to have Oak Grove restored and open again. It was always in ruins as long as I've known it, but my grandmother could remember when the Bennett family still lived there. She used to tell me stories about the grand parties they'd have at the holidays."

"I wish I could talk to her about it. Our oral history file about the plantation is woefully slim. I think anyone who was alive when it was still occupied is probably long dead. The last family member passed away in the 1940's."

"You know, you might think about visiting Miss Rachel over at Rolling Hills. She's over a hundred now, and she just might remember something."

"Is she . . . does she have her wits about her?" I couldn't think of a more delicate way to ask if the elderly lady was still sharp enough to help me at all.

"Most of the time, yes. The Daughters of the South went out to visit her at Christmas, and she remembered all of us."

"I'll keep that in mind. Thanks, Mom. This could be a tremendous help."

I could hear the pleasure in her tone. "Well . . . I'm glad. Listen, why don't you come over for dinner tonight? I have a pork butt in the slow cooker and I bottled barbecue sauce last weekend. I'm doing pulled pork with coleslaw. And I'm going to stop by Kenny's for your daddy's favorite pie."

I didn't answer right away. All I really wanted to do was go back to the office, finish up my work for the day, and then go home for a long soak in a cool tub. But I hadn't gone over for my weekly dinner yet, and I decided I might as well do it tonight.

"Okay, Mom. What can I bring?"

"Not a thing, baby girl. Just your smiling face. Your daddy's going to be so tickled that you're coming. You can tell us more about the plantation and what you're planning to do . . . it'll be fun."

"Sure. I'll see you about six?"

"That's perfect, honey. You drive safe, now."

I swallowed another sigh. "You, too, Mom. Tell Reenie and Smith I said hey, okay?" I knew both of the vets who were my mom's employers.

"I'll do that."

I hit the end button, turned the air conditioning up a little higher, and then I focused on my driving until I'd reached the historical society office.

Chapter Five

Lincoln

"WELCOME TO BURTON, LINC."

Around a long wooden table, a bunch of men raised their mugs of beer to me. There was a murmur of agreement before we all drank deep, and then those murmurs were replaced with hums of appreciation. Mason had given us his best tonight, and it tasted damn good. The fact that my mug was filled with root beer didn't change my appreciation. Mason hadn't even blinked when I'd chosen the soda over the alcohol; he hadn't pushed or asked questions.

"So is this some kind of club? Tell me I don't have to run naked through town or something even worse for initiation." I glanced over at Sam Reynolds, who was staring deep into his drink.

"Nah." Flynn Evans set down his beer with an audible thump. "Nothing that official. It's more of a survival tactic. The ladies—that's my wife, my sister, *his* wife—" Flynn hooked a thumb toward Sam. "—and Mason's wife . . . they insisted on having girls' nights every once in a while. We decided that means we get boys' nights, too. The women couldn't complain, because it was their idea first."

Mason chuckled. "Yep. So on the nights they get together, we run herd on all the kids. And then we get our own night, when I close down a little early so we have the run of the place."

The place he referenced was his bar and night club, the Road Block. Mason was a hometown boy who'd moved to Nashville, made it big in the music business as a talent agent, married a rising star . . . and then lost her in a tragic accident. I could definitely relate to that.

Left alone with a baby daughter, Mason had moved home to Burton and opened up his own bar, where he continued to showcase both up-and-coming talents and provide the locals with a place to drink, dance and hang out. Along the way, he'd also found a new love, apparently, since he was married again and had added a son to his family.

"Well, I appreciate you including me. Thanks, Sam and Alex, for inviting me. And I'm grateful to Meghan and Ali for taking the kids tonight." I took another long swig. "Even though I'm not a local. Nor do I have a woman participating in girls' night."

The blond guy to my right elbowed me. "Hey, no problem, Linc. I'm not a local anymore, and I for sure don't have any woman. At girls' night or anywhere else." Alex Nelson smirked.

We all laughed, and I shook my head. "I'll give you the

woman part, Alex, but you're a Burton boy, even if you *are* just in town for a visit. I've been to your parents' house. The whole living room is wall-to-wall Alex Nelson, from birth to last week. There's no escaping it."

"He's not wrong." The man next to Sam nodded. I was pretty sure I'd heard him called Smith, but I hadn't yet figured out if that was his first or last name. "But I'm definitely not a local. Hell, I'm not even a Southerner. I'm from Boston."

"A fact we have graciously decided to overlook." Alex leaned in close to me, muttering in a sotto voce that went real South real quick. "Our grandfathers are rolling in their sacred graves at the idea that we are consorting with a damn Yankee, but we have evolved, you see." He laid on the accent extra thick, and I had to laugh.

"Aww, there are no labels." Will Garth, a tall rangy dude who ran the town's newspaper and printing service, spread his hands over the table. "No rules. When it comes to the Road Block hang-out, it's anything goes."

"He's right." Sam spoke at last. "Nothing formal. Just fun." He drained the last of his beer and slid the mug down the table. "Mason, want to hit me again?"

I thought I noticed a momentary twinge of concern in Mason's eye, but he snagged the mug without missing a beat. "Sure thing, Sam. Anyone else need anything while I'm up?"

"I'll take another, too." Alex lifted his mug. "I'm not behind the wheel tonight, in case you were worried. Flynn is playing designated driver for both Sam and me."

"Which means this beer was my one and only." Flynn gave a long, exaggerated sigh. "So just an ice water, if you don't mind, Mason."

"Got it. Hey, Linc, mind giving me a hand with these? I've been working behind the bar so much, I'm out of practice with serving tables."

"No problem." I stood up, holding Alex's empty glass, and followed Mason across the rough-hewn oak plank floor to the bar. While he busied himself with Flynn's ice water, I eased onto a stool.

"So how's it going over at Oak Grove?" Mason cast me an assessing glance. "I heard construction started a few weeks back."

It didn't surprise me that he knew. I'd already figured out that the Road Block afforded its owner the opportunity to catch all the hottest news in the area. Most of our crew hung out here on Friday nights, spending some of their hard-earned salary, and I was sure they talked about what was happening on the Oak Grove project.

"Yeah, we're underway. Took us a little while to clear out the driveway, but now we're moving along. All the plaster on the first level is out now, and we've secured the second floor so we can start up there. The plumbers arrived today, and we'll be working on insulation, too."

"Uh huh." Mason nudged another root beer in my direction. "And everything's been going smoothly? With the locals and with the historical society?"

"Sure." I frowned, confused about why he was asking. As far as I knew, the society was happy with our progress so far.

"And with Jenna?" Mason didn't meet my eyes as he wiped the top of the already-pristine bar. "She's doing okay, too?"

Understanding washed over me. In the five weeks I'd been in Burton, an unusual number of people had subtly and not-so-subtly inquired about Jenna Sutton. Some asked if she was handling the job well, while others used pointed questions that made me curious about why some in this town seemed to view her as so fragile and unstable.

I'd been working closely with her since our first walk-through of Oak Grove. I knew that she was nervous about the project being the first one she was running on her own, but she was handling those nerves with admirable ease. I myself didn't always feel completely confident about being the contractor; I'd had way too many sleepless nights, worrying that I'd made the wrong call or was forgetting something crucial.

We'd shared our anxiety from the beginning, with Jenna teasingly referring to us as building virgins whenever neither of us was certain about something related to the job. I liked that she was willing to ask me questions when she wasn't sure about something. I'd dealt with my share of arrogant, know-it-all owners and consultants, and it was refreshing that what Jenna and I had was evolving into more of a partnership.

"Jenna's doing more than okay. She's handling this restoration like a pro." I took a drink, wiped my upper lip and cocked my head. "Want to tell me why you asked me that?"

Mason shrugged one huge shoulder. The dude was seriously ripped. He reminded me more of a linebacker than a musician, although I'd been assured by more than one person that he was a talented guitar player and singer.

"Just wondering. You know Jenna is Rilla's cousin, right?"

I chuckled. "Pretty sure everyone in this town is related to everyone else. But yeah, now that you mention it, I think I heard Jenna talk with some of our guys about her cousin being married to the owner of the Road Block."

"Yeah. Well, Rilla's protective of her. And so am I. We all want her to do well with this. She needs a win, you know? A real strong one."

"I feel like I'm missing something here." I leaned back a little, studying Mason. "Is there anything you want tell me?"

He crossed his arms. "Honestly, I'm surprised you haven't heard anything yet. You know small towns. Everyone talks about everyone else." He paused for a moment, and I sensed he was debating with himself.

"I'm not comfortable with gossip. But I also think you need to be aware of some of Jenna's history, if only because eventually, some less charitable busy-body will end up telling you her version, and it might help to know the truth before that happens."

"Okayyyyy." I drew out the word. "Not sure I'm following you, Mason."

He bent over, resting his elbows on the bar and dropping his voice. "Couple of years ago, Jenna was hung up on a guy. Now that doesn't sound like such a big deal, but you gotta understand—Jenna's the youngest of four girls, and she was maybe just a little bit spoiled. A little immature. When she decided she wanted—this guy, I think she figured he'd fall into her lap like everything else in her life."

"That doesn't sound at all like her." The Jenna Sutton I

knew was serious to a fault and meticulously responsible. She never even mildly flirted with any of crew, and she had an air about her that discouraged too much familiarity, even while she was pleasant and friendly. I couldn't imagine her chasing after anyone.

"No, she's changed pretty radically. One of the reasons was that the man she set her sights on wasn't looking for anything serious or even the least bit permanent. He was a real player in those days. Now, he's changed quite a bit since then, too, but back then, he was a real love-'em-and-leave-'em dude."

The picture was beginning to be clearer. "So Jenna was one he left."

Mason nodded. "Yeah. In a big, bad, hurtful way. Now don't get me wrong. He didn't do anything without her consent. She went after him, and from what I hear, he tried to put her off, but what young guy is going to keep turning down a pretty girl who so clearly has the hots for him? But what happened after, that was on him. Jenna expected roses and declarations of love. Instead, he made it clear she was just the latest in a long line of easy fucks."

An unexpected and unreasonable anger bubbled up in me. I'd known guys who didn't care where they were sticking their dicks as long as it was under a skirt, but I'd never been one of them. I'd been with Sylvia since we were in high school, and after she'd died, my love affair had been with a bottle, not the unending stream of ready pussy that was offered to me nightly at the bars I frequented. I couldn't understand men who treated any woman that way.

"This asshole lives around here?" I tried to think of anyone I'd met who might fit this profile. Mason had said the jerk had changed, but I couldn't think he could be that different. What was that saying about tigers and stripes?

"No." Mason waved his hand. "He moved away. What happened with Jenna shook him up, and it made him a different man. A better man. So at least something positive came from her breakdown."

"Wait a minute. Breakdown? She fell apart over a guy blowing her off? That sure doesn't seem like the Jenna I know." Not that I knew her *that* well, of course; our interactions were strictly business, even if they were friendly. We weren't braiding each other's hair and telling secrets, but I did feel like I had a sense of who she was.

"Like I said, she wasn't the same back then. I don't think anyone realized how devastated she was until—well, it all ended up to be okay, and she got some help, and she's turned things around. But that kind of humiliation in an everyone-knows-everyone place like Burton isn't easy to bounce back from. People talk too damn much, and other people's shit is their favorite topic. So she's not the same girl anymore. She's closed off, she's quiet and she keeps to herself—a lot. Hell, before all this, she was at my house as much as she was at her own, because she and Rilla were close. She babysat for us all the time. Now, we're lucky if we see her once a month."

"So you needed to check on her with me because you and your wife feel like Jenna's cut you off?"

Mason hesitated. "In a way. It's more than that, though. I guess . . . I feel responsible for what happened that night, with Tr—with the man she slept with. See, it happened here.

At the Road Block. On my watch, you could say."

"Here? They . . . uh, hooked up here?" I knew it happened. I'd heard my crew talk about some of their adventures, sometimes trying to one-up each other on the most public place they'd nailed a chick, in their words. But I couldn't imagine actually doing it, and I definitely didn't see Jenna down for that kind of action. Yeah, maybe she'd changed a lot, but no one changed *that* much.

"Well, maybe not technically here. They connected here. He took her home from here. Still, I let it happen. I can't help feeling like it's partly my fault." He looked unhappy, his mouth tight and his eyebrows drawn together.

"Uh huh. How old was Jenna then?" I was trying to do the math in my head. I knew she looked young, but I wasn't sure of her exact age. I'd figured mid-to-late twenties, based on the job she had and how efficiently she did it. I assumed she was just one of those people who had a baby face.

"She was twenty-one. It was actually her birthday that night."

"Okay, so she was of age. She was an adult. She's not your daughter. She made her own decision. That means it wasn't your fault, Mason." I shifted on my barstool. "And while I'm pointing out truths, maybe you and the rest of her family aren't giving Jenna enough credit. Maybe you're not seeing who she is now. Because from what I can tell, she's a lot stronger than you think. She might be different than the girl you remember from before—and I'm not claiming that I know her better than her family and friends—but one thing I can say. Jenna's not as fragile and breakable as you all seem to think. Did you ever think that treating her like she's made of glass might not be helping her?"

Mason stared me down for the space of several moments, and it occurred to me that if I didn't know him at all, this dude could be seriously intimidating. Then he sighed, closed his eyes and slumped. "I kind of want to hit you right now, you know that? I'm thinking it would make me feel better. But there's another part of me, the part that might arguably be the more rational side, that says maybe you might have a point. Maybe you're onto something."

I lifted one shoulder. "Hey, I might be way off-base. I'm speaking from personal experience, more than anything else." I raised my glass of root beer. "I don't know how much of my story you've heard through the grapevine that seems to run from the Cove up here to Burton. I had a real rough stretch after my wife died."

Mason gripped my forearm. "I did hear a little something about that. Guess we have a few things in common, huh?"

"Yeah, at least one thing I'd never wish on my worst fucking enemy. When your wife died, Mason, what did you do? How did you handle it?"

He looked pained. "I cursed God, I cursed man, and I got real angry. But I had Piper. When I think what might've happened to me after Lu was killed, if it hadn't been for my baby girl . . . she saved my life. It was because of her that I came back here, started up this place and found a life again. And if it hadn't been for that move, I never would've met Rilla and had Noah, too." His eyes were glued to the floor. "I don't talk about her so much anymore, but I still miss Lu. It's hard, you know . . . to say, God, I wish it hadn't happened. I wish she was still alive and with me. But if she were, I wouldn't have Rilla and the baby and the life that I love right now. That's an impossible choice."

"Yeah." My voice was hoarse. "I get that. But you see, man, you got angry, but you didn't swan-dive off that cliff. You didn't abandon your baby girl; you made a new life for her, with her, and you stepped up. Me, I had two reasons for keeping on, you know? Becca and Oliver were little. They'd just lost their mama, and they needed their daddy. But you know what I did? I gave them away. Left them with their grandparents, so I could drink my life away without guilt. Well, without any *more* guilt, I should say, because I was eaten up with that shit. I was on a fast-track to oblivion. I was heading straight to an end that would've made my kids orphans."

"But you didn't." Mason spoke low, with intensity. "I mean, here you are."

"Yeah, but it came damn fucking close. If it hadn't been for Ryland, I don't know what I would've done. I made the choice, ultimately, to go into rehab and to stop drinking, but when I came out, Ryland had my back. He gave me a job. He gave me the space I needed to heal. But there were others, guys from our crew who'd known me before, and definitely my in-laws, who acted like I was always one bad day away from falling off the wagon. They walked on eggshells around me, and worse, they taught my kids to do the same. It just about drove me crazy."

A deep furrow appeared between Mason's eyes. "You think we're doing that to Jenna?"

I spread my hands. "Hey, I don't know. I've only been

around her at work, when we're with people from the society or my own crew. I haven't seen how her friends treat her, or what it's like around her family. You'd be the better judge of that."

"Yeah. And it's just like you said—eggshells." He grimaced. "She always looks so . . . pained around us. Millie and Boomer don't like to hear about anything negative when Jenna's around, and they get mad if anyone steps out of line about that."

"Like I said, I don't know the whole situation. Just a thought."

"Hey, Mason. You get lost over here with our refills? Need a refresher course in building a beer?" Sam ambled over to us.

"Sorry, bud. Linc and I got talking. I've got your drink here." Mason handed the filled mug over the bar. "Everything okay, Sam? You're not usually a second-beer guy. And you've been kind of quiet tonight."

Sam sipped his beer, not meeting Mason's gaze. "Yeah, I'm good." When none of us spoke, he blew out a deep breath. "Meghan went to a specialist today, in Savannah. You know, a . . . woman doctor-type. They'd run some tests last time." He glanced at me. "She had a miscarriage a couple of years ago, and we've been, you know, trying ever since. But no luck. And the news today wasn't great."

Mason clapped a hand on his friend's shoulder. "I'm sorry. I didn't realize it, Sam. I just figured you and Meghan weren't ready for kids yet."

"We haven't talked about it much. Ali knows, and Maureen does, too. We've been trying not to worry, because you know . . . we're young. We've only been married a couple of years, and we were careful before that, and hey, no one's going to complain about the fun of trying. But finally Meghan thought she might as well go get checked out."

"What did the doctor say? Surely there's something they can do, right? You hear all the time about all the advances and shit." Mason braced his hands on the bar, watching Sam.

"Yeah, I guess they could, but they can't find anything wrong. No reason, physical or otherwise, why I can't manage to fucking knock up my wife."

His voice rose, and the conversation at the table across the room died abruptly. There were several long moments of silence, and then chairs scraped as the others joined us, some of them taking seats on barstools and the rest gathering around.

Flynn was the first to break the silence. "Sam . . . bro . . . why didn't you say something?"

Sam snorted. "Not exactly the kind of shit you want to broadcast, you know? Both for Meghan's sake and mine."

I noticed glances exchanged around the room. "You got checked, too, right?" This time it was Alex asking. "So if everything's working fine with Meggie, you're sure it's not your swimmers?"

"Yeah, I got checked." His face turned a deep red. "Most humiliating fucking experience of my life. But the doctor said everything was good. My swimmers aren't having any issues, thank you very much."

"Hey, it had to be asked." Alex gave his friend a full-body nudge. "And I feel your pain. I just went through that myself, actually, a couple of months back."

This time, the quiet was astonished and deafening. "Uhhh . . . what?" Flynn stared at his friend. "Why in the hell would you be at a fertility clinic? Does Cal know you're cheating on him with your hand and a cup?"

Everyone laughed at that, the tension easing a little, as Alex rolled his eyes. "Yes, of course Cal knows. It was his idea, if you want the whole story. We're, uh, looking into having a baby, and the doctor we're working with wanted to check both of our swimmers before we made a decision about who was going to be up to bat first."

"Up to bat? What the hell kind of craziness is that?" Sam still sounded rough, but I saw a spark in his eyes and a half-smile forming on his face.

Alex gave a long, exaggerated sigh. "Look, do you really want me to get into the down and dirty nitty gritty with you guys about this?" He scanned the room, and when no one objected, he shook his head. "Fine. Don't forget you asked for it. Cal and I have been talking about kids since we moved to the Cove. We don't want to rush into anything, but at the same time, we're tired of waiting. We talked about adoption, and it still might be something we do. But first, we're going to try it this way. We started the process this past spring, and we found a surrogate we both love. Cal and I figured that one of us would donate for one kid, and the other of us would give our guys for another. That way, we're both furthering our family trees, and we both get that experience." He picked up a nearby beer and gulped it down. "Not saying our way is the right way, but it's how we're doing it."

"Huh." Will, sitting on a stool, wagged his head. "I never really thought about it much. But hey, congrats, Alex. What did you decide, and when is one of you going to get this gal pregnant?"

Alex laughed. "Turned out both of us have viable, uh, product. So we finally decided we'd go in alphabetical order. I'm going first, and it's going down—or in?—this fall. The surrogate's name is Kelly, and she lives in the Cove. So we'll be able to see her during the pregnancy, and we hope she'll be part of the baby's life."

"It's a brave new world." Smith grinned. "And when did we all go from talking baseball, hot music and hotter chicks and start discussing sperm counts and babies? I think somewhere along the line, I got old and no one told me."

Flynn poked him in the ribs. "Smith . . . you're old, dude. Now you've been told. Accept it."

"Sam." Mason spoke over the chuckles that followed. "Listen. We all talk big, and we bluster a lot, but we all know how important this is. And if you need to talk to anyone about it, don't hold back. That's part of why we're here for each other, right?"

There was a general murmur of consensus. Sam ducked his head, though I couldn't tell if it was in embarrassment or emotion. Maybe a little of both, I decided.

"And just remember this," Flynn called out. "When you do manage to, uh . . . what was refined and romantic way you put it? Oh, yeah—fucking knock up your wife. When you do that, and the baby's keeping you up all night crying, or you're stuck changing diapers—we're most definitely going to be here to remind you that you asked for this. I, for one, have no problem singing the I-told-you-so song."

Sam slugged his brother-in-law in the arm, as Mason

ducked under the bar and pulled out a bottle.

"Gentlemen, I think this calls for some of the good stuff. I don't break out the high quality booze for you jackasses often, but tonight I'll make an exception." He brought down glasses and poured Scotch into each of them in one smooth move, not breaking his stride even when he stopped before the last one and added club soda to it instead of the alcohol. He handed that one to me.

Each of the men picked up a drink, and Flynn cleared his throat. "To all of us here—the fellowship of the jackasses. May we always be stronger together, brave enough to conquer sperm cups and wise enough to listen to our women."

"Hear, hear!" Will called, and we clinked our glasses together as I wondered how I'd gotten lucky enough to be accepted into this solidarity of brotherhood.

CHAPTER SIX

Jenna

"T HERE'S REALLY NO PLACE LIKE a small town on the Fourth of July." Rilla smiled at me as we spread a red and white striped cloth over a picnic table. "Sometimes I feel like I've stepped right into a Norman Rockwell painting, you know? The red, white and blue bunting everywhere . . . flags waving . . . the parade and the picnic, and everyone gathered to have a good time."

"Have you considered volunteering at the Burton Board of Tourism?" I teased my cousin. "You could write up what you said just now and we'd get a huge influx of visitors, just for the holiday."

"Actually, I have considered it." She grinned. "I've been doing some pro bono PR work for the board, and we have good ideas. Problem is, we need to have somewhere for all those tourists to stay when they come flocking to Burton. Right now, they'd have to go to the hotel all the way in Farleyville. We could also use a few more eating establishments. We have Kenny's, Smokey Joe's and Franco's—plus the Road Block, of course—but they'd be swamped if we got any kind of decent response to my ads."

"Once Oak Grove is finished and ready for visitors, we're going to be pushing for more advertising from the state and the county. Having a hotel in Burton would be a draw for that, too. You should talk with Joanna Phelps, our PR rep over at the historical society. It would be great if the two of you could work together to promote both the town and the plantation."

"Not a bad idea." Rilla side-eyed me. "So everything's going well over there? At Oak Grove, I mean?"

"It really is." I was ebullient at the progress we'd made so far and at the fact that I hadn't made any serious faux pas yet. "It's been absolutely amazing to see it progress from this falling-down old house to something that will remind people of what used to be."

"You sound like you love what you're doing." Rilla patted my arm as she came around the table to retrieve napkins from the picnic basket. "It's good to hear that."

I paused, considering. "You know, I really do. I don't think I've been this happy since . . ." My voice trailed off. "Well, for a long time. I feel like I'm really doing something constructive. No pun intended."

Rilla's face broke into a huge smile. "Why, Jenna Sutton, did you just make a joke? Oh, my gosh. This is a red-letter day."

I dropped down onto the bench. "What's that supposed to mean?"

"Oh, nothing, really." She began folding napkins into triangles. "You just haven't been very, um . . ." Rilla cast her eyes up as she searched for the word. "Relaxed, I guess. Light-hearted. What's a word that means *liable to make jokes*?"

"Clown-like?" I raised one eyebrow.

"Noooo." She shook her head. "I'm not criticizing, Jenna. I'm just saying it's nice to see you smile. To hear you talk about your work with such passion and—joy, I'd say. We've all been so worried for so long that it makes me happy to see you happy."

Knowing that my family worried about me wasn't exactly a news flash. But over the past two weeks, I'd begun to notice a slow change in how some of them acted around me. Mason and Rilla were less reticent about teasing me. They'd pushed me to accept a dinner invitation and then treated me like they used to—giving me a hard time about silly things and not backing down when out of habit, I began to shut down. They'd even asked me to babysit, and I'd had a fun night with Piper and Noah, which reminded me of how much I'd enjoyed those kids.

My sisters were different, too. Courtney and her husband Ian, along with their son Duncan, had stopped by my house one night unexpectedly and taken me out for ice cream. Carla had taken to calling me more regularly. Even Christy, who seemed to have pulled away from me the most in the aftermath of the Trent situation, had asked to meet me for lunch one day.

It was a subtle shift, but I noticed. I didn't know what had happened to change them—or maybe it was me? Maybe it was the shot of confidence from the work I was doing at the plantation? I wasn't sure. But I liked it. The more they were themselves around me, the more I felt free to let down my guard and be who I really was now—not the Jenna from Before, but the new Jenna. The Now Jenna. The one who'd been through shit, come out the other side and was ready to start living again.

I wasn't sure when I'd made that decision—the one to start living again. It had happened slowly, but I was pretty sure it had something to do with the Oak Grove project. I woke up each and every morning, excited about what was planned for the new day. I couldn't wait to go out and see the work that had been finished since my visit the day before. I liked the fact that I knew what I was doing, and I enjoyed the people who were working with me.

Of course, it hadn't escaped my notice that Linc Turner played a big part in this difference. It wasn't anything huge or overt; it was more in the way he treated me. He never acted as though he doubted I could do what I said I would. And when I expressed concern about my ability to accomplish a task, he offered both encouragement and help. At the same time, Linc never made me feel weak or helpless. He never made me feel *less*; on the contrary, when I was with him, I felt infinitely *more*.

I'd worried at first that maybe I was starting to crush on him a little bit. That would have been disastrous. First of all, look at how my last foray into crushdom had gone. Not well. I wasn't eager to stroll down that path again. And then there was the fact that we had a professional relationship, one built on mutual respect. Of course, there was the age difference, too, which wasn't a little thing, and the fact that this guy, no matter how nice he was to me and how wonderful he made me feel, was a widower with two children. The idea of tackling that particular mountain of complications made my stomach turn over. No, Linc Turner wasn't meant for me that way—in a romantic way—but I surely did appreciate what he'd done for my confidence level.

I'd even been excited about the town's huge Fourth of July gathering and celebration. The last two years, I'd stayed away, not able to face the thought of being with the people who whispered about me. I'd had no desire to celebrate anything. But this year was different. When my mom had brought up the picnic, I'd jumped in with both feet, offering to help with the table set-up and decorations.

"Hey, earth to Jenna!" Rilla caught my attention. "We need to put up this bunting on the gazebo. Give me a hand?"

I reached around a tree to grab the step stool my mom had sent out with Rilla and me. Boomer's Auto Repair sponsored a good part of the town's Independence Day celebration, which gave us a prime spot on the green to decorate and on which we would have our picnic and watch the parade and fireworks. We'd been occupying this ground on the Fourth as long as I could remember, and I was past master at planning the splashes of red, white and blue. But in years before, I'd done the work with my sisters. This year, Rilla had insisted on helping me, which didn't seem to have upset Carla, Courtney and Christy at all.

I balanced on the top rung of the small ladder, reaching to attach the eye of the bunting to the hook I knew from long years of experience was up there. Focusing, I stuck my tongue out of the corner of my mouth and closed my eyes, feeling for the hook. Lost in concentration, I leaned just a little further and heard Rilla's shriek of panic moments before I felt the unsettling sensation of my footing falling away from me as the step stool teetered.

I didn't even have time to cry out. I knew for certain, in one still-cognizant part of my mind, that I was about to fall and hit the ground pretty hard. I was conscious of letting go of the bunting, aware that it would definitely rip if I clung to it, and this was an old decoration that my mother treasured. I'd just felt a surge of fear-induced adrenaline when a pair of strong hands gripped my waist and a familiar voice murmured, "I got you. You're okay."

And then all I knew was the heady feeling of a hard body pulling me close, holding me tight, and arms wrapped around me. I relaxed into the embrace, blissfully aware of nothing but this sense of security.

"Jenna! My God, are you all right? Are you hurt?"

Rilla's voice cut into my reverie. Suddenly, I realized I was clinging shamelessly to the arms that had rescued me—arms that belonged to Lincoln Turner.

I pushed away, trying to find my rhythm of breathing again and hoping he didn't feel my heart pounding or feel the heat my body was giving off. His hands were just above my ass, and God, *God*, I wanted them there and lower and everywhere.

"I think she's all right. Probably just a little shaken. Maybe got the breath knocked out of her." Linc's voice was very close to my ear. Slowly he lowered me to the ground, keeping his hands on my hips.

I kept my hands on his arms, still a little breathless. I told myself it was for balance, that I was still shaky from the surge of adrenaline. It had nothing to do with how solid Linc's muscles felt under my fingers. I willed those fingers to stay still and not to trace the tendons on his forearms . . .

"My God, Jenna, you scared the crap out of me!" Rilla grasped my shoulders and pulled me away from Linc. I was inexplicably annoyed with her for taking me away from him, while at the same time, I thought vaguely and stupidly that I really must have frightened her, since she never took the name of the Lord in vain.

"Sorry." I managed to choke out one word. Swallowing hard, I willed my heart to slow down and cleared my throat. "Sorry, Rilla. I thought I could get it attached there, but I must've had the step stool over a little too far."

"Yeah, well . . ." She glanced over my shoulder. "Thank God you saw her falling and could get here. I was frozen in place—I couldn't make myself move."

I laughed a little, the sound still shaky in my own ears. "I would've crushed you, Rilla. I'm glad you didn't try to catch me." For the first time, I let my eyes meet Linc's, praying he didn't see there what was going on in my treacherous body. "Thank you for catching me. I really thought for a minute that I was going to end up broken on the ground."

"You're not broken, Jenna." He murmured the words so low that I wasn't sure I'd heard him. For several heartbeats, he gazed at me steadily before breaking away to smile at Rilla. "Hey. I'm Linc Turner. You must be Rilla Wallace, right? Mason's wife?"

"Guilty on both counts. And Jenna's cousin." Rilla extended her hand as understanding dawned on her face. "Oh! Linc. You work with Jenna out at the plantation job, right? You're the contractor."

"My turn to plead guilty." Linc's large hand engulfed Rilla's small one. "I'm real glad to meet you. I got to know your husband pretty soon after we moved to Burton. He's a great guy."

"One of a kind, for sure." Rilla glowed as she always did when she spoke of Mason.

Linc turned his neck, scanning the area, and then waved in the direction of the sidewalk. "I was walking with the kids when I spotted Jenna about to go splat. I took off running, and they probably think I'm crazy."

Becca walked toward us, accompanied by a smaller boy with dark red hair and blue eyes. He ran to Linc, coming to a sudden halt and standing with his hands on hips, reminding me of a diminutive Peter Pan.

"Dad, there's horses. I saw them on the street, right after you ran away. There were like, ten. Maybe fifteen. And they're all dressed up, decorated with bows and stuff."

Rilla laughed. "That's the horse brigade. They'll be part of the parade later on. And then there's more horses pulling the canons, and mules when the Sons of Burton come by, dressed like soldiers from the War Between the States." She looked up at Becca, who was watching all of us, an unreadable expression on her face. "The Daughters of the South dress up in beautiful antebellum gowns, too. That's one of my favorite parts."

"Becca and Oliver, this is Miss Rilla. And this is Miss Jenna, who's working on Oak Grove plantation with me.

You've heard me mention her." Linc winked at me, and I was pretty certain my insides turned completely over.

"Uh, Becca and I met already. Over at Kiki's." I smiled at her. "Have you been back for cookies?"

The girl nodded, but she didn't answer me out loud.

"Where are you going to watch the parade and eat your picnic?" Rilla crossed her arms over her chest. "Do you know the best spots? Or are you meeting friends?"

Linc shook his head. "We were just kind of winging it, this being our first year. I figured we could buy something to eat and just perch on a curb somewhere. What would be your recommendation?"

"I'm biased, of course, but I think right here is the perfect place. And you don't need to worry about food, because Aunt Millie and the girls always make way too much. There will be plenty. Please, do join us."

I was grateful that Rilla was extending the invitation, because even if I'd wanted to, I wasn't sure I could've managed it yet. I was still coming down from the double whammy of near-death (okay, well, maybe near maiming. Near concussion?) and the way my body had reacted to Linc's hands on me. I hadn't been this shaken in a long time.

He glanced at his kids. "Well, I don't want to intrude—"

"Please. There's no such thing as intrusion in Burton on the Fourth of July. Everyone's going to be milling around, visiting with their own families and other friends and neighbors." Rilla bent over and spoke conspiratorially to the children. "There's going to be a bunch of kids here, too. My daughter Piper is a little bit younger than you two, and Noah's still a toddler. But Ali and Flynn have Bridget, and my cousin Courtney has a boy about your age, Oliver."

"Bridget's going to be here?" Becca's eyes lit up. "Daddy, can we please stay?"

Linc chuckled. "They met Bridget last month at Meghan and Sam's house, and the girls hit it off right away. Meghan's been kind enough to let the kids come out on a fairly regular basis, since the farm is on the way to the job site. So they've all become buddies."

"Then that decides it. You have to stay." Rilla gave one definitive nod. "And you can sing for your supper, as it were, by hanging up the bunting Jenna was risking her life to attach. Do you mind?"

"Not at all." Linc stood on the first rung of the mini-ladder and looped the eye over the hook on his first try. I grimaced. *Show off.* Rilla clapped her hands.

"Wonderful. Now Jenna, do you mind if I run back home to help Mason finish getting the kids ready? I need to pick up my baked beans, too. I think all we have left here is setting out the plastic ware and the cups."

"I've got that. See you in a bit."

Rilla waved and took off down the grass toward where she'd left her car at my dad's shop. I watched her go and then began to rummage through the bags, hunting for the rest of the supplies.

"Dad, can I go back and look at the horses? Please? I promise I won't get too close or anything. I'll just stand back and look."

"Hmmm." Linc rubbed his jaw. "It's just around the block?"

"Uh huh." Ollie nodded vigorously.

"Bec, do you mind walking over with him? Not that I don't trust you, son. But there're a lot of people in town, and I'd feel better if the two of you stuck together."

Becca heaved an exaggerated sigh of long-suffering. "I guess, if I have to . . ."

"You do. But you have my undying gratitude for your sacrifice. I'll never forget it."

"Daddy, sometimes you are so lame." Becca huffed a little, but she grabbed her brother by the arm. "Come on. Let's go see these freaking horses. But we are staying far back, you hear, Ollie? Horses can be dangerous."

I hid a smile, ripping open a bag of plastic forks. Linc ambled over and sat down on the bench that was attached to the picnic table.

"I hope you don't mind." He sprawled on the seat, stretching one arm along the table. "The kids and I crashing your family's party, I mean."

"Of course not." I fussed with setting up the forks. "You're all welcome. The more, the merrier. Our picnic is your picnic."

He laughed. "Any other trite saying you want to toss my way?"

"No." I shook my head. "But I really don't mind at all. If you don't, I mean. My family can be a little large and overwhelming. So buyer beware and all that."

"Got it. But I don't mind large and overwhelming. It'll be good for my kids, too. They haven't had a lot of interaction since we moved, aside from the visits to the Reynolds farm. They could use some people interaction."

"Then they're in luck. This is the place to find people,

and lots of them." I jammed a fistful of plastic spoons into a cup I was using as a makeshift holder. My hand was shaking just the tiniest bit. I hoped Linc wasn't watching too closely. I'd been alone with him plenty of times before, but it had always been in a work environment, where we each had a role to play. Here, in the middle of the green, as the town began to come to life and prepare to celebrate, I felt strangely vulnerable.

And then there'd been what had happened when his hands had gripped my waist and held onto my hips. I hadn't had that kind of reaction to a man—to anyone—ever. I let my memory slip back into the danger zone and consider Trent, how it had felt when he had touched me. Had there been the same heat? The same zing? I didn't think so.

"Jenna, are you sure you're okay?" Linc frowned at me. "Your cheeks are all flushed, and you were muttering to yourself."

"Yes." I stepped back. "Yes, thanks, I'm fine. Just thinking about what I still need to do. And sometimes when I think hard, I talk to myself."

"Uh huh." He nodded, watching me with a teasing light in his eyes. "Okay."

"Do you think it's too early for a beer?" I blurted out, wiping my hands on my denim shorts. "I mean, it is a holiday, right, and it's so freaking hot out here."

Linc cocked an eyebrow at me. "It's just now ten o'clock, Jenna. But you do what you want." He took a breath and then added, "I don't drink, though. I'd take a bottle of water if you have one."

I reached into the cooler and took out two bottles of

water. Handing one to Linc, I dropped onto the bench about a foot and a half away from him, leaving plenty of space. "You don't drink at all? I didn't know that. I'm sorry."

"Why should you be sorry? And why would you know it? I don't go around with a T-shirt that says, *Hello, my name is Lincoln, I'm an alcoholic.*"

"You are?" It seemed so far from possible that I stared at him, and I was pretty sure my mouth had dropped open.

"I am. Recovering, of course." He took a long drink of the water, and I watched in fascination as his throat worked, swallowing, his huge Adam's apple bobbing. "It's not a very interesting story. After Sylvia was killed, life felt pretty pointless. I decided the best way to numb the pain was with whiskey, or with whatever I could drink that made me forget."

"The kids?" I thought of those two sweet faces, alone and motherless, while their father drank away his grief.

"Left them with my in-laws. They were never in any danger—they were just without either parent for about six years."

"Linc." I reached across and touched his hand before I thought better of it. "I really am sorry. That whole time must have been excruciating."

He stared at where my fingers met the back of his hand, but he didn't move. "It was tough. But we all made it through, and I like to think I grew as a person." He released a bark of laughter on a long breath. "Damn, I hope to hell I grew. Otherwise it was a long time wasted."

I flattened my hand so that my palm pressed lightly over his hand. I felt the bumps of his knuckles against my soft and sensitive nerves. "Nothing is ever wasted if you lived through it." I was echoing my therapist, although I wasn't about to share that. One deep and dark secret shared at a time was plenty, I thought, although I suspected Linc's alcoholism wasn't anything he tried to hide. It simply hadn't come up in our interaction up to this point. I hadn't had occasion to offer him a drink until now.

Which reminded me. "I don't usually drink much, either. I don't know why I said what I did about the beer."

"Please don't feel like you can't have a beer or some wine around me—or anything at all. It's really okay. If I can't deal with that kind of temptation, I have bigger problems." He flipped his hand over so that now our palms were against each other. My heart began to pound, and I ran my tongue over my dry lips. I couldn't tell if this was anxiety or pure, hot need.

"I'll try to keep that in mind." I spoke just above a whisper, afraid to break the spell.

"Jenna—" Linc leaned toward me a little, not breaking the contact between our hands. I looked up at him through my eyelashes and waited for him to continue.

"There you are, Jenna! Good heavens, it's so hot already, I just about busted a blood vessel carrying this stuff from the car, and your father—" My mom stopped in mid-sentence and stared at me. And at Linc.

Without thinking how it might look, I yanked my hand away, holding it in my lap, and jumped to my feet. "Here, Mom. Let me take some of that. I thought Daddy was helping you tote all this over. Why didn't you text me? I would've come to help."

"I did try to call you, but it went right to voice mail." My mother hadn't moved yet.

"Sorry. It's in my bag, and I think the ringer's still turned off from work yesterday." I set the hamper of food on the table and turned around, taking a deep breath. "Mom, this is Linc Turner. He's the contractor from the Oak Grove project?" I sounded as though I was asking her instead of telling her, and annoyed with myself for being so wishy-washy, I shook my head. "I mean, he is. He and his kids were looking for a place to eat and watch the parade, and Rilla invited him to join us."

"Well, isn't that nice?" Mom moved finally, but her gaze stayed on Linc's face. "Of course, you're welcome to celebrate with us. We love to have more faces around the table." She shrugged the heavy canvas bag off her shoulder and let it drop to the bench. "Will your wife be joining us?"

Astonishment spread over Linc's face, and I could've gladly sunk into the ground and disappeared. My mother, who was the kindest, most gracious woman I knew, who would never hurt another soul if she could help it, had a pinched expression around her mouth and something dark in her eyes.

"Mom." I ground out the word between clenched teeth. "What's your problem?"

Linc had recovered enough to answer her. "Ah, my wife passed away six years ago, Mrs. Sutton. But my children are around here some place. They were looking for the horses that are going to be in the parade."

My mom's face turned the same color as the patriotic shirt she was wearing—minus the blue stars. "Oh my Lord," she whispered. "I had no idea. I am so sorry. That was so rude of me. So thoughtless. I do apologize."

"No apology necessary, ma'am." He stood up, and I could see a line of tension in his shoulders. "Can I help you carry anything else? Any more trips from the car?"

"Ah, my husband is just now coming with the chairs, and he could likely use a hand. He's just about a block that way, unloading a pickup truck that says 'Boomer's Auto Shop' on the side."

Linc sketched a salute and began a slow jog in the direction my mother had indicated. When he was out of range, she sank onto the bench. "Oh, my goodness. I have never been so embarrassed. I don't know what came over me. That poor man."

"Why on earth did you say that to him, Mom?" I sat down next to her. "You made it sound like an accusation of some sort. As though he was doing something wrong."

She shook her head. "I didn't know his wife was dead. You'd mentioned him to me, and you said he was older and had kids. I automatically assumed a wife. You didn't say he was a widower."

"Why would I? He's someone I work with. I don't give you the marital statuses and history of every person I meet through my job. Geez, Mom."

She sat forward, grabbing for my hand. "It just threw me, because here I come walking up, and there *you* are, holding hands with a man I don't know—"

"We weren't holding hands, Mom. God."

"Don't cuss, Jenna. And it sure looked like it, from where I was standing, and then you jump up like I'd caught you with your hand in the cookie jar, and you introduce him as a man I'd assumed was married. So it wasn't such a big leap for me to think I'd just found my daughter holding hands with a married man!"

"We weren't holding hands!" I raised my voice and then thought better of it, glancing quickly down the sidewalk to make sure Linc and my dad weren't nearby. "And honestly, Mom. What do you think of me? You jumped to the conclusion that I was messing around with a married man pretty dang fast. You're my mother. Aren't you supposed to believe the best of me?"

She wheeled on me, and words came tumbling out of her mouth faster than either of us expected. "Well, you can hardly blame me, all things considered!"

We both sat for a moment in stunned silence, and then I stood up. "I think I see Rilla and Mason. I'm going to help them with the kids."

"Jenna. Wait—" My mother rose, too and reached for me. I shrugged her off and walked away.

CHAPTER SEVEN

Lincoln

I T TURNED OUT THAT THE Fourth of July in the town of Burton, Georgia, was the biggest ticket around. I couldn't believe how crowded the square was, how many people were watching the parade with child-like rapture, and how much food was on just about every table. It reminded me a little bit of tailgating at a college football game, when fans tended to drift from vehicle to vehicle.

And it was an all-day affair. The kids and I had been downtown since that morning, and as the sun was beginning to set, the party was still going strong. Around the square, some people had broken out guitars, banjos and mandolins, and there were sing-alongs happening all over the place. I saw some heavier drinking going on, but for the most part, it was low-key; no one was falling down drunk. Yet, anyway.

Becca and Oliver were having the time of their young lives. My daughter was staying close, I'd noticed; she made sure I was in sight at all times, but she was enjoying herself with Bridget Evans. Since she'd been spending so much time out on the farm, I'd noticed that she'd begun to relax a little. There wasn't quite so much fear. Ollie played a pick-up game of catch with a bunch of kids, between repeated trips back and forth to the food table.

"This is so good, Mrs. Sutton." He lifted a huge sugar cookie in one hand and mumbled around crumbs. "Thank you for letting us eat with you."

I was proud of my boy's manners, even more so when Jenna's mother hugged him to her. "You just eat as many of those cookies as you want, honey. You are so very welcome." As Oliver ran off, grinning, she looked up at me. "You have done a wonderful job with those children, Linc. You ought to be proud of them."

I shook my head. "I am proud of them, for sure, but I can't take credit. My in-laws had them for the last six years. I had to travel so much for my job that it was just more sensible to have Becca and Oliver in one place, steady. I'm very grateful to Sylvia's parents, for the love and energy they gave their grandkids."

"Still. You can tell things about a child's raising, and you have a part in that." She patted my arm, and I worked hard to keep a smirk off my face. Millie Sutton had spent the better part of the day trying to make up for what she'd said when we'd just met. I could tell she felt horrible about it, and I'd tried to be gracious, to put her at ease. I didn't know why she'd acted like she had, but I was willing to let bygones be bygones and give her another chance. Hell, I was all about the second chances.

I cast a glance around the part of the green that the Suttons, Wallaces, Reynolds and Evans had claimed as theirs for this day, my eyes seeking Jenna. By the time I'd come back with her dad that morning, both of us loaded down with chairs, she'd been busy helping Rilla and Mason wrangle their kids. I'd watched surreptitiously as she'd held their little boy, who looked to be about a year and a half or so. She dipped him down, and as the little guy squealed in delight, she blew raspberries into his neck, making him giggle. I was struck by this new Jenna, open and glowing, so different from the work Jenna, when she was smiling and pleasant but contained, and even from the flustered Jenna I'd encountered when the kids and I had first arrived.

I hadn't been looking for her, at least, not consciously. Becca and Oliver, revved up by the signs they'd seen around town advertising the big Independence Day celebration, had been up since just after sunrise, nagging me to get ready so that we could go. Once we'd arrived downtown, their eyes were round as they took in all the sights, heard the music coming from everywhere and encountered the crowds.

"Where will we sit, Daddy? Is there a spot where we can lay out a blanket?" Becca had tugged at my arm.

"Yeah, and what're we going to eat? I'm hungry." Ollie had rubbed his stomach.

"When are you not?" I'd tapped the bill of his ball cap. "I don't know, guys. Remember I've never been here for the holiday either. I'm figuring it all out, too." We'd reached the edge of the green and paused. "Let's see if we—" I'd broken off as movement caught my eye. Across the grass, a familiar figure had stood on the highest rung of a step stool, her arms extended. The basic male in me had immediately admired the length of tanned legs under denim shorts and the way her ass filled out said shorts. On the heels of those not-so-pure thoughts came the realization that the legs and ass belonged to Jenna Sutton. Before I could decide whether or not to approach her, to say hello, something else happened. In a split second, I'd taken in the situation: the girl standing up on the small ladder, reaching up to attach one side of the flag decoration, had overestimated her ability and balance and was about to tumble onto the ground.

Without saying anything to the kids—there wasn't time—I'd sprinted toward her, my heart thudding in fear that I might not make it in time. My hands had caught her by the waist just as she completely lost her footing.

And then . . . something else occurred. I'd touched Jenna before, here and there, since that first handshake. It was never serious, just casual brushes as I handed her something or pointed out a part of the house. Nothing had stirred in me before. But now, with her firm body in my grasp, plenty was stirring.

My fingers spanned her small middle, and then, as I held her tighter, my hands slid around to rest just above that very fine backside, pressing her to me under the guise of keeping her steady and safe. The rack I'd judged at our first meeting to be pretty nice was now smashed against my chest, and her hands were like vice grips on my arms. The heat of her entire body burned into me and started a fire I didn't want to extinguish . . . unless it was with her mouth on me and mine on her body.

She was breathing hard, from the near-miss of falling,

I assumed. And then something shifted, and she relaxed against me, sagging in my arms, and for a moment, it was perfect. It was the missing piece I hadn't known I needed, sliding neatly into place.

"Jenna! My God, are you all right? Are you hurt?" A diminutive woman with long blonde hair rushed toward us, her hand on her heart. Jenna pushed away from me slightly, but she was still trembling.

I glanced up, forcing my eyes away from Jenna even as I kept her close. "I think she's all right. Probably just a little shaken. Maybe got the breath knocked out of her." I lowered her to stand on her own, but I couldn't quite make myself let go of her yet, my fingers still gripping her hips.

Jenna must've still been a little shaky, since she kept her hands on my arms until the other woman pulled her away, wrapping her in a quick hug. I only half-listened as Jenna stuttered out an apology for scaring us, not paying close attention until she raised her gaze to look me fully in the eyes. There was something there, something akin to terror and fire and raw emotion—more than a little almost-fall off a ladder should've caused.

"Thank you for catching me. I really thought for a minute that I was going to end up broken on the ground."

I spoke the first words that came to my mind. "You're not broken, Jenna." My mind flew back to my conversation with Mason the week before, when we'd talked about Jenna and how her family and friends treated her. As though she could read my thoughts, vulnerability and surprise flashed across Jenna's face.

I finally forced myself to look away and introduced myself to the other woman, who I'd figured out was her cousin Rilla, Mason's wife. Within a few minutes, she'd invited the kids and me to their celebration. Accepting hadn't been a hardship, not when it would mean hanging around with Jenna.

Rilla had left us not long after that, and my kids, who'd given their enthusiastic endorsement to partying with the Sutton and Wallace clans, had run off to check on the horses Ollie had seen earlier. Jenna had seemed flustered once we were alone, and I wasn't sure if it was because she was still getting over her near-fall or whether she wasn't comfortable being on her own with me . . . which was stupid, because we'd been alone together plenty of times at work. Or maybe it was something else entirely. Maybe she'd felt the same thing I had when I'd held her against me.

I hadn't meant to go all confessional on her, telling her about my past and my drinking, but it had come pouring out. She'd reached out to touch my hand, and it had felt as though every nerve in my body was focused on the small spot where we were connected. It had taken a ridiculous amount of nerve for me to flip my hand beneath hers, so that our palms pressed together. I couldn't remember the last time I'd been this turned on, which was ridiculous, because Jenna was sitting a solid two feet away from my body, and we were barely touching each other.

She'd jerked away from me when her mother had arrived, and I hadn't missed how she'd held the hand that had been under mine, as though it burned. Everything had gotten weird after that; I'd heard wonderful things about Millie Sutton from everyone in town, but she certainly didn't seem happy to meet me. She was stiff, nearly hostile, and then she asked about my wife, which floored me.

Still, I'd managed to maintain an even tone as I'd explained to Mrs. Sutton about Sylvia's death. The lady's face had gone red, and I'd seen regret and embarrassment there. Offering to go help her husband carry chairs had given us both a chance to recover, I'd figured.

But from the time I'd come back with Boomer and the chairs, I'd realized that Jenna was avoiding me. She positioned herself at the opposite end of every group, and when I sat down at the picnic table, she jumped to her feet and mumbled about checking on something. She and Ollie had played a game of lawn darts, and I had smiled at my son's trash talk as well as her answering jibes. Becca stuck with Bridget most of the day, but the two girls had accompanied Jenna to the far end of the green to check out the Daughters of the South, who were apparently allowing pictures with visitors now that the parade was over.

As the day wound down, I was aware that Jenna had separated herself not only from me but also from most of her family. I'd met her three older sisters and the husbands who belonged to two of them, as well as Jenna's nephew, who had been Ollie's companion most of the day. I'd seen the same expression in every eye when Millie Sutton had introduced me as the contractor on the Oak Grove job—or as Mrs. Sutton put it, "Jenna's plantation project." It was a mix of surprise and wariness, as they took measure of me, and it made me wonder about what Jenna's family really thought about her.

Now, in the gathering dusk, I finally spotted Jenna sitting in a lawn chair, apart from the rest of the group, on the other side of the gazebo. I meandered in her direction, trying to keep it casual, so that no one would guess that I was seeking her out. I didn't care for myself, but the last thing I wanted to do was to make things more difficult for Jenna with her family.

She was sitting in the low chair with her knees pulled up and both arms wrapped around them. I knew the moment she spotted me, because her shoulders went stiff, and she glanced away. I ignored that and dropped to the ground next to her seat, stretching out my legs in front of me.

"Hey. You kind of disappeared." I bumped lightly against the chair. "Everything okay?"

She was guarded, I could tell, with all her shields up and every defense at the ready. The smile she gave me was forced. "Sure. It just gets to be too much, sometimes, and I need a little space. A little quiet. Some alone time, you know?" Those last words were pointed, and I knew they were meant to push me away.

"Yeah, I get it." I settled myself down, just so she would know I wasn't going away. "You've got a big family to start with, and then you add in Meghan and Sam, Ali and Flynn and all the Evans, Rilla and Mason . . . it's a little overwhelming, isn't it?"

"It can be." She sighed, and I sensed a little corner of the wall crumbling away. "It's hard when you're the different one, too. Everyone else can handle the crowds, the loudness and—well, just everything. I'm the one who can't deal with it." There was bitterness and not a little frustration in her tone.

127

"Well, that right there is some bullshit, Jenna." I spoke matter-of-factly. "There's nothing wrong with you or how you deal with things. And you need to stop listening to anyone who tries to tell you that."

She gave a harsh bark of laughter. "Yeah, that's easy for you to say. It's not so much what they say. It's how they act. How they treat me. I'm not stupid. I might be weak sometimes and maybe a little unstable, but I know what they're thinking, and what they probably say when I'm not around."

"Of course you're not stupid. Remember, I've been working with you for over a month now. You're probably one of the most astute and capable project managers I've ever known. And I'm not just saying that to make you feel better. I hope you know me well enough by now to realize that I don't lie and I don't sugarcoat. If you were fucking up the job, I'd be the first one to call you out."

Her lips twitched. "Thanks."

"Sometimes the people who're closest to us are the least capable of seeing the truth about who we really are. I don't know all the history of you and your family, Jenna, but I know who you are now. And I like what I know."

Jenna snorted and began to answer me when a shadow fell over both of us. A man stood on the other side of her chair, hands in the pockets of his shorts. He had light blond hair, cut short, and wide brown eyes that made him look like a startled cow. I didn't like the way he was checking out Jenna, in that predatory, proprietary manner.

"Hey, Jenna. Thought I'd find you around here."

She flickered up a glance at him but then stared straight ahead. "Hey, Nick." Her voice was curt and dismissive. Inside I was cackling with relief.

"Haven't seen you around much this summer. What's going on?"

"I've been busy with work. I have a huge new project for the historical society, out at Oak Grove." She still didn't look at him.

"Yeah, I've heard about that. You probably know your uncle Larry made me the weekend manager." He paused, obviously waiting for her congratulations or some other positive reaction.

Jenna lifted one shoulder. "Hmm. I didn't know. I haven't seen Uncle Larry in a while."

"Oh." The word hung there for a minute. "Well, we were hoping that the contractor on the plantation project might come to us for some of the supply orders. We were kind of thinking maybe you'd suggest they use us."

"You're in luck. This is the restoration contractor right here." Jenna inclined her head toward me. "But I'm not suggesting or recommending anyone or anything. That would be unethical. You're welcome to talk to him, though." One side of her mouth curled. "Linc, this is Nick Hoffman. Nick, Linc Turner."

He spared me a quick glance. "Hey. Ah, tonight's probably not the time to talk business—"

"You're the one who brought it up," Jenna pointed out.

"—but maybe we can get together next week and talk about your needs and how Wexler's Hardware might be able to help." Nick finished up without acknowledging Jenna's interruption. He dug into his pocket and handed me a card. "Give me a call."

I shoved the cardboard rectangle into my own pocket without looking at it. "Sure. Thanks. My company negotiates our supplies for all of our ongoing jobs, but I can let them know about your store." That was kind of not the truth. I had a lot of leeway to make my own calls about supplies, but I didn't like this guy, and until I knew what he was to Jenna, I wasn't going to commit to anything.

"Okay." He nodded and then turned his focus back to Jenna. "So, Jen, want to come over with me and watch the fireworks? I've got a sweet spot. Very private."

"No, thanks." She shifted in her chair, angling her body toward me. "I'm watching them with Linc. I'll see you around, Nick."

He didn't move right away, but stood staring down at her, his jaw clenched. Finally, he growled out, "Whatever."

As he stalked away from us, Jenna's body slumped down in the chair. "Sorry about that. I kind of used you to get rid of him. But you don't need to stay here with me. I'm fine on my own."

"I know you are. But I'd like to watch the fireworks with you, if that's okay."

She looked over at me, the difference in our height negated by the lift of her chair so that our eyes were level. "Yeah, it's fine."

For a few minutes, we sat in companionable silence. I picked up a blade of grass and began peeling off its fibers one by one. "So . . . Nick. Who's he?" I was pretty sure he wasn't the guy Mason had told me about, the man who'd slept with Jenna and then blown her off. I hadn't gotten that vibe from Jenna or from him. Plus, he didn't fit the image of a man-whore.

Jenna rolled her eyes and blew out a breath. "Nick is a mistake. One of several in my past." She flashed a glance over to me. "It's a long story, and not a fun one."

I squinted up at the sky, which still was mostly pink, painted with the colors of the setting sun. "They won't do the fireworks until it's full-on dark, right? My kids are roasting marshmallows over at the fire pit, with Rilla and Meghan. I've got nothing but time." I paused. "If you want to tell me, you can. You don't have to. We can talk about something that makes you more comfortable, if you want. The weather. The plantation. Recite the Declaration of Independence."

She gnawed the edge of her lip. "You might not like me much after you hear it."

I spread out my hands. "Earlier today, I told you that I was a recovering alcoholic who'd abandoned his kids to their grandparents for six years, because I couldn't fucking man up when I lost my wife. Believe me, sugar, nothing you have to say is going to make me think less of you. Judgement isn't my thing."

The crickets and cicadas chirped over the undercurrent of voices and songs and laughter. Jenna was silent for so long that I assumed she'd decided against telling me when she began to speak.

"I was a flighty kid. I didn't take anything seriously, not school or boys or my parents. I think I was probably a little spoiled. I dated some in high school, but not any one guy for long, mostly because I didn't want to spend the time or energy on any of them. My best friend was Lucie, and I was close to her, but ultimately, I threw her away, too. That's another ugly part of the story." She swallowed. "After graduation, I started going to the community college because I didn't know what else to do. I babysat for Rilla and for a few other people. And then the fall before I turned twenty-one, I started working for my uncle Larry, at the hardware store."

"Ah. That's where you met Nick?"

She shook her head. "No, he wasn't there yet. Uncle Larry just had one full-time, year-around employee and then he hired me part-time, and . . . there was another guy who'd been there on and off for a few years. He did seasonal farm work, but when that was over, he'd stay in town and work for Uncle Larry."

This was the guy. I could hear the cautious, raw tone in her voice. My hands curled into fists. I wanted to pummel that man. I waited for her to say his name.

"Trent—that was him—he was older than me, but he never treated me like a kid. We joked around a lot, and I thought we were friends. No, we definitely *were* friends." She nodded. "But I was young and stupid. Naïve. I thought we were more than friends, or that we could be. In my head, I built up this elaborate fantasy about what Trent felt for me and what our future would be. Everything he did, every little gesture or smile or whatever, I took to mean so much more than it was." She took another deep breath. "It wasn't his fault. Trent had no idea what I was thinking. He probably thought I was a little bit silly and immature, but he never led me on. With distance and a lot of therapy, I can see that now."

I choked back what I wanted to say, which was that no guy was that oblivious. If he knew that Jenna was crushing on him and didn't do anything to gently let her know the truth, he was guilty of avoidance, at the very least.

"I'd decided that Trent was waiting for me to be twenty-one. So the night of my birthday, my friend Lucie and I went to the Road Block. I was so focused on getting Trent to notice me, to see me for the grown-up I thought I was, that I was horrible to Lucie. She was the only one who knew how I felt about Trent, and she was trying to tell me the truth, to get me to see what was real, but I didn't want to listen, and she ended up walking out." Jenna played with a loose thread on the chair's nylon webbing, wrapping it around her finger. "I haven't talked to her since that night. I figured I'd see her the next day and apologize, but then, uh, it didn't happen. By the time I was in a place where I was capable of being her friend again, she'd moved to Savannah." She inhaled deeply. "Anyway, once Lucie was gone, that left everything open for me to go after Trent and I did. I threw myself at him."

My heart broke for the humiliation I heard in her voice. I wanted to reach up and take her hand, but I sensed she didn't want what she would see as my pity.

"He kept putting me off, but I was persistent. And I was drinking. He didn't know it, but I was downing a lot of alcohol." She slid her eyes to me. "When I said earlier that I don't drink much, I wasn't lying. It's mostly because of what happened that night. I never want to lose control like that again."

I nodded. "I can understand the feeling."

"The long and short of it is that Trent took me back to the room he was renting, and we . . . uh, we slept together. I had never—" She closed her eyes. "It was my first time.

133

He didn't know that. He didn't even know it after. He let me sleep there that night, but then he told me in the morning that I'd better go home. There weren't any declarations of love. No early-morning cuddles. It wasn't what I'd pictured. Instead it was cold and shameful and . . . cheap. I left that room feeling like the worst kind of slut."

I couldn't stop myself from laying a hand on her arm. She glanced down at where I touched her, but she didn't move away.

"I didn't tell anyone what had happened, and after a little recovery, I decided Trent just didn't know how I felt. He thought I'd just been using him, the way all the women in town did. So there was a party I knew about, three days after we'd hooked up, and I'd heard Trent was going to be there. It was back at the Road Block, and I showed up and went right for Trent. I acted like we were together. Pulled up a chair next to his, hung all over him . . . I think I probably embarrassed the hell out of him. He tried to make a joke out of it, shake me off him, but I wasn't letting go. He finally took me aside and said I needed to cool it. When I still didn't get the message, he got louder and, um, clearer. He told me that I was a one-night stand, and that he'd only slept with me because he felt sorry for me, after I'd made such a big deal about coming onto him. A pity fuck, he called it, and then he said, 'And honey, you weren't good enough for me to give you a second ride.'"

"God, Jenna, where is this guy now? Why the hell didn't your father beat him? If you were my daughter—" I shook my head. "He wouldn't have the equipment left to do what he did to you to any other woman."

She attempted a smile. "Oh, well, when it eventually came out, my dad went after him. If it wasn't for Mason and Sam, my dad might've done something terrible. At least, that's what I heard. I wasn't there. By that time, I was, um, away." She twisted the hem of her shorts between two fingers. "I had kind of a breakdown, and that's when it all came out. The whole town was talking about it, about me, and Trent ended up leaving, probably to keep away from my dad as much as anything else." She paused for a few beats. "He came back last year, and being the coward I am, I left town and went to stay with my grandmother in Charleston. But I heard he'd gotten married and was turning his life around. I'm glad for him. Really, I am. Trent wasn't the bad guy in this situation."

"That's a matter of opinion." I hoped my tone made it clear exactly what my thoughts on the subject were. "And you're not a coward, Jenna. But where does Nick come into this?"

She groaned. "Oh, that part's just embarrassing. After Trent left town and I started to recover a little, Uncle Larry hired Nick. He'd just moved to Burton. We met at Uncle Larry's house, and he asked me out. At that point, I was still so numb . . . I said yes mostly because saying no was too much effort. And somehow I ended up sort of dating him. I fell into it, without any real decision. I never felt anything for him. I guess someone had told him what had happened to me, because he never pushed me. Didn't try to kiss me, at least not at first, and he probably thought he was giving me space. But it was like a weird, bizarro-world version of what had happened between Trent and me, reversed, except

I never slept with Nick. He was sure we were going to end up together, though. Positive that we were meant to be. When I broke things off, for good, he got real mad. Not just at me, either. I heard he went off on Trent one day at the Road Block, when Trent was back in town."

I hmphed. "You know, I don't think I like Nick very much, but I can give him some props for going up against Trent."

"Oh, Linc." She sighed again, and her head drooped back against her chair. One hand fluttered over to cover mine where it still rested on her arm. "I appreciate that you're standing up for me, but honestly, I had to let go of any resentment I had toward Trent. I was in therapy for a very long time, and that's the most important thing I took away. I had to see where I'd created this situation for myself. I had to take responsibility."

"That I understand. It's part of the twelve-step program I'm in. I couldn't blame Sylvia for driving when she was too tired—that isn't what made me drink. It was just an excuse. All the people in my life wanted to give me an out, an excuse, but I couldn't keep doing that if I wanted to recover. And I did."

"Exactly." Jenna nodded. "My dad and mom want to blame Trent. My therapist—well, I saw several, but my favorite one—she said that I didn't have to blame myself, but I had to accept responsibility. There's a difference. Blame is a negative action, while responsibility gives you power over a situation. It gives you a choice. It's easy to say things happen to me, but I'd rather think I can make things happen."

There was an assurance and confidence in Jenna as

she spoke that blew my mind. I wondered if her family had heard what I did—that Jenna had not only recovered from what had happened with Trent, she had risen above it and used it to become a better person.

"It seems like you're in a place to move on. Is your family, um, supportive of that? I got the sense today that there's still some tension."

She lolled her head to the side and opened her eyes. "They would say, yes, that they've been nothing but supportive. And in one way, that's true. But they all still see me as Jenna Before. Somewhere deep inside, my parents, at least, feel like I let them down. I made bad choices, I screwed up, and for the rest of my life, I know they'll always be waiting for the other shoe to drop. No matter what I do right, it's like they're always waiting for it to go wrong, for them to have to scoop up the pieces again and put me back together."

"Does all this have anything to do with what was going on with your mom earlier? When she first got here? She seemed a little . . . upset. Not that she hasn't been great to me all day," I hastened to add. "She and your dad are both awesome. They've been real friendly and welcoming. But at first, your mother wasn't happy. That was clear."

A faint pink stained Jenna's face. "That was a complicated situation, but let me just assure you, it had nothing to do with you. It all went back to my mother assuming that if there's a bad choice to make, I'm going to make it. I'm sorry you got caught in the crossfire."

"Hey, no worries. I wasn't upset." I was caught by her hazel eyes, large and luminous, watching me. "I've got thick skin. But have you talked to your parents? Your sisters?

Maybe thought about some family counseling?"

She bit the edge of her lip and shook her head. "No. I try not to rock the boat. I just stay in the status quo, and I do what I can to keep them happy. Dinners at home once a week. Answering phone calls and texts. Just maintaining, you know?"

"I do know. I lived in maintaining town for a few years, after I stopped drinking and got my job back, started working regularly."

"But you're not there anymore?"

I laughed softly. "Not really. After a while, it gets boring. You get restless, or at least I did. And someone comes along to make you want to move out and on. To start living again, not just keep treading water."

Jenna quirked an eyebrow at me. "That sounds very much like something my therapist used to say to me all the time. 'What's life without risk?'" And I always said that life without risk is safer and steadier. More predictable."

"Uh huh, and what did the esteemed doctor have to say about that?"

She grinned, and my heart stuttered as something so real and light glimmered in her eyes, maybe for the very first time since I'd known her.

"She'd say it was okay to feel that way until someone comes along who's going to make me want to be brave again."

"Yup," I whispered. "That's it exactly."

"Who was it for you?" Jenna spoke low, too, and neither of us looked away from the other. "Who made you brave?"

I exhaled long. "Basically, my kids. They'd been there all along, but Ryland kicked my ass into gear. He told me I couldn't just leave them with Sylvia's parents forever. That's what Hank and Doris—those were my in-laws—that's what they wanted, really, I think. Syl had been their only child, and Becca and Ollie are their only grandchildren, of course. They wanted the kids to replace who they'd lost. But Ry convinced me I needed to take them back and make a life for the three of us. He'd been bugging me for a long time to take the partnership, and once I finally gave in, it opened the door for us to base Kent and Turner here. All of that pushed me into living again. I'm not treading water anymore."

"Hmm."

I wasn't sure if she was aware of it or not, but Jenna's fingers had begun stroking the back of my hand. It sent shivers up my spine and reminded other parts of my body that I wasn't dead yet. I shifted, moving a little closer, so that my face was near hers.

"Do you think maybe you're ready to move out of maintaining and into real life, Jenna? Are you ready to be brave?"

She swallowed, and I could see the rise and fall of her throat. "I don't know. Maybe. I want to . . . try. I think."

"Let us be part of that, the kids and me." I took a risk and repeated my move from earlier, turning my hand and capturing her fingers. She froze, but she didn't pull away from me. "We can help you start moving on. Let us into your life. Open that door." I paused for a breath, as something occurred to me. "It would be good for Becca, too. She's stuck in her own form of limbo, where she feels like if she can keep everyone safe, life is controllable. I'd like her to realize it's okay to start being brave again."

"What does that mean? Letting you into my life. You

mean . . . we'd be friends?"

I wanted to laugh at that. *Yeah, friends was a start, but it wasn't where I wanted to end.* I wasn't sure if I was ready for anything else. I hadn't been looking for anything else. But the idea of possibility, with this woman, kind of intrigued me.

"Sure. Beyond just work friends. I want you to step out of your safety zone, and we'll help you do it."

"How far out of my safety zone?" She frowned, suspicious.

"Let's say coming over for dinner. Hanging out with us. Inviting us to your place. Having a social life and interaction beyond and outside of your family."

Jenna was thinking about it, I could tell. Uncertainty and eagerness battled behind her eyes. I waited to see which would win.

"Okay." She nodded. "I can't promise anything, but I'll give it a shot. It won't be easy. I've been shutting people out for a long time."

"I know. But this is good, Jenna. For all of us. And we'll move slow, as slow as you need."

"All right." Her fingers curled around my hand, holding tight. "Thank you, Linc. Thank you for listening. Thanks for not making me feel like an idiot."

I fought the urge to lift her hand to my lips. *Baby steps.* "Any time, sugar."

Above our heads, there was a sudden explosion, and color filled the black sky. I moved a little so that my back was against the side of Jenna's chair and leaned, looking up. She was close to me, our hands were linked, and although I hadn't yet dared to take the time to figure out what the hell I was doing here, there was no place else I wanted to be.

CHAPTER EIGHT

Jenna

THE DAY AFTER INDEPENDENCE DAY was a workday. I was scheduled to make my regular visit to the Oak Grove work site before I went to the office, and to my annoyance, I was nervous. Again. After weeks of being at ease with Linc and all the crew, today I was shaky with nerves. I knew it was because of the conversation I'd had with Linc the night before; I'd spilled nearly all my deep, dark secrets, and facing him after that made my stomach roll.

Linc had been wonderful, supportive and so sweet. He hadn't treated me like a moron or assumed that I had to be handled carefully, but I was worried about how he'd be after a night to think it over. Was he going to regret his offer to help pull me back into real life? Part of me hoped he did, and just left me alone. Another part, growing increasingly louder, wanted him to carry through.

I arrived at Oak Grove a few minutes later than I normally did. Linc's truck was in its usual spot, along the tree line, and as I climbed out of the car, I heard him whistling. Taking a deep breath, I made myself walk across the gravel and up the porch steps.

Linc must have heard my footsteps. He stuck his head out the front door opening—they'd removed the actual door for safety's sake while the bulk of the interior work was happening—and grinned at me.

"Hey, sugar. Mornin'. Ready for your tour?"

It was the same way he greeted me every day, and I began to relax a little. I'd gotten used to his teasing endearments; although I could tell he tried to rein himself in, he often peppered his speech to me with *darlin's*, *honeys*, and *sugars*. I'd learned not to take offense, because I knew it didn't mean that he took me any less seriously. In fact, I'd been impressed by the level of respect with which all of Linc's crew treated me. There was no derision or sarcasm if I asked a dumb question, and they were patient with me, answering in careful detail.

"Sure. Feels funny, having missed a day." I stepped through and smiled, as I always did. Seeing this plantation come back to life was the highlight of every day.

"Nothing was done yesterday, so you didn't miss a thing. But they did put in the chair rail in the dining room on Tuesday after you'd been here, and the baseboards are up in the parlor. The plumber's nearly finished upstairs, and the electrician is going to come by early next week for his walk-through. He should be starting next month, I think."

"This is amazing." I ran my fingers over the smooth

wood. "I can't wait to see it painted. I know that's a long time coming." I tossed Linc an apologetic glance. "I'm just saying . . . eventually."

"Yeah, I hear that. One step at a time, darlin'. These rooms that don't need plumbing can have some of the cosmetic stuff set up early, so it gets us thinking we're nearer to the end. But we still got a long way to go."

"True. Oh, the security company called on Tuesday. They want to come out and look at everything before they give us an estimate. Do you think we should have them here the same time the electrician comes? I know a lot of what they do will be in conjunction with how the boxes are set up."

"Not a bad idea. I'll let you know the exact time the electrician's coming, and you can set it up. Now, come here. I have a little surprise for you."

I tilted my head as I followed Linc back into the front hallway. "What kind of surprise? I'm not a big surprise kind of girl. I like safety and predictability, remember?"

"I know that, sugar. Don't worry, this is a good one." He stopped at the foot of the stairs. "Remember the railing that was up here before? The one we had to remove because of the rotting?"

"Yes." I sighed. "Don't remind me. It broke my heart to have to take that down."

"Well, prepare to have your heart unbroken." Linc leaned down and picked up a piece of paper that was lying on one of the steps. "Check this out."

On the paper was a sketch—a rough one, yes, but I could tell what it was meant to be. "Oh! Linc! That's the banister. Who did it? What does it mean?"

He stuck his thumbs in the belt loops of his jeans. "I took a picture before we tore it out, and I sent it to one of my friends back in Crystal Cove, along with the description from your research. Cooper's a master carpenter, and he does all kinds of custom pieces for our restorations. He did this sketch, and if you approve it, we'll go ahead and commission him to do the work. He said he'd even come up here and install it, gratis. So what do you say?"

"Oh, my God, Linc! Yes, of course. I'm so excited. I thought we were going to have to go with some generic piece of wood there . . . this is going to be perfect. Thank you so much." Without thinking, I stood on my toes and wrapped my arms around his neck in what was meant to be a quick hug.

The minute I pressed myself to him, I knew I'd made a mistake. Heat suffused my body, and I could feel my pulse beating in every sensitive nerve. My instinct to flee kicked in, and I made to step back, hoping Linc would just pretend me hugging him was a normal, everyday occurrence.

But no such luck. Before I could move away, he slid his arms around my waist, pulled me against him, and gave me a tight squeeze. "You're very welcome, darlin'. I'm glad you like the idea."

I didn't have anything to say or any way to say it. I was too busy being flooded with sensation, with the feel of Linc's hard chest and the way my body seemed to fit against his. As though he could sense I was just about to melt or implode, he let me go, trailing his fingers along my hips as I took one step backward.

"I'm sorry about that. I don't know what made me . . . I mean, we're at work. I know how to behave. That was inappropriate."

"Jenna. No one is here but you and me. The crew isn't going to get here for another half-hour at the soonest—considering most of them were probably partying late last night, might be a little longer than that. You hugged me because you were excited about something good. That's what friends do, and no one would've thought anything of it."

I wrapped my arms around my middle. "Maybe. Still, I don't want to blur boundaries. I'm kind of sensitive about that—about my ability to read people and not assume things."

Linc nodded. "I understand that. But part of me being your person—the one who's going to drag you back into life—is that you have to trust me. I will always be honest with you, Jenna. If I feel like you're stepping over lines, I'll tell you. And you can always ask me if you're not sure. We're not going to pussy foot around shit, okay?"

"Okay." I nodded. "I'll try to trust you. I won't promise it's going to be easy."

"Of course it isn't. If it were easy, you'd have done it long ago." He crossed his arms over his chest, making me remember what it felt like to press against that muscled wall. "Now, would you like to come over for dinner tonight? I thought I'd pick up pizza from Franco's. The kids and I have become regulars there."

I opened my mouth to say yes, but instead, other words came tumbling out. "I don't know if tonight is a good night. With the holiday yesterday, I have a ton to catch up on, and—and maybe the kids won't be comfortable. I think Oliver likes me okay, but Becca doesn't seem sure. And maybe we should take some time to think this over."

"Jenna." Linc cocked his head and looked down at me with what might have been amusement. "This is one of those times when you need to trust me. If you don't have pizza with us tonight, what will you do?"

I could've lied and said I would eat with my parents or one of my sisters or even Rilla and Mason. But we'd promised honesty, so reluctantly I admitted, "I'll go home after work, eat some soup from a can and watch old episodes of *Veronica Mars*. In my sweatpants."

"Sweatpants this time of year? You'll roast."

I smirked, finding it funny that out of everything I'd just recited, Linc had picked up on my planned attire. "I live on the second floor of a duplex, and they never bothered to separate the climate control system when they changed it to a two-family home. The owner lives downstairs, and she is apparently going through—well, let's just say she has a lot of hot flashes. She keeps the house at about sixty-five degrees. I'm always cold when I'm at home."

"Ah. Well, when you come for pizza at our house, I suggest shorts, because I can't afford to keep our air conditioning that low. Plus the kids like to eat outside on the deck, even when it's hot. There won't be any *Veronica Mars*, but I can get quippy like Logan, if it'll make you smile."

My eyes widened. "You know Logan? Did you watch *Veronica Mars*?"

"Not voluntarily," Linc snorted. "After Ryland met Abby and moved in with her, I used to stay with them sometimes.

Abby is a huge fan and watches the damn series over and over. She can recite entire episodes. I was forced to watch it against my will, and I absorbed some of it, apparently."

"Oh, that's the best. We can talk about Duncan and Lily and Mac and Wallace—"

"What about Piz?"

I made a face. "Ugh. I can't stand him. I totally ship Veronica and Logan. All the way."

Linc closed his eyes. "Oh, my God. I've opened a terrible can of worms and there's no way to stuff them back in, is there?"

"Absolutely not. Now what time tonight, and what can I bring?"

"Six and . . ." He twisted his mouth. "Do you have anything in the way of desserts handy? The kids love cookies and all that crap, but I can't bake for shit."

"Sadly, neither can I, but I have a friend who can. I'll bring something fabulous. And I'll see you at six."

<hr>

"Well, if it isn't my favorite customer, back again. Does this make it . . . what, twenty-eight days running? Wow, a solid month of almost daily visits. Color me impressed, sweetie pie."

I rolled my eyes. "Okay, Kiki. Get it all out. I'll wait."

"Hey, I'm just thrilled. This new relationship of yours means I can afford another mixer. But you have forced me to up my game. Coming up with something new to send with you over to the Turner house is my new daily challenge."

"It hasn't been *every* day." I felt silly quibbling the details when Kiki was pretty much right on the track. In the just over a month since Linc had first invited me for pizza at his house, I'd spent almost every evening with the Turner family. It wasn't always dinner; sometimes we met on the town green for a game of softball or to hear one of the local bands that played on Thursday nights during the summer months.

Linc and the kids rarely came to my house, although they'd stopped by to pick me up a few times. My little apartment wasn't quite ready to accommodate three extra people, particularly two kids, and especially Ollie, who was a typical nine-year old boy, never still. My landlady hadn't ever had reason to complain about anything I did in my upstairs part of the house; I had a sense that one of the reasons for that was my total lack of life up until now. She wouldn't love hearing Oliver running over her head.

I had insisted, though, on keeping things even as much as I could. I brought over pizza several times, and I treated for dinner at Kenny's twice. And since that very first night, I always, always brought them some small treat from Kiki's bakery. I was pretty sure it was that habit that had cemented the easy friendship I had with Oliver now. He greeted me with a hug each time, and then followed that up with the question, "What kind of dessert did you bring?"

Linc had scolded him about it at first, but when he realized it had become part of our banter, he left it alone and just shook his head.

If only cookies or pastries could have won over Becca so easily. The young girl still regarded me with caution, if not occasional hostility. I tried to respect her feelings without pushing by including her in every invitation and conversation but never complaining when she chose to decline or ignore me. And when Linc had apologized to me about her behavior, I'd assured him I wasn't hurt. Honestly, with everything Becca had been through in her young life, I felt that she was entitled to a little rebellion when it came to more change.

As though she could read my thoughts—and who knew, maybe she could; this was Kiki, after all—the baker reached across the glass display case and patted my arm. "Try not to worry too much about Becca. She'll come around. When she's in here with me, she talks about you sometimes, and she always has something positive to say. She likes you, but she's afraid to acknowledge it, to you or even to herself, I think."

I shrugged. "It's no big deal, Kiki. It's not like I'm going to be part of her family or anything. I'm just a friend of her father's, and eventually, she'll either like me or not. I thought maybe I could help her in some way . . . but maybe that was naïve, considering I'm still so screwed up myself." I sighed. "Regardless, I'm glad she has you in her life. I think every girl needs a Kiki in her corner."

I'd expected a quip or a laugh in response, but instead, Kiki frowned. She hesitated a moment before she spoke. "Do you have a few minutes, or are you in a hurry today?"

A zing of trepidation spiraled down my middle. "Um, I have some time. Linc is cooking, but they don't expect me for a while yet."

"Good." She skirted the counter and went to the door of the shop, where she flipped the OPEN sign to CLOSED and turned the lock. Coming back over to me, she pulled out a chair and pointed to the one opposite. "Sit down. I think we need to talk some things over."

"Okay." I sat, my stomach clenching. "What's up? You're kind of freaking me out."

"I know. I'm sorry about that. I've been waiting for an opening to have this conversation with you, but it doesn't seem to be coming, so I'm going to make my own." Kiki laid her hands flat on the table between us. "Jenna, I want to talk about Trent."

I recoiled a little in surprise. "What about him?"

She leaned forward a little, seeking my eyes. "I need to apologize to you, about how I acted after . . . well, all around the time that you were suffering the most. When you probably needed someone, I wasn't there for you. And Jenna, I am truly sorry. I made a decision without really thinking about it . . . well. You knew that Trent and I were friends, too, didn't you? He'd been coming here since he was a little boy, and he was so lost. So unloved and neglected. Of all my kids—" She flashed a quick smile at me. "Yes, I think of you all as my kids. All of you who I have been privileged to have in my life, some for a long time and others only for a season—you're all partly mine, in some sense. And some need me just a little, while for others, I'm the only steady person in their lives."

"He mentioned you once, at work." I hadn't thought about this for a long time. "I said I'd been by the bakery, and he told me you were the most wonderful person in this whole town. He said you were the only one he could trust and depend on, from the time he was a little boy."

"I'm glad he felt that way. I always wished I could do

more. I actually thought about trying to get approved as a foster mother, so I could take him in officially. But I had Sydney, you know, and I had to put her first." Kiki had raised her niece from babyhood on. "But it broke my heart, because no one ever put Trent first. He was shuttled around, returned to his loser of a mother—"

"Kiki!" I'd never heard her speak of anyone so bitterly.

"I'm sorry, but in this case, it was true. She did everything she could to destroy his life, whether it was intentional or incidental. Anyway, Trent will always hold a special part of my heart. And when I heard what had happened . . ." She exhaled long and closed her eyes. "I couldn't figure out how to support both of you. I knew you had your parents, who are and have always been wonderful. You had this loving family who was wrapping you in their arms. Trent had no one but a town ready to crucify him for being the very person they'd made him to be."

I nodded. "I can understand that."

"There was some guilt, too. After all, I knew how you felt about Trent. I'd picked up on those intense emotions, but I never thought it would go that far. I didn't pay attention to the warning signs—and if I had, maybe I could've headed you off. I'm sorry, Jenna. I let you down on so many levels."

"Kiki." I reached across the table and covered both of her hands with mine. "You don't have to apologize. I never felt you let me down." I paused, trying to figure out how to put my feelings into words. "What happened with Trent and me was a result of who I was back then. Before. There are a lot of things I wish could be different from that time, but ul-

152

timately, if it hadn't happened, I wouldn't be who I am now. And I'm starting to realize that I like the Jenna After more than the Jenna Before."

"God, you sound healthy." Kiki smiled. "How did that happen?"

"A lot of therapy, months of hibernating from the world and people who wouldn't let me give up. You're one of those. Even when we weren't necessarily talking all the time, I've always known you have my back."

"I'm glad." She squeezed my hands. "Speaking of people you can count on . . . any improvement on things with your mom and dad?"

I shook my head. "Not really. We're doing what's become status quo with us: we don't talk about anything important. We ignore what happened on the Fourth of July; neither of us mentions it. I don't know if she told my father about what she said to me or not, but he just seems confused about why there's so much extra tension now. He did ask me what was going on with Linc and me, and I explained that we were friends, helping each other out. I'm not sure he understands, but he's not giving me any grief about it, so . . ." I lifted one shoulder. "For now, that's about all I can ask."

"You're going to have to force the issue eventually." Kiki sat back in her chair. "Your parents are good people, Jenna. They love you, and they want the best for you. I think sometimes they don't understand you, but it doesn't change the fact that they will always be in your corner. I hope you know that."

"I do know it. We need to figure out what our relationship looks like now. I feel like they're still trying to be the parents they wished they had been to me before—and now I need them to accept who I've become. It's going to be a long path, I think, but I have faith that eventually, we'll find our way."

"Good. And now let's talk about Linc." Kiki folded her arms over her chest. "Were you being honest with your father when you told him you were just friends?"

"I didn't say *just* friends," I corrected. "I don't want to make friendship sound less important than it is. Linc is dragging me out of limbo, out of the place where I was just existing instead of living. I'm grateful. I'm not sure that anyone else could've done it, because on some level, I suspect everyone who knew me before is trying to make me back into the old Jenna, the one they're comfortable with. Linc didn't know that old Jenna. He doesn't have expectations; he pushes me, yes, but I trust him."

"Uh huh. And on no level are you interested in jumping his bones?"

I'd have thought that after all these years of knowing Kiki, I'd be used to the outrageous things she said. But still, I couldn't stop the heat that spread over my cheeks, just like I couldn't quite figure out how to answer her.

"Honestly, Kiki. The things you say."

"You sound like Sydney. And that's a stall tactic right there. Trying to divert the conversation from the fact that you are, indeed, hot for Lincoln's rocking bod."

"Does Troy know that you're looking at other guys? I can't think he'd like it." Kiki's lover Troy Beck was probably one of the least jealous guys I'd ever seen, but I couldn't resist jabbing at her anyway.

"Troy knows I'm his. I'm totally taken, but I'm not dead. I can admire the male form on a level of pure appreciation, not one of lust. And stop trying to change the subject. Do you or do you not think Linc is completely fuckable?"

"Kiki!" I pressed my hands to my face. "Stop. I'm trying *not* to think of him that way. Linc has been so good to me, so kind and . . ."

"And I didn't miss the way he was looking at you when you all came into the bakery last week. He wants to lick you up like one of my strawberry parfaits. The guy is jonesing for you, Jenna. There's not a question in my mind about that."

My heart was thumping so loud in my chest that I was sure Kiki could hear it. "I think you're imagining things. He never . . . I mean, we never . . ."

"He might never, and you might never, but that doesn't mean you both don't want to. And why in the hell shouldn't you?"

"Oh, only about a thousand different reasons. First of all, we work together. Second, we're friends, and I don't want to mess that up. It's important to me. Third, I'm not sure I'm ready yet. And finally, there's the age difference. Linc's thirty-four. I'm twenty-three. Eleven years is a big gap."

Kiki laughed, throwing her head back and clutching her middle. "Oh, sweetie, you're not going to go there, are you? With me? Honestly?"

I stuck out my tongue at her.

"Jenna, I'm currently shacking up with a man who is over twenty years younger than I am. For us, it isn't just the years—it's the fact that I'm the older one. The world tends to look the other way when the man is the senior partner, so to speak, but when it's the woman—well, I'm a cougar. I'm preying on innocent younger men." She rolled her eyes. "My point is, the age difference excuse isn't going to fly with me. Plus, I'd say your experience puts you at least at the same emotional level as Linc."

"Okay, well, even if I concede that point, there are the others that are perfectly valid."

Kiki cast her eyes upward. "Bullshit. You work together. So what? Some of the best couples meet through their jobs. You're friends. That's the absolute best foundation for a lasting romantic relationship."

I cocked my head. "Did you and Troy become friends first?" I was fairly sure I knew the answer to this question, but I wasn't certain. They'd met while I was out of town, living in Charleston with my grandmother, and by the time I came back to Burton, she'd already gone on tour with him.

"No. Our relationship began when he fucked me senseless against the wall in a dark hallway at the Road Block. We didn't even know each other's last names. Hell, he didn't even know my real *first* name. But we got to be friends after that."

"Ah." Well, that was more information than I'd needed. I wondered if I'd be able to look Troy in the eye the next time I saw him.

"As to your claim that you're not ready—Jenna, darling girl, no one is ever ready. Not one of us. When Troy and I hooked up, I wasn't looking for anything more than casual sex. I needed an itch scratched. I wanted a long, hard—"

"Okay, enough." I clapped my hands over my ears. "I don't need any more visuals, thanks very much. Geez, Kiki."

She chuckled. "Anyway, my point is that if you spend your life waiting to be healthy and whole before you consider falling in love, it'll never happen. Falling in love, finding that right person—that's part of what makes us whole. Not that you need a man to make you complete . . . or shit, maybe you do. My feminist roots are screaming about that, but maybe there's something to it. I would've told you I was perfectly happy before I met Troy, but I learned that loving him made my life better on an entirely new dimension. More complete. I could have lived the rest of my days pretty content, but everything is so much better now that he and I are together. Does that make any sense to you?"

"Strangely, it does." I pushed back my chair. "Which is probably a sign that I need to get my cookies boxed up and go, before you've gotten me totally brainwashed."

"No brainwashing. Just pointing out something you're already feeling." Kiki stood up, too, and went behind the counter to get the cookies.

"Kiki." I leaned my hip on the metal part of the display, carefully avoiding the glass which I knew smudged much too easily. "If I did . . . have feelings for Linc . . . how would I know what to do? I really have no idea. I don't have moves to make. The last time I decided to go after a guy, the consequences were kind of disastrous."

She paused in the act of tying string on the long box, tilting her head and pursing her lips. "I think, in this case, you just need to accept how you feel. You need to be honest with yourself, and stop trying to talk yourself out of it. And then wait. In this case, with your history, I don't recommend you making the first move. But I do believe that we give off

157

vibes, and if you're open to the idea of a relationship, Linc's going to pick up on that. Given the look in his eyes the last time I saw him, I'd lay good money that it won't take him long at all to make his feelings known."

She pushed the packaged cookies over the counter to me, her eyes twinkling. "And honey, when that happens, you hold on tight and enjoy the ride."

CHAPTER NINE

Lincoln

"HEY, LINC." JERRY LANG STUCK his bald head through the doorway of the master suite, where I was on my knees, checking the flooring. "We got that counter set, and the electrician finished in the living room—uh, parlor—and dining room. He left about forty-five minutes ago. You good for the rest of us to take off?"

I sat back on my heels. "Sure." I pulled my phone out of my back pocket, dusted off the screen protector and checked the time. "I didn't realize how late it was. Yeah, get going, and I'll see everyone back here Monday. Thanks for all your work."

"No problem, boss." Jerry withdrew, but before he could get very far, I called him back.

"Hey, Jerry."

He leaned in again. "Yeah, boss?"

"You see Jenna anywhere around? She was supposed to be here to take a look at the kitchen. I thought she'd be on site by now."

Jerry shook his head. "Nah, I haven't seen her. Once the guys and I clear out, it's only going to be you here." He grinned. "You okay with that? I know it's against the, uh, protocol to have anyone on the job by himself."

I rolled my eyes. "Yeah, Jerry, I'm okay with that. It's more for the beginning of a job, when someone could be hurt, and besides which, I'm the boss. The buck stops here. I promise, I'm not going to sue myself if I'm stupid enough to fall down the steps or nail my foot to the floor. Also, Jenna should be here any minute. Then I won't be alone."

"Yeah, I'd say not." Jerry quirked an eyebrow, and I didn't like the gleam in his eye. "Not hardly."

"What the hell's that supposed to mean?" I stood up, rising to my full height, my eyes narrowing. I'd known this man for many years; he'd come over with Ryland and me when we'd left Leo Groff's company and joined on with Ryland in his new venture. Since he wasn't part of the finishing team, I hadn't worked very much with him until this job. I liked him, and I respected him. But damn if I was going to let him cast dispersions on Jenna's name. I knew how sensitive she was about what people thought.

Jerry backed down, and the gleam I'd objected to extinguished. "Oh, nothing, boss. Just . . . you know. We all like Ms. Sutton. It's nice to see you . . . uh, I don't know. You seem happy around her. Been a long time since I've seen you smile so much. I figure having your kids back is probably part of it, and that's great, but seems like you kind of light up a little when Ms. Sutton's here. I'm not trying to say anything wrong's going on. But it makes all of us guys happy to see you with a bounce to your step again."

I nodded, letting my shoulders drop. "I appreciate that, Jerry. I do. But Jenna and I are friends, and I don't want anyone doing or saying anything to make her uncomfortable, got it? I know how the guys are when they latch onto something. I know you'd never do anything to hurt her feelings. Not on purpose."

"I got it, boss. None of us would ever make her feel bad. I'll make sure of that."

Glancing out the window, I rubbed the back of my neck. "Thanks, Jerry. Now go on and enjoy your day off. See you Monday."

I stood still, listening to the clump of his boots down the steps. There were voices downstairs as the rest of the men gathered their tools and stomped out of the house. Within a few minutes, all was silence.

Glancing down at my phone again, I frowned. Jenna had promised to be at the plantation by five, when everyone would be on their way out, so that she could check out our progress without getting in anyone's way. She was always punctual, and she would have texted me if she'd known she was going to be late. Since it was Saturday, she hadn't been working at the historical society; last night, when she'd left the kids and me after what had become our regular Friday night pizza and movie extravaganza, she'd mentioned housecleaning and maybe a visit with her cousin Rilla.

I could've texted to check on her, but I didn't want to distract her if she was already on the road. So I pocketed my phone again and finished checking the edge of the floor. We were moving along in the upstairs rooms, and I was satisfied with our progress overall. There were a few minor bumps, some hold ups that might delay us a little, but—and I hated to say it, even to myself, in the sanctity of my own head—so far, this job had been amazingly smooth.

Jenna had felt we were sufficiently far along this week that she had brought in her boss and their PR manager, so that they could get an idea of where we stood. I'd been gratified at their surprised exclamations as they toured the house and examined what we'd done so far. Jenna told me later that they'd been thrilled and excited about how well Oak Grove was developing, returning to what it had been so many years ago.

I heard the sound of a car crunching over the gravel, and I stood up fast to look out the window. Jenna's small blue compact rolled to a stop just behind my pickup truck, and as I watched, the driver's door swung open. Her long legs unfolded from the front seat, and then she emerged, her brown hair caught up in a high ponytail. She was wearing khaki shorts and a tank top, and even from this distance, I could see how the cotton hugged her boobs.

God Almighty. For the last month, I'd been ignoring the way my body reacted each and every time I saw Jenna. I wasn't stupid; I knew it was more than just basic chemistry and biology. I saw women all the time, and none of them ever made my balls tighten, my cock go hard and my fingers itch to touch them. I was constantly finding excuses to touch Jenna, though, all in non-sexual ways, of course. I'd brush her arm reaching for a napkin when we ate together. Press my leg against hers when we were all on the sofa watching a movie. Take her hand to help her up and hold it just a beat longer than necessary.

But I hadn't let myself think about why I needed to do it, why she made me yearn. I refused to acknowledge the dreams I'd been having with increasingly frequency, dreams that featured Jenna Sutton in a starring role and left me aroused and frustrated. I wasn't ready to think about the ramifications of wanting Jenna. Each time I was tempted to say something, to make a move, I had a ready list of reasons why it wouldn't work.

First of all, there was our work relationship. As I'd said to Jerry, I didn't want even a hint of gossip about us to muddy the waters while we were working together on this project. It was too important to her for there to be any snide talk about the historical society project manager banging the contractor.

And then of course, there was the difference in our ages. Eleven years felt like a damn long time when I considered it in the cold light of day. I never saw Jenna as that much younger than me; she was mature and steady, and she always seemed to be older than just twenty-three. But other people would see it, for sure. There was also the fact that I had two children. Becca and Oliver were the greatest kids in the world, and I loved them more than my own breath. But expecting someone who was barely out of her teens to take on parenting two almost-adolescents would be wrong. It would be asking too much.

Finally, but definitely not the least of my worries, was our friendship. I'd promised to be her friend, the person she could trust above anyone else to be truthful. In the last month or so, watching Jenna come out of her shell and come back to life had been a beautiful thing. She was more spontaneous now, less contained and less anxious. I'd heard her laughter more often, and each time, it made my heart expand. I was terrified that if I changed our relationship now, it might destroy the progress she'd made.

I watched now as Jenna slammed shut the car door and bent to look into the side view mirror, fussing with her hair. Seeing her smoothing one hand over the dark strands and then reach into her purse for something she put on her lips struck me as two distinct realizations swept into my mind.

Jenna was fixing herself up before she came to see me. She wanted to look good for me. If that was the case . . . maybe, just maybe, Jenna was feeling the same temptation about me that I was feeling about her. I'd noticed over the past week or so that she'd been different. More than once, I'd had the sense that she was watching me with knowing eyes, that she'd been dressing a tad more—not provocatively, because Jenna always looked classy. But her shirts clung just a little more, her skirts were a tiny bit shorter. Could she be trying to subtly tell me something?

On the heels of that heady thought came a second, more sobering realization. *I was guilty of treating Jenna the same way her family had.* By assuming that she was too fragile to handle a shift in our relationship from friends to—well, more than friends—I was taking away her choice. I was assuming she'd fall apart. And that was so wrong that I felt a little sick.

She was heading into the house now, a little skip in her

step, as though she was eager to see me. Suddenly nervous, I rubbed my hands down the front of my jeans and took a deep breath before I headed down the stairs to meet her.

Just as my boots hit the bottom steps, Jenna appeared at the front door. Her eyes met mine, and she smiled. In that moment, I knew. I knew with a certainty that I hadn't felt since the last time I'd kissed Sylvia goodbye. I knew that despite all the obstacles we might face, all the reasons not to go forward, I was going to have this woman. Or more accurately, we would have each other. There was a sense of inevitability as well as anticipation. I wanted to pull her into my arms and kiss her until neither of us had breath left. At the same time, I wanted to take her by the hand and tell her every secret thought I'd ever had and share every hope for our future. I wanted more than just her body; I wanted her heart and her soul.

"Hey." She paused there, tilting her head, looking at me quizzically. "Everything okay?"

"Yeah." It was all I could manage to get out.

"I'm sorry I'm late. But I have a good excuse." She came further into the house and rested her hand on the sanded newel post between us. "Rilla and I went out to the farm today to see Meghan. We figured we'd stop by the stand, pick up some vegetables and peaches . . . you know. I was going to text you and offer to get Becca and Ollie and bring them over here with me, to save you the stop at Meghan's. But while we were visiting, Becca came into the kitchen, crying."

"What? Why?"

Jenna laid her hand on my arm. "Don't panic, she's fine. She just . . . umm . . ." Her face pinked a little. "She officially

165

entered puberty today. Her cycle started."

"Oh." If I'd thought I was speechless before, now I was really dumbstruck. I'd had a sense that this was coming, but I'd been living deep in a river in Egypt called Denial. "Oh, God. Well . . . what did you do?"

Jenna shrugged. "It was fine. I handled it. But the point is, when Becca came into the kitchen all upset, she came to *me*. She didn't go to Meghan. She wanted my help. She needed *me*." Happiness shone out of her eyes.

"Babe, that's terrific." The endearment, more intimate and full of meaning than my typical *darlin's* and *sugars*, slipped out without me thinking about it. But if Jenna noticed, she didn't give any sign, other than maybe a slight hitch in her breath before she spoke again.

"I left Ollie with Meghan and the other kids, and I took Becca to the store to get the supplies she needed. And then I took her to a coffee shop, and we sat and talked for over an hour. She was so scared about what this means . . . even though I know they prepared her for this in school, and God knows everything's on the internet these days, she still needed to hear the facts from someone she trusted."

"And that someone was you." I absorbed a little bit of Jenna's joy, coming the rest of the way down the stairs, and rubbing her upper arms. "Thank you, Jenna. I can't tell you how much this means to me. I was dreading what was going to happen when it, um, started. I didn't know what to say or do. I'm so glad she had you."

"Me, too." Her smile stayed put as she sighed. "Anyway, I had to go back to the farm because I'd driven Rilla and the kids there, so I had to take them home and then come over here. Becca decided she wanted to hang out with Bridget. Ali invited her to stay overnight. Oliver wasn't sure he wanted to be, and I quote, 'with all those girls,' but Flynn lured him into going over to the Nelsons' farm to see the new colt. He promised they would do manly things—said he needed Ollie to save him from being overrun by females." Jenna rolled her eyes, and I laughed.

"Well, I'm glad you made it. I was starting to worry when you didn't text."

Jenna leaned against the windowsill. "Sorry. By the time I realized that I wouldn't get her by five, I was already driving. I didn't want to take more time to pull off and text."

"That's okay." I offered her my hand. "Want to come see the kitchen? The guys got the counter installed, I hear."

"You mean, the sideboard." She cast me a teasing glance, and I grunted.

Originally, the kitchen hadn't been a part of the main house. The cooking had been done in an outbuilding, set yards away, but that had been destroyed years ago. The historical society had made the decision not to recreate that structure, but instead to approximate a kitchen inside the house. Since they planned to hold fund-raising events at Oak Grove eventually, it made sense to install a working kitchen that would resemble as closely as possible one from the mid-nineteenth century. We made concessions to functionality, but overall, I thought the plan was pretty brilliant.

What the guys and I referred to as a counter was seen by the historical society as a sideboard. It was made of butcher block, and we'd installed it somewhat lower than a traditional modern kitchen countertop, but it would work, from both points of view. We were carefully adhering to the guidelines laid out by the health department, so that it could be approved for food preparation.

"Oh, Linc . . ." Jenna ran her hand over the wood. "It's perfect. It has the look of a sideboard that was used for years, like someone kneaded endless loaves of bread, chopped a million different vegetables, peeled mountains of potatoes . . . can't you just see it?"

"Um . . . yep." At this moment, I couldn't see anything but Jenna. The end of her ponytail brushed over the tanned skin of her back where the tank top dipped, and I wanted to push her hair aside and kiss her there. Her shorts cupped that perfect round ass so well that I wanted to skim my fingers just beneath the hem. I wondered if I would find her wet and ready for me.

"Linc?" She turned, resting her lower back against the counter—uh, sideboard—and folding her arms over her chest, which meant her tits were resting on top of those arms. At that moment, all the blood in my brain headed south, and I could only remember three pertinent facts: Jenna was the woman I wanted. We were alone in this building. And my kids were not going to be at home tonight.

"Yeah?" I rasped out the word.

"I was talking to you, and it was like you zoned out. I lost you for a second." One side of her mouth curled into a smile.

"Um . . ." *Oh, yeah, I was smooth.* "No, you didn't lose me. I was just thinking." I took a step closer to her.

Jenna's eyes widened a fraction, but she didn't flinch. "Really? What were you thinking about? Something else in the kitchen?"

I shook my head. "Not really." Another step forward, and I was so near her that she had to look up to see me. I became painfully aware that her breathing had sped up. When I glanced down, I could see the tops of her breasts, just below the neckline of her top, their rise and fall rapid.

"What are you doing, Lincoln?" she whispered.

I rested my hands on her arms again, caressing her warm skin lightly with my palms. "I'm making my move, Jenna. I'm taking things between us to the next level. And unless you have a strong objection, I'm going to kiss you right now."

Her chin lifted up, and the tip of her tongue ran over her lips, which parted slightly. "And if I have objections?"

I slid my hands up to frame her face, brushing my thumbs just under her mouth. "I will never do anything that you don't want, Jenna. I promise. If you don't want me to kiss you, all you have to do is say no, and I'll back off. I won't say that I'll never try it again, but I'll never force you into something that makes you uncomfortable."

She swallowed, and I felt the motion of her throat under my hands. "And if I have no objections . . . and I don't want you to back off . . . what will you do?"

"This." Without giving her time to second-guess herself or me, I lowered my mouth to hers, touching first her upper lip, then the bottom, before I angled my head and deepened the kiss. Jenna stood very still until I coaxed her to open to me, my tongue delving between her lips. Then she lifted her arms to twine around my neck, making a noise in the back of her throat that went straight to my dick.

Slow, I reminded myself. *Slow. Just a kiss, because this is what she needs. This is what we need.*

And so I contented myself with exploring the inside of her mouth, stroking my tongue over hers, tracing the interior of her lips. I held her face as though it was the most precious thing I'd ever touched, because it was.

She pressed closer to me, and the feel of her sweet tits against my chest nearly drove me over the edge. But I forced myself to keep my hands cupped around her cheeks. I could have stood there and kissed her into eternity. My entire world shrunk to the intoxicating feel of her lips against mine and the intriguing small sounds she was making—part groans, part sighs.

When I lifted my head a little, just to take a deep breath, Jenna threaded her fingers through the hair at the back of my neck and ran her tongue over her kiss-swollen lips.

"Linc?" Her voice was low and thick with desire. "Maybe . . . should we talk about this?"

"Hmmm." I nuzzled her ear, breathing in her sweet scent, so uniquely Jenna. "We can. We will. We'll talk about whatever you want, as long as I can keep my arms around you while we do it. And then after we talk, I'm taking you to my house and cooking you some dinner. Just the two of us."

"That sounds wonderful. Perfect. But—" She cleared her throat and stared at a spot on my shoulder. "I—I don't want—I don't think I'm ready for—to stay the night with you. To . . . you know. Not yet."

"Hey." I nudged her to meet my eyes again. "Jenna, I

don't expect that. I just want to kiss you. I want to touch you, hold you. I want to talk with you while I'm cooking, and then eat with you and maybe, just maybe, make out on the couch for a little while before you go home. That's all."

"That's all." She laughed, breathlessly. "That's all. Linc, that's enormous to me. I'm not saying I don't want it, too," she added quickly. "Just that it's more than I can take in. I'm not sure what to do here. My growth is completely stunted when it comes to things like relationships and dating. I feel like I'm using muscles that have been dormant for a very long time."

"Don't worry, babe." I kissed the top of her head. "We'll take it slow. All of it. You tell me if I push too far or too fast. Okay?"

"All right." She leaned against me, her head on my chest. "I trust you, Linc."

I swayed a little, as though we were dancing to music only the two of us could hear. "I've been trying so hard not to do this, Jenna. I wasn't looking for a relationship. Not even something casual, and believe me, honey, what I'm feeling here is pretty damn far from casual. I didn't want to push you into anything, or change the friendship we have. I don't want you to feel like I'm betraying that. So if you don't feel the same way I do, it doesn't have to change what we had. What we have."

"Linc? You're not pushing me. I've been hoping you'd do this for a while. I just couldn't be the one to say it or to make the first move. I'm sorry. After—after Trent, it was something I couldn't do."

"I get it." My voice was muffled against her hair.

"I'm not a real good bet." I could feel the movement of her lips against my chest and the vibration of her voice through my body.

Chuckling, I stroked down her back. "I know your history, Jenna, and you know mine. We're both going into this with our eyes open. And talk about a questionable prospective—I'm a recovering alcoholic with two kids. You're the one who should be having second thoughts, babe."

"I'm not, though." She sounded so certain. I couldn't believe that this woman, who could have any guy in the world, was in my arms.

"Should I ask why you're so sure?"

Her shoulders rose and dropped. "I don't trust my own judgment. Not anymore. But from the minute we met, I liked you. I felt comfortable with you. And then even after you found out about my history, you opened up your life to me. You shared your kids." She stroked my arm below the sleeve of my T-shirt. "I like you. I like the way you are with me, with the crew and with Becca and Oliver. I like your long stories, and I even like your corny jokes."

I grinned. "Well, there you go. I like my corny jokes, too." I wrapped the end of her hair around my finger and tugged gently. "I liked you right away, too. And I like how brave you are, how honest you are, and how you treat my guys like they're your equals, not just men who're working for you. I even like . . ." I closed my eyes. "Watching *Veronica Mars* with you. Okay, I admitted it."

She was quiet for a few minutes and then she lifted her head. "Will you kiss me again, Linc? Please?"

"Baby, you never have to ask me twice." Holding her

as close to me as we could get with our clothes still on, I sealed my mouth over hers again, losing myself in the wonder and pure joy of her kisses.

CHAPTER TEN

Jenna

THE LAST TIME I'D HAD a boyfriend, I was a junior in high school. I'd gone out with Levi Brandon for all of six weeks, which was a record for me. Our relationship had consisted of holding hands in the hallway between classes, sitting together at lunch, and weekend dates to the movies in Farleyville or for pizza at Franco's. Levi had tried to convince me to go with him and all our friends to one of the lakes just outside town, but I knew my parents would freak out about that. I had three older sisters who knew what happened at lake parties, and since they were all out of school, they weren't shy about filling in my parents on the dirty details.

I'd been secretly relieved that I had an excuse to turn him down. Levi was fairly popular and a fun guy, but he didn't make my heart beat faster when he kissed me, and I didn't get butterflies in my stomach when I knew I was going to see him. By the end of six weeks, I was bored and tired of being someone's girlfriend. Levi was getting possessive and talking about the future. When he mentioned applying to the same colleges, I'd laughed out loud, and that had been the end of that. Heartbroken I was not.

After that, I hadn't met another boy—or man—who interested me enough to consider more than one or two dates, until Trent came along. One of my therapists had pointed out that my lack of relationship experience had made me even more susceptible to falling hard for him, because I'd imbued him with all the qualities I hadn't found in any other male. I wasn't sure I bought that, but I'd certainly fallen hard for a guy who hadn't given me any signals that he felt the same way, so maybe that doctor was onto something.

In the weeks following my first kiss with Linc, though, I more than made up for the rapid heartbeat and stomach butterflies I'd been missing out on during my younger years. I woke up each morning with a delicious sense of anticipation, knowing that I was going to see him at some point during the day. And when I was driving out to the plantation for my regular walk-throughs, my stomach fluttered until I saw him, at which point I had to bite back a huge smile and fight the urge to leap into his arms.

We were keeping our new status on the down low, for now at least. Neither of us wanted to complicate the Oak Grove project with speculation about what Linc and I might be doing when we had meetings, and we were careful not to even touch during business hours.

And then there were the kids, too. Becca and I had begun to forge a friendship, and I didn't want to jeopardize that by letting her know I was making out with her dad most evenings. Linc and I both felt that Oliver wouldn't really care one way or the other, but we wanted to ease both of them into the idea of us.

Kiki was the only one who knew the truth because, of course, she'd guessed the first time I'd stopped in to the bakery after our kiss. I knew she wouldn't say anything, not even to her niece Sydney.

We had to be careful and circumspect, but I had to admit that for now, at least, there was a certain thrill in a secret relationship. I still hung out with the whole family several times during the week. It was a struggle not to touch Linc on those nights, to pretend that we were still only friends. On rare and wonderful occasions, the kids would spend the night out at Meghan and Sam's farm or at Ali and Flynn's house, and then Linc and I spent hours on his couch or mine, kissing and touching, going just a tiny bit further each time.

I still wasn't ready for sex yet. I felt guilty about it, because I knew Linc was beyond ready. He never said anything, never pushed, but there was more than one night when he left my house walking funny, and I often felt the evidence of his desire for me against my leg when he held me.

I was thinking about that as we sat at my apartment one evening. Ali and Sam had recruited both the kids to help with the second peach harvest. It meant early mornings and late nights, so they were sleeping at Ali's house for three nights. I felt like a kid who'd been given an unscheduled school holiday.

"You know it's not that I don't love Becca and Oliver,

right?" I was sitting on the floor in front of the sofa, putting together some of the Oak Grove research for the booklet we planned to sell as part of our fundraising effort. Linc was sprawled behind me, his feet propped on the arm of the couch. "I always enjoy my time with them. But being alone for three evenings?" I laid my head back on the sofa cushion, looking at Linc upside down. "Not going to lie. It's pretty sweet."

"Hey, babe, you're preaching to the choir." He leaned over to kiss me, his chin brushing against my nose. "I'm all over this. Matter of fact, I was thinking of hiring the kids out to other farmers who might need help with their harvest. 'Bout time they started pulling their own weight, right?" He winked at me, and I laughed.

"As if. We'd both be missing them too much." I sat up again and reached for a folder. "Oooh, this is the transcript of that diary I've been waiting to get."

"But speaking of the kids being away . . ." Linc shifted on the sofa, swinging his feet around to the floor as he sat up. "I talked to Hank and Doris today."

"Oh, really?" I knew Sylvia's parents had been trying to work out a way to see Becca and Oliver. I couldn't blame them for missing their grandkids, but I also understood that Linc was concerned about interrupting the kids' adjustment to Burton and life with their father.

"Yeah. I finally convinced them that it wasn't a good idea to send Bec and Ollie to Texas by themselves, and that I can't take the time off right now to make the trip with them. So they've decided that they're going to come here next week, before the kids start school. Doris offered to take them to

Savannah, do some school shopping and some sightseeing. It sounds like a good compromise."

"It does," I agreed. "How do you feel about that?"

Linc slid one leg behind me to sit on the other side of my shoulder, so that my back rested between his hard thighs. "I feel really good about it. First of all, it'll be fun for Becca and Ollie to show their grandparents their new home and to explore Savannah a little. And second, I was thinking that maybe . . . you might want to come spend that weekend with me. No pressure," he added hastily. "I'm not saying we have to do anything you're not ready to do. But just to sleep in the same bed and wake up together—that would be pretty much heaven."

"Wouldn't you worry someone would see us and say something?" I bit the side of my lip. I wanted this. I really did, but I was also still nervous about the idea of sleeping with Linc. No, come to think of it, sleeping with Linc didn't bother me. It was the prospect of having sex with him. There were times when I yearned to be that close to him, but then in my mind, I heard the echo of Trent's words. *Honey, you weren't good enough for me to give you a second ride.* I couldn't bear the idea of disappointing Linc, or of not being good enough for him. It would kill me.

"Nope. But if it would make you feel better, I'll pick you up, so your car won't sit in my driveway all weekend. No one will have to know. But I'm not ashamed of you, and I'm not ashamed of us."

"I'm not, either. But I want us to decide how we tell the kids. I don't want them to hear from someone else. And I should probably say something to my family before we go public."

"I agree. So—we take a weekend to be together, without anyone knowing or bothering us, and then we'll figure out how and when we want to tell everyone who's important to us."

"Now that sounds like a plan I can get behind." I snuggled down more securely between his legs, perusing the pages before me, as Linc leaned back, flipping through the channels on the television.

"This diary is absolutely fascinating. I'm so glad we were able to get a copy of it from the museum in Marietta." I squinted, reading the exquisite penmanship.

"Remind me of what it is?" Linc glanced over my shoulder.

"It's the journal of a cousin of the Bennett family. She lived with them for the first two years of the war, and she talks about Oak Grove back then, what it was like and about all the family members."

"How did you find out about it?"

"Actually, it was my mom, by way of Miss Rachel. She had some really old photographs that her grandmother had left to her, and one had this cousin's name written on the back. Miss Rachel remembered hearing something about her, so we did some research, and lo and behold, we found out who she was. Turned out that she was very active in the historical society up around Marietta and had left them all her diaries and letters. They were happy to make copies and send them to us. We're hoping she can tie up some loose ends about the family." I flipped over to another page. "Aha! This is what I was talking about. We know there were six children in the family during the war, and we've traced the histories and descendants of all of them but one—Lydia. She just kind of vanishes after 1863, but this cousin is writing about her here . . ." My voice trailed off as I read.

"Well, don't leave me hanging. What does she say? Did Lydia do something scandalous to get written out of the family Bible?" Linc played with a strand of my hair, twisting it around his finger.

"Oh, my God." I read the last paragraph over again, my heart thudding in my ears. "Uh, yeah. She kind of did. But it's so sad." I laid down the paper and turned my head to look back. "Linc, she killed herself. Her cousin writes that Lydia's fiancé died at Gettysburg, and when Lydia found out, she drowned herself in the creek."

"Huh." Linc frowned. "Yeah, that's sad." He was quiet for a few minutes. "But I've got to admit, it also pisses me off a little bit. Suicide makes me angry. It's such a waste. When I think about all the people who died in that war, and how many people struggle to stay alive even now, with cancer and heart attacks and accidents—no, I can't imagine anyone making a choice to end his life."

"I can." I spoke over the lump in my throat. For weeks now, I'd been pushing down a growing concern that someone in town was going to spill the last—and only—secret I was keeping from Linc. The night of the Fourth of July, when I'd shared the whole story about Trent, it hadn't felt like the right time to add on the final shame. *Oh, by the way, in the aftermath of the humiliation of being publicly dumped and having my heart stomped on, I tried to take a bunch of pills and kill myself.* I'd assured myself that it was okay to dole it out in small doses. But there was no way I could let this pass without telling him. Before, it was a lie of omission. This would be an out-and-out failure to be honest.

"I can imagine it. I can imagine feeling like there's no other way out. I can imagine knowing that I've disappointed the people who are most important in my life. I can imagine having all the hopes and dreams I'd built up revealed to be the stupid fantasies of an immature girl. I can imagine knowing that everyone in town is whispering about me and dreading the moment when those whispers make it around to my parents and my sisters." I took a deep breath. "I can imagine feeling like stopping the pain, any way I can, is a far more appealing choice than letting it continue to hurt. I can imagine taking a bottle of pills, lying down in my bed, and consoling myself that me checking out is going to make things easier on everyone."

I was trembling, and to my surprise, I tasted salt on my lips from the tears that were spilling down my face. There wasn't any sound in the room except for my own uneven breaths.

"Jenna." Linc whispered my name. "Jenna . . . why didn't you tell me?"

I shrugged, keeping my back to him so I didn't have to see the betrayal I was certain must be in his eyes. "I don't know. At first it just . . . it seemed like I'd laid enough of my shit on you that night we talked about everything. And then the longer it went on and no one told you, I guess maybe I thought I might not have to say anything. It's not something I like to discuss, as you can probably imagine."

I sat on the floor, his legs still flanking me, and I waited.

I waited for him to accuse me of lying to him, for him to jump to his feet and walk out, for good. I waited for him to call me a coward.

Strong arms slid over my ribs and lifted me into his lap. Linc gripped my chin so that I had no choice but to look into his eyes. But where I expected to see condemnation and judgment, I saw only love and compassion.

"Jenna . . . babe. Don't ever be afraid to tell me anything, okay? I want all of you. Every bit, broken or whole, pretty and shiny or what you might think is ugly. I'm not afraid of anything you are." He pressed a hard kiss to my lips and used his thumbs to wipe the tears from my cheeks. "Jenna, I know I haven't said it yet. I keep hoping you feel it, that you know it anyway, but I haven't said the words out loud because I didn't want to scare you. But maybe you need to hear them as much as I need to say them right now."

"Say it." I breathed out the two words. "Please. I need to know."

Linc smoothed back my hair and framed my face with his two large hands, just as he had the first time he'd kissed me. Staring deep into my eyes, he spoke slowly and clearly.

"Jenna, I love you. I love you. I know this is new, and I know there's a shit ton of reasons why we don't make sense and why we might not work, but I don't care about any of them, because I am so fucking deep in love with you that nothing else matters. I want a future with you. I don't know what that's going to look like, but we'll figure it out together. As long we love each other—" He paused. "That was not my subtle way to get you to say you love me, too. I'm not pushing you. If and when, you'll say it in your own time. I just—"

"Lincoln. Would you hush a minute and let me talk?" I laid one finger on his mouth, smiling a little through my tears when he pursed his lips to kiss the fingertip. I took a deep, shuddering breath and went for broke. "I love you. This is me saying it in my own time, not because you told me or because I feel like I have to say it now. I don't. I want that future, too. I want to be with you always, and figure out a way around all those things that stand in our way. I know it's not going to be easy, but if at the end of the day, I end up with you, I don't care how difficult it is."

Linc kissed me again as the last word left my mouth, and this time there was nothing fast or hard about it. He nudged my lips apart and swept his tongue over me, teasing until my own tangled with his. Desire thrummed through my blood, making my breasts feel heavy and my core ache.

With a little moan, I shifted so that I straddled his body, letting the most needy part of me rub against the hard ridge beneath the fly of his jeans. Linc answered with a loud groan and slipped his hands under my T-shirt, cupping my boobs through my bra, his thumbs brushing over my sensitive nipples.

We'd come this far before. Linc had touched me over the material of my bra, even slid his searching fingers into the cups to rub my nipples into peaks. But tonight, I wanted more. I wanted to give him more. Not sex—I wasn't there yet. But I knew I could make him feel good. I could make sure that when he left my house tonight, it wouldn't be with a bad case of blue balls.

With hands that shook only a little, I reached for the button of his jeans. Linc jerked in surprise when the backs of my fingers brushed the firm plane of his stomach. He broke our kiss and frowned at me.

"Jenna. What are you doing?"

I wriggled back so that I was in a better position. "I want to touch you, Linc. I want to . . . make you feel good." Drunk on the heady mix of love and pent-up desire, I went for broke. "I want to make you come."

"Babe—that's—that would be incredible, but you don't have to do that. Not tonight." He captured the hand that was attempting to tug down his zipper.

"Lincoln." I twisted my wrist loose. "Please let me do this. I want to. God, I want to touch you." I traced the line of his jaw and then followed my finger with my lips, dropped small kisses there. "I'm terrified to disappoint you when it comes to sex. I don't want to let you down. But just now, I'm feeling brave and bold, and I want to put my hands on you." The zipper finally began to give way. "I want my mouth on you. Letting me make you come will be the best gift you could give me. Okay? Please."

Without waiting for his answer, I dropped to the floor again between his legs, this time facing him. Linc watched me, indecision warring on his face, but when I closed my hand around his cock through the tight cotton boxer briefs, he seemed to make up his mind. Lifting his hips, he helped me ease his jeans partway down his legs until I had the access I wanted.

I'd been thinking about this for a while, and I'd done my research. I knew what to do in strictly technical terms, but when faced with an actual erection rather than a hypothetical one, all of my rational thoughts fled. Timidly, I stroked him once, and then twice, all of the time watching his face closely.

Linc hissed out a breath and arched his neck. "Jenna. My God. If you only knew how many times I've dreamed about you doing this . . ."

That gave me courage. I rolled down the boxers, revealing his long, thick shaft. The head was round and flared, and a small bead of moisture shone at the tip. I touched him there, and Linc jerked his hips upward, closing his eyes. I circled him with my fingers, giving a few experimental pumps of my hands, and then I rose on my knees and took just the head between my lips.

Words poured out of Linc's mouth, but none of them made any sense. He stroked my hair with one hand as my tongue circled the ridge of his cockhead. I was surprised to realize that as much as I was focused on giving him pleasure, I was incredibly turned on, too. I slipped my free hand down between my legs, touching myself, moaning as the friction increased.

Feeling even bolder, I slid my mouth lower, taking more of him within me. He pulsed beneath the ministrations of my tongue, lips and hand, and I moved up and down, unconsciously mimicking the way that he thrust himself deeper into my mouth.

"Jenna—baby. I'm coming. Move your mouth. I don't want to—" He didn't have to explain anymore. I knew my own limitations, and while I might have someday been all right with him orgasming in my mouth, tonight was my very first blowjob, and I felt that finishing him off with my hand was perfectly okay.

Judging by the way he cried out my name as he came, I'd have said Linc agreed.

I crawled back up into his lap, laying my head on his chest as his heart thudded beneath my ear. I wanted to ask him if that had been okay, if I'd done a good job—no pun intended—but I was afraid to know the answer.

"Jenna, that was fucking amazing. God, baby. It was beyond anything I ever dreamed. You astound me. Just when I think you can't surprise me, you do something that blows my mind." He grinned. "And not just my mind, apparently."

"Hmmm." I moved restless against him. "I'm glad it felt good. You were the recipient of my very first oral sex."

"No shit?" I was immensely gratified by the surprise in his voice. "Babe, you rocked it. You rocked me." He smirked, and I narrowed my eyes.

"What? What's funny?"

"Nothing. I was just remembering something you said the day we met, out at Oak Grove. You told me that you were always thorough, no matter what you did. Even back then, that kind of made me hot for you." His hand wandered down to squeeze my ass. "Now, I can say for sure that I'm all for your type of thoroughness." He slid one fingers just barely under the waistband of my pants. "Can I return the favor? Let me make you come, too."

I was on the verge of saying no. Not that I wasn't on fire for him—I was—and not that I didn't want him to touch me—I did. But there was still that part of me that was afraid.

"Just let me touch you. Nothing else. I promise, baby, I'll make you feel good." Even as he spoke, his hand went around my back to unclasp my bra, freeing my breasts. My heart pounding in my ears, I lifted my arms one at a time to let him ease me out of it, so that I was bare beneath the large T-shirt.

Linc cupped one boob, and then he nudged me to sit up a little. He lifted my shirt, and the expression on his face when he looked at me was nothing short of reverent.

His mouth closed around one small pink bud, and the feel of him sucking on me was beyond any words I knew. I moved, bringing myself closer, letting him take more of me. When his lips moved to the other side, his hand skimmed down my stomach and beneath my yoga pants.

I wasn't wearing anything underneath, since the yoga pants tended to show panty lines no matter what. So when his fingers ventured under the waistband, they found me wet and ready for him.

Just the feel of his touch on my most sensitive parts threatened to push me right over the edge. I moaned, long and loud, as Linc slipped one long finger into me and used his talented thumb to rub against my clit. His mouth continued to suck my nipple, and mindless, enormous pleasure took over.

I rose up, keeping his lips on my breast as I rode his hand. The most exquisite pressure built low in my abdomen as I climbed higher and higher, everything in me focused on where his fingers moved relentlessly. It all culminated in one long, roaring crescendo that had me shouting Linc's name as my channel clenched around his finger.

I collapsed onto his body, panting and exultant. I managed to turn my head long enough to meet his eyes.

"That was the most . . . wow. Oh, my God. Thank you.

Thank God. Thank whoever it was who invented sex and . . . oh, my God."

Linc shook beneath me as he laughed. "Jenna Sutton, have I told you how much I love you?"

I smiled sleepily, raising one hand to smooth over his bristly cheek. "You did, but feel free to tell me again as often as you like. Also, feel free to make me come as often as you like, because that was fucking amazing."

Before I could take another breath, he'd flipped me beneath him on the couch, his face close to mine.

"Just remember, baby, you asked for it." He began to kiss down my neck to my chest.

Oh, yes, I did. And I'd do it again.

CHAPTER ELEVEN

Lincoln

DORIS AND HANK ROBBINS HADN'T always been my biggest fans. After all, I'd been a punk-nosed kid from a family of cowboys when I'd met their seventeen-year old daughter in high school, and three years later, I'd persuaded her to marry me and go on the road with my job, working for Leo Groff. Sylvia was their only child, and I'd torn her away from them.

Still, they were the only family I really had left. My own mother had died when I was sixteen, leaving me with an often-absentee father and two older brothers. Without a woman to tie us together, we'd drifted apart, and I was lucky if I spoke to any of them even once a year. But Doris and Hank . . . even when they disapproved of our plans, they had our backs. Doris was there when Becca was born, and again when Ollie came barreling into the world.

And when the shit hit the fan and I couldn't handle life

after my wife's death, they'd parented my kids until I could man up and do it myself. I'd forever be grateful for that. I'd been aware on some level that Doris had wanted to take legal custody of Becca and Oliver, to continue raising them, but Hank had put his foot down. It was because of him that I'd been able to take back my children. The day I'd left with them, he'd laid a hand on my shoulder, looked me in the eye and said, "Son, you're their father. You're responsible for every little thing in their lives now. Again. Don't fuck it up."

Short, sweet and to the point. I liked it.

Still, I was a little unsettled by the idea of them coming to my new town, to my new house, to see us. Maybe part of me was afraid they'd find something lacking in how we did things and insist on taking my kids away again. I was slightly worried that I'd lose Becca and Oliver's allegiance again, that they'd tell me they wanted to go back to Texas. After all, living with their grandparents, they'd had the focused attention of two doting adults twenty-four/seven. Hank was retired from his job with the telephone company, and Doris had never worked outside the home. With me, in Burton, the children were often juggled between friends, out to the Reynolds' farm or over to Flynn and Ali's house. They were too old, really, for a babysitter or childcare, but too young to be left on their own while I worked. A neighborhood girl who was in her late teens came over sometimes to sit with them when I had to be in the company office, and that had worked well this summer, but I knew I'd have to put some kind of regular routine in place for the school year, when they'd need a predictable schedule.

So when Hank and Doris's familiar extended cab pickup pulled into our driveway early on that Friday morning, I fought back the urge to grab hold of the kids and beg them to love me more. Becca, who'd been watching at the front window, cried out, "Gramma's here!" and flew out the front door, her brother hot on her heels.

I hung back a little, watching Doris jump out of the truck and fold her grandchildren into her arms. She held Becca at arms' length, and I could guess that she was exclaiming over how much my daughter had grown up since May.

It was true. Becca had begun to blossom into a miniature young woman, no longer a little girl. Under Jenna's tutelage, she'd started wearing a bra—something I didn't want to know about but had gladly paid for, since Jenna was the one who'd taken her shopping for it—and she now had what she called night-time skin care, when she washed her face with some creamy stuff and then smoothed some kind of oil over it. Sure, she was still a kid who loved to run all over the fields with Bridget out on the farm, but the inner prissiness she'd had before was maturing into something more.

And Oliver . . . he'd gotten taller, too. He looked sturdy and healthy. Watching my children interact with their grandparents, it hit me that they'd not only survived the first months of life with me, but they'd actually thrived. I hadn't fucked it up. So far, at least.

After a few minutes, I wandered outside to join them in the driveway. Hank met me halfway, pumping my hand and telling me about their drive to Georgia from Texas.

"Thirteen hours, and the worst traffic we hit was in Atlanta. God almighty, what a mess." He shook his head.

"Lincoln. Come over here and give me a hug." Doris wrapped her arms around me and squeezed. "You look good. All of you look good and healthy." She hugged Becca to her side again. "Oh, I'm just so happy to see y'all. Now take me inside and show me around. This is a lovely neighborhood, Linc. And the house is just precious."

And so the morning went. I'd told the guys I wouldn't be on-site until later, which was a good thing, since the kids insisted on giving their grandparents a tour of the town. We stopped in at the bakery for coffee and Danish, and Kiki fussed over Doris and Hank, telling them what a wonderful young lady Becca was and how much everyone in Burton loved all of us. We stopped in at the library, where Becca had made friends with Cory Evans, the librarian and Flynn's mom, and had a picnic lunch from Kenny's on the green.

Finally, I drove out to Oak Grove, with Hank and Doris following me, kids in their truck, so that they could see what I was working on before they all left for their weekend in Savannah. As I bumped into the yard, I spied Jenna's car and smiled. She'd known I was going to be absent from the site; I assumed she was there to keep her eye on things. Ever responsible and vigilant, my Jenna was.

"Hey, Dad, Jenna's here!" Ollie shouted as he slid down from his grandparents' truck.

"Yeah, but I don't think she has any cookies for you here, bud." I tapped him on the head, grinning.

"That's okay. I'm still full from lunch." He rubbed his stomach.

I pretended to stagger back. "It's happened. It's finally happened! We managed to fill Ollie up!"

He rolled his eyes as we all laughed. "I could eat a cookie if she had one," he mumbled. "I'm just saying I'm not, like, starved."

"Linc, this is amazing." Doris shaded her eyes as she gazed up at Oak Grove. "I looked this place up on line and saw what it looked like before. I know you're not finished, but even so . . . it's come a long way."

"Thanks." I was proud of what we'd done here so far, pleased with my crew's hard work and how, together with the historical society, we were realizing the vision we shared for this piece of history.

I gave them the grand tour, going through the downstairs rooms and pointing out what we'd added, what we'd restored and what we'd had to adapt. All the while, I kept one eye open for Jenna, listening for her voice and waiting to find her.

She wasn't on the first floor, but when Ollie clamored up the stairs ahead of us, I heard her call out his name.

"Ollie, hey! What're you doing here? I thought you were heading to Savannah today."

We all followed the sound into one of the smaller bedrooms, where Jenna knelt on the floor in front of a window, sandpaper in her hand. Our eyes met across the empty space, and I felt naked, vulnerable, as though Hank and Doris and both kids could see our connection.

"Gramma, this is Jenna." Becca dragged her grandmother over to Jenna. "She works at the historical society, and she did all the research about Oak Grove. She knows everything about it. And she's my friend, too." There was a heap of meaning behind that one word, and I knew Jenna

193

felt it as much as I did. Her breath hitched a little, her lips parted, and she smiled up at my daughter.

"Jenna, I've heard so much about you." Doris offered her hand as Jenna rose to her feet, her eyes shooting to me in question. "Becca told me what a great help you've been to her. Oh, heck with shaking hands—come here and give me a hug, honey."

I hadn't realized how tense I'd been about my in-laws meeting Jenna until that moment, when relief washed over me. Jenna embraced Doris, her eyes closing as the older woman squeezed her tight.

"What're you doing, Jenna?" I cleared my throat and pointed to the sandpaper still in her hand. "Did they put you to work?"

"Oh." She glanced down as though surprised to find the paper there. "Jerry told me that the painters are coming Monday for the upstairs, and they were worried about having this sanding done, since they're all working on stuff on the first floor. I figured I'd lend a hand."

Hank chuckled. "This one's a keeper, Linc. Any gal who'll pick up sandpaper and pitch in is one you don't want to let get away. Maybe think about hiring her for your crew."

A slow smile spread over my lips as Jenna's face flushed the prettiest shade of pink. "Not a bad idea, Hank. I'll have to take it under consideration. Not a bad idea at all."

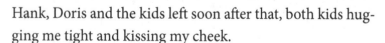

Hank, Doris and the kids left soon after that, both kids hugging me tight and kissing my cheek.

"Daddy, will you be all right, alone all weekend?" Becca's eyes were anxious. "I don't want you to be lonely without Ollie and me."

I touched my daughter's cheek with one finger. "Sugar, I'll be fine. I'm going to catch up on some work and probably watch a ton of old movies on TV—the kind that you and your brother hate. You go and have a wonderful time. Don't you worry about me one minute."

Jenna left Oak Grove at the same time, remarking that she needed to get back to her office now that I was back on site to be in charge. I noticed that she was careful to keep her good-bye to me casual as she walked out with the kids and their grandparents.

For the rest of the afternoon, I fought to stay focused on the job at hand and keep my mind on work, and not the upcoming weekend. Jenna and I hadn't specifically talked about what was going to happen, except in the vaguest terms. I'd given the crew a rare Saturday off; we were ahead of schedule, and it wasn't unheard of for us to give our guys a break now and then. No one would think anything of it, and I didn't even feel the smallest twinge of guilt. I'd been working damn hard, and I deserved this time with my girl.

I forced myself to stay at the plantation until after five, when the rest of the crew took off, yelling back and forth to each other about their plans for the evening. Most were heading over to the Road Block, and I smirked, thinking Mason might have his hands full tonight. Of course, if anyone could handle them, it was Mason Wallace. I had a feeling he'd knocked together his share of hard heads.

"Hey, boss, you gonna join us?" One of the carpenters paused in the doorway.

I shook my head. "Thanks, but I'm beat. Too old to keep up with y'all anymore. But you go on and have a good time." As he turned to leave, I added, "But not *too* good a time. I am not leaving my house this weekend to come bail any of your sorry asses out of jail. Got it?"

"Message received, boss." He raised his eyebrows at me. "You have big plans this weekend?"

I let one side of my mouth curl up. "Could be. Now get on out of here, so I can go home."

I was just stepping onto the porch when my phone vibrated in my pocket. I pulled it out and checked the screen.

Come home, Linc. I'm here waiting.

It was from Jenna, and I smiled, almost involuntarily as I tapped out a response.

My house? I thought I was picking you up at your place.

After a few seconds, her reply appeared.

Change of plans. Come home.

She didn't have to tell me twice. Or, hell, maybe she had, but . . . fuck it all. I was already half-sprinting to my truck, jumping into the driver's seat and ready to break all the speed limits between here and her.

———◆———

There was no sign of Jenna's car when I rolled into my driveway. I guessed she'd pulled into the garage, which was an excellent idea; it wouldn't broadcast to the neighbors that I had a weekend guest staying with me. I climbed out of the truck and went into the house, noting that the front door wasn't locked. Jenna had a key for when she helped me out with the kids, so it didn't surprise me that she'd used it to come inside.

I stood for a minute in the dim light of the entryway, taking a moment to calm myself before I went to her. I wasn't sure if sex was on the table this weekend. Or on the bed . . . or anywhere else I'd fantasized about taking Jenna. Time alone together had been pretty rare since the night she'd given me the blowjob at her house, but what we did have was hot and intense. Something had shifted that night, both in Jenna herself and between the two of us. I wasn't sure if it was that she'd finally been completely open with me about her suicide attempt—which had shaken the hell out of me—or if it was her growing confidence in her own sexual abilities. I knew what Jenna had said about not blaming Trent for what had happened between them, but I could've cheerfully castrated the man for making this beautiful woman doubt her own desirability. Moving forward, I realized that it was my job to give her back that faith in herself, in who she was and in how sexy she could be.

"Hi."

Jenna stood in the kitchen, visible through the arched entryway. She wore a short green dress with thin straps over her shoulders and a skirt that fluttered just below her ass. Her feet were bare, and her hands were clasped behind her back as she watched me with huge eyes.

"Hey." As sexy greetings went, there were better.

"What're you doing, just standing there? Are you afraid to come in?" She tilted her head, a teasing smile tugging at her full lips.

"No, not afraid. Just . . . thinking." I took a deep breath. "God, Jenna, you're so fucking beautiful."

She blushed prettily, her smile growing. "Thank you. But how can you tell from all the way over there? Don't you want to come closer?"

"I do. God, I really do. But I got to admit something, even if it makes you think less of me."

"Never going to happen. I shared all my deepest secrets with you. You can trust me."

I took one long stride closer to her. "I know I can. But still . . ." I stepped again, so that I was within touching distance, but I didn't lift my hand. Not yet. "But still, I have to tell you, babe. I'm terrified. Scared absolutely shitless."

Her lips parted a little. "Why?" It was barely a whisper.

"Because I want . . . this . . . us . . . to be perfect. I want everything to be exactly right. I want to make you happy and bring you more fucking pleasure than you've ever known. I want you to realize how important you are to me, how much I want you, how much you turn me on . . . how much I am dying to touch you." I raised my hand and skimmed the backs of my fingers over her cheeks. "How much I want to be inside you." With one more step, I was nearly on top of her, and I bent my neck to brush the merest breeze of a kiss over her lips. "How much I love you."

The last syllable had hardly left my tongue before Jenna surged up onto her toes, angling her mouth across mine, consuming me in a kiss that ignited a fire low in my belly. I gripped her hips, easing her body even closer, mindful of being careful and gentle. I didn't want to hurt her or frighten her, and I forced myself to rein in my own raging desire.

Jenna's hands were knotted in my T-shirt, holding herself to me. She lifted them behind my neck, twining her fingers together there, and broke her lips away from mine just long enough to move her mouth to my ear.

"Lincoln . . . don't treat me like glass. I'm not going to break. Love me like a woman."

I growled deep in my throat. "Babe . . . I thought we should take it slow."

She trailed her lips over my cheek. "Slow can come later. For now, I need you to show me I'm whole and . . . a woman you don't need to protect. A woman you can love without boundaries or without holding back."

And just like that, she'd stripped me bare, again. She'd astutely realized that I was putting her in a position I shouldn't, assuming she needed me to lead the way and teach her, when of course, I was learning from her.

I gripped her ass, kneading the globes, and lifted her so that her long bare legs straddled me. The fabric of her dress bunched under my hands, and to my utter shock, I felt bare skin.

"Jenna. Babe, are you commando?"

She nuzzled my neck, her tongue darting out to taste my skin. "Hmmm, if commando means I'm not wearing panties, then yeah. Yeah, I am. Absolutely commando."

"Oh . . . my . . . God." I punctuated each word with hard kisses to her lips. "Bedroom. Need to get you to a bed. Now."

I started walking toward the stairs, pausing at the first step. "Babe. This is not me coddling you or treating you like less than the fucking incredible woman you are, but I need to ask. I need to be clear, make sure we're both on the same page. Are we . . . uh, is sex on the table?"

She laughed, which made her tits bounce under her

dress. Oh, fuck me, she wasn't wearing a bra, either.

"I thought we'd start out in your bed, but yeah, the table could work for our second course." She held my chin between her fingers and sealed our lips together in another blistering kiss. "Or the third."

It made me grin that our minds followed the same lines, the same corny puns. "The bed it is."

I made it up the steps and around the corner into my bedroom faster than I ever had before. I bounced Jenna onto my bed and then sat down on the edge of the mattress to untie my boots. Standing up, I pulled my T-shirt off with one arm.

Jenna had crawled to the middle of the bed and propped herself up on her elbows to watch me. "Take it all off. The jeans. Everything. And do it slow."

I quirked an eyebrow and unbuttoned my pants. "Little demanding, Ms. Sutton?"

She lifted one shoulder. "I like what I like."

Slowly I tugged down the zipper. "And is this what you like?" Under my boxer briefs, my cock was hard. I shook the jeans the rest of the way down my legs and kicked them away.

Jenna licked her lips, and I almost lost it right there. "It's a start. Lose the underwear. I want all of you, Linc. All of you, completely mine, right here."

My dick sprang up when I shed the boxers, long and straining toward her. She lifted one hand and beckoned to me.

"Come here. I want you."

I knelt on the bed, dropped onto my hands and moved

toward her, my eyes on the top of her legs where the hem of her dress teased. One thin strap had fallen off her shoulder, and the way she laid thrust her breasts forward.

I couldn't decide what part of her I wanted to touch— and taste—first.

Jenna made it easy when she wriggled a little, knocked the other strap down. Her dress dipped over that delectable rack, the cotton clinging enough to reveal her hard nipples. As she watched me with bright eyes, I lay alongside her and covered one of those stiff peaks with my mouth, wetting the material of her dress.

She hummed deep in her throat, writhing as though the feeling was too much. While I kept my mouth on the first nipple, I eased the side of her dress down and used my fingers on the other boob. Jenna arched, pushing more of her breast into my mouth, and I greedily took everything I could.

My cock, lying between us, throbbed with the need to be inside her. I couldn't remember aching like this before. When I couldn't hold back one more nanosecond, I raised my head and met her eyes.

"Can you get this fucking dress off, or do I have to rip it?" I smiled, echoing her earlier words. "I want all of you, Jenna. All of you, completely mine, right here."

Her eyes darkened, the pupils dilating. "Then by all means. Let's get it off." She sat up, yanked the bottom of the dress from underneath and slipped it over her head.

For a long mind-blowing moment, all I could do was look at her. I'd always thought Jenna was hot. But seeing her laid out naked before me, she robbed me of the ability to breathe, as well as the capacity for rational thought. If I'd gone blind in the next minute, I would have been perfectly content with that view as the last thing I ever saw.

"Are you going to just sit there staring, or are you going to touch me?" She laid one hand along my cheek. "You're giving me a complex."

"I was just thinking that you are fucking gorgeous. I was thinking that if I have my way, you're the last naked women I'm ever going to see in my life, and I'm so okay with that, it's ridiculous."

Her lips parted slightly as her gaze went luminous. "That was probably the most beautiful thing anyone has ever said to me."

I traced a line down the center of her chest, between her breasts, to the soft roundness of her stomach, the dip of her navel, and then, finally, between her legs. She slid them apart, giving me greater access, and I delved that single finger into her folds, wet and waiting for my touch.

She moaned as I circled her stiff and swollen clit, her lower body rising to meet my hand. I watched her face, fascinated by the flush of her skin and the way her eyelids drooped at the same time that her mouth fell open. I moved my fingers to her opening, sliding two into her slick and tight channel and using my thumb to press on her clit. She went off like a rocket, hips canting toward me, fingers gripping my forearm as she moaned my name along with several other unintelligible words.

My dick was more than ready to join the party, but I made myself stay with her, stroking her down until her breathing had evened a little. When she was limp, I reached to the nightstand and fumbled in the drawer to find a condom. I'd had to buy a new box, since I hadn't had the need for them for a while.

Jenna opened her eyes to see what I was doing, and a shadow passed over her face. For the first time since I'd come into the house, I saw worry cloud her expression.

"Babe. Talk to me." I rolled on the condom and caressed her hairline. "What's wrong? Are you with me here?"

"I'm with you. I'm just—" Her throat convulsed as she swallowed. "The condom. It took me back. Promise me, Linc. If I do something wrong, please tell me. Help me. Don't let me . . . do this wrong."

"Baby." I lifted her hand and wrapped her fingers around my erection. "Feel this? You did this to me. You. No one else. I go around half the time with a semi because I'm either *with* you, or I'm imagining *being* with you, or I'm thinking about when I *was* with you. There is not one thing you could do right now that wouldn't make this the best night of my life."

She blinked and nodded slowly. I hesitated, wondering what I could do to convince her. Then inspiration struck.

"Come here." I slid off the bed and pulled her by the hand.

"Where are we going?" Her forehead knit together.

"Just trust me." I dragged her over to the corner of the room, to the full-length mirror that Abby had insisted I needed and so had bought for me. Holding Jenna in front of me, I wound my arms around her waist.

"Look at this, Jenna. This is me. Linc. And you. No one else. Just us." I skimmed my palms up to cup her breasts. "Me touching you . . . here." Keeping one hand on her boob,

I brought the other down to cup her sex. "And here. It's me who just made you come. It's me who's going to fucking combust if I don't get inside your sweet pussy real soon."

"Lincoln!" Her voice was filled with shock, but I saw the twitch of her lips.

"Sorry, babe. You make me say all the sexy words, because you, Jenna Sutton, are so fucking sexy." I used my long middle finger to touch her clit, still sensitive from her last orgasm. "I'm not treating you like you're fragile, darlin'. I swear I'm not. But you need to be reminded that in this bedroom, between us, is only us. Now bend forward a little."

She frowned at me over her shoulder. "What?"

I gave her ass a light smack. "You heard me. Bend a little."

She tilted, sticking that sweet rear out. "Okay. Now what?"

"Now . . . watch. Keep your eyes on the mirror."

She did as I asked, her gaze meeting mine. I held my cock in front of me, sliding it between her cheeks and nudging her silky opening with the head.

"All right?" I ground out the words, because I was trying to keep myself from thrusting into her.

"Yes," she gasped. "But—more. I need more."

"And baby, I'm here to give it to you. Keep looking ahead." Holding her hips still, I plunged forward, seating myself in her impossibly tight channel.

"Oh. Linc. God. Linc." Her eyes drifted shut. "Feels so— so good."

"Don't. Move," I growled. If she so much as pulsed around me, it was going to be all over fast. I sucked in a couple of deep breaths and tried to think about anything other than how fucking good she felt. After a minute, I felt like I was a little more in control. Barely. "Okay. Open your eyes, sugar. Watch me. Watch me fucking you. Watch me loving you."

I pulled her back tight against my chest, reaching up to rub her nipples between my fingers as I swiveled my hips, moving inside her, drunk with every sensation that was overwhelming me. She was watching us, watching my hands on her and God, I'd never seen anything sexier, ever.

"I want you to come again." I knew I might be asking too much, but why the hell not go for broke? I pinched one nipple hard and whispered into her ear. "Touch yourself, babe. Watch in the mirror as you touch your clit, as I rub your nipples and take you from behind."

Her teeth sank into her bottom lip, but one of her hands ventured lower, tentatively. Her two fingers slid over her clit, and when they touched me where we were joined, I almost thought I was finished.

She began to move her fingers faster, clenching around me. I couldn't last much longer, I knew. But I wanted to finish, to come inside her, with my mouth on hers. I pulled out, gritting my teeth, and turned her around, scooping her up and taking her back to the bed.

"God, Linc. I'm about to explode here. I need you. Please. *Please*."

I didn't waste time speaking. I simply slid back inside her and pumped, my balls tightening and the base of my spine tingling.

"Baby, I'm about to—God, Jenna. God, I love you. Love

you so much, babe."

When the climax hit, it rolled over like a tidal wave. My body went stiff, one hard muscle as I poured myself into this woman. Love like I'd never known filled me, and I knew that no matter how many reasons there were that we shouldn't work, we would. I couldn't live without Jenna in my life, in my arms, and in my bed.

And I was going to do anything and everything to make sure that happened.

CHAPTER TWELVE

Jenna

Linc: Hey, babe, whatcha doing?

I grinned down at my phone screen as I walked along the sidewalk on the main street of Burton. Glancing behind me, I stepped to the side, leaning against a brick storefront to answer Linc.

Jenna: Left work, stopping to see Kiki before I go home. How is the school open house going? ;)

Linc had spent the better part of our morning meeting out at Oak Grove bitching and moaning about having to go to the kids' school for the annual autumn open house. He'd tried to talk me into going with him, at which suggestion I had laughed until I cried.

"You've got to be kidding. No way, no how. But you have fun."

The phone buzzed again.

Linc: Boring as hell. What do you think about homes-

chooling?

My heart skipped a little. Linc had been doing this more often lately, asking for my input when it came to the kids. We hadn't told Becca and Oliver yet about our relationship, so I felt uncomfortable with having opinions on anything that affected them.

My finger hesitated over the keyboard before I answered.

Jenna: I think that's not a decision that should be based on your dislike for school open houses.

His next text came swiftly.

Linc: I was afraid you were going to say that. Shit.

I shook my head and started walking again.

Another vibration and another text. I read it as I approached the bakery.

Linc: Do you think sexting from the classroom is a problem?

I frowned.

Jenna: Why? Are they saying it is? In sixth grade?

As far as I knew, Becca wasn't even interested in boys yet. Or if she was, she was still at the age where she was playing it close to the vest, not letting on.

Linc: Not the kids. Me. God, I'm horny. And I'm bored. So I figured we could take care of both problems at once. What are you wearing?

I laughed, skimming my hair out of my eyes.

Jenna: Lincoln Turner! Shame on you. In school. I'm not going to tell you I'm wearing your favorite skirt . . . that white top you told me made you hot . . . and that's it.

Of course, that wasn't strictly true. I'd been at work after all, so I was quite respectably wearing underwear. But he didn't need to know that.

Linc: Killing me, babe. Killing. Me. And when you know I can't come over tonight. Wait, you mean you had nothing on under that today when I saw you? Damn, babe. Fucking killing me.

Our time together on school nights was rare anymore, since the kids had hours of homework and an earlier bedtime. It was a rare evening when Linc could make a good excuse to go out and come over to my place, even if he could get someone to stay with Becca and Oliver. The result was that we were both perpetually horny. I'd decided that I was addicted either to sex or to Linc; since our weekend together, I couldn't get enough of him. It was definitely good for my ego that any time I touched him, in any way, he was raring to go. I was beginning to own my sexuality. And I'd have been lying if I'd said it wasn't damn fun.

Pausing just outside the door to Sweetness and Bites, I tapped in one more message.

Jenna: Sorry. ☹ About to go into Kiki's. Call me later?

Linc: Yup. Tell K I said hey. Love you.

There was little that could light up my face more than those words from Linc. I tucked away my phone and floated my way into the bakery, practically glowing.

And ran smack into Trent Wagoner.

As small a town as Burton was, it was pretty amazing that I hadn't seen Trent since that last horrible night at the Road Block, when he'd rejected me so thoroughly and so loudly. Of course, I'd lain pretty low after that, and following my suicide attempt, I'd been in the hospital and then only left home to see my doctors and therapists. Trent had high-tailed it to Michigan not long after, which made it somewhat easier for me once I did venture away from my house; at least I didn't have to worry about running into him at every turn.

He'd come back to Burton a week after my twenty-second birthday. I'd still been living at home then, and we'd just finished breakfast when Rudy Buskill, a police sergeant who was a friend of my dad's, knocked on the door. He hadn't come inside, but I'd heard what he had to say anyway. Trent's mother had been arrested for solicitation two nights before, and last night, Trent himself had arrived and bailed her out. Rudy didn't know the details, but as he understood it, Trent was planning to stay in Burton until he could get his mom straightened out. Rudy had come by to give my dad a head's up, just in case.

I'd retreated to my bedroom after Rudy left, but it wasn't far enough away not to hear my parents' discussion. My father was still furious, and he warned my mother that if he ran into *that scum,* as he termed Trent, he'd make him sorry he ever showed his sorry face in this town. I heard worry in my mom's voice.

"Boomer, if you lay a hand on that boy, the only one who's going to get into trouble is you. Use your head. Just— just stay away from him. Likely Donna Wagoner will end up getting arrested again and they'll lock her up. Then her boy will leave. Just stay clear of him, you hear me, Boomer?"

I made up my mind then. By noon, I'd called my grand-mother and made arrangements, packed a bag and in-formed my mother I was going to Charleston to stay indefinitely with Grandmother Wexler. I'd seen the relief in my mom's eyes, even though she'd tried to hide it. And I didn't return to my hometown until I'd learned that Trent and his new wife had moved to Nashville. Trent had gotten a gig playing guitar with Crissy Darwin, a rising folk singer who'd just signed with a record company. I felt fairly safe that he wouldn't be coming back to this town any time soon.

But here he was. I realized, as I stood frozen in the open doorway, that he must've been about to leave the bakery. He had a box tied with string tucked under one arm and one hand on the door.

I couldn't move. I couldn't speak, and I couldn't tear my eyes away from his face. He looked the same, I thought—but then no. His face was leaner, and the hint of cautious wariness that had always been part of his expression was gone. He looked . . . happy. Relaxed.

At first, he also seemed mildly puzzled, as if he couldn't quite place what I was doing here, as though I was the one who was out of place. And then the slight smile left his face and was replaced by a mix of regret and embarrassment.

"Jenna." He managed to speak first. "I, uh . . . how are you?"

"I'm fine," I replied automatically. "I didn't know you were back in town."

"We're passing through. I'm on tour with Crissy, and we're heading to South Carolina. Elizabeth—my wife— wanted to stop and see some friends she made when we lived here last year." He paused before adding, "We're not staying. Crissy's visiting Mason, and the tour bus is out at the Road Block. We're hitting the highway tonight."

"That's nice." I took a step back. "Well, I should get out of your way and—"

"Jenna." Kiki had emerged from the kitchen, and she glanced from Trent to me. "Come in. Don't go running off. Close that door, and turn the sign. We can shut down for a little bit, give you both some privacy. I think you two have some unfinished business to talk over."

"Kiki, I'm sure Trent doesn't have time to catch up with old . . . well. I'll stop back later."

"Jenna Sutton, I told you to close that door. It isn't going to take long. And I don't think this meeting was accidental."

I stepped inside, turned the sign and crossed my arms over my chest. "Okay, Kiki. Now what?"

"Now I'm going to leave you two alone to finish what you need to work out." With that, she disappeared back into the kitchen.

I rolled my eyes and huffed out a breath. "Sorry about her. She's damned pushy."

"Don't I know it." Trent rubbed his jaw ruefully. "But she's also pretty wonderful. I couldn't come through Burton without stopping to see her." He shifted on his feet, his eyes going to a spot somewhere behind. "Listen, Jenna. I'm actually glad I got to see you. I've wanted to talk to you for a long time. To tell you how damn sorry I am for how I handled—well, everything. From the night of your birthday, right on through what happened at the party. It was all my fault. I was an idiot, and more than that—I knew better. I knew I shouldn't have taken you home on your birthday. And I knew I should've talked to you the next day and told you it had been a mistake. But I didn't, and for that, and for everything I said later—I'm so sorry, Jenna. You were a good friend to me, and I let you down in a big way. I can't ever make that right."

I didn't feel like reliving that time of my life. The last thing I wanted to do was rehash something I'd put to rest. But I could tell that Trent needed to say the words.

So I nodded once. "Okay. Thanks for saying that. You didn't have to. It was my fault—I threw myself at you, I put you into a terrible position, and then I made it even worse. But it was a long time ago, and I got over it. You should, too." I let out a long breath. "I heard you were married to a nice girl. You—you're happy?"

"Very." He imbued that one word with a ton a meaning. "Elizabeth is who I needed. She's who I was meant for, and the crazy thing is, she loves me, too. We work, the two of us. What we have works."

"I'm glad." And I was. It was wonderful to realize that.

"How about you? What're you doing these days?" Trent smiled. "I always thought you could do anything in the world you wanted. You had smarts and charisma for miles."

"I'm working at the county historical society. I'm a project manager for restorations. Right now we're restoring Oak Grove, that old plantation outside of town."

"Know it well." Trent grinned, and I remembered Kiki saying the plantation used to be a place where kids went parking. Yeah, I was sure Trent was one of them.

"Ah, well, it's coming along nicely. You wouldn't recognize it, I bet."

"I hardly recognized you, Jenna, to tell you the truth. You look good. Like you're at peace."

I considered his words. "I am. I spent a long time figuring out where I went wrong, learning more about myself than any self-respecting twenty-three-year old woman
needs to know ... and I treaded water for a long time, hanging in limbo." I thought of Linc's description. "And then I
found someone to pull me out and make me want to live
again."

"I'm glad." He repeated my words back to me. "I don't
want you to worry, Jenna. I won't be back in Burton very
often. You don't have to dread running into me again."

"I don't. I mean, I wouldn't. This is your hometown, too,
Trent. I understand it might not hold a lot of happy mem-
ories, but you should be able to come back when you want.
We're okay, you and me. I promise."

Trent nodded. "Thanks. I'm glad Kiki made us do this.
It's good to have some, uh, what do they call it? Closure?"

I laughed. "Yeah, I guess so."

"I'll see you around, Jenna. Be well."

"I will. You, too. Good luck on the road."

With a parting smile and one last wave, Trent left the
bakery. As soon as the jingling bell above the door stopped
shaking, Kiki appeared from the kitchen.

"Well, that went well."

I shot her a reproving glance. "Kiki, that's some iffy shit
you were playing with there. Yes, it was fine. But with the
history between Trent and me, leaving us alone together
might've been disastrous."

"Pfft." She waved her hand. "You're both in a good place,
and it was time you mended these last fences. Now you can
move forward, freed from some of your past. Feels right,

doesn't it?"

I pulled out a chair from one of the small tables and sat down. "I guess it does. But in return for having set me up, you can plate me up one of those chocolate croissants and pour me some tea. It's the least you can do."

Kiki put her hands on her hips and cocked her head. "Set you up? Why, whatever do you mean, Jenna?"

I stuck out my tongue at her. "Don't bullshit me, Kiki. You know very well just what time I come in here after work. You could've very easily made sure Trent was gone before I came by. So, yes. I smell set up."

She sighed. "Even if I did, and I'm not saying that's truth, I had the best of intentions. And like I said, it worked."

"Doesn't change that you were messing with a potentially tricky situation. So make sure you warm that croissant before you bring it to me, please."

She stared at me for a minute before grinning and tossing up her hands. "Whatever you say. Geez. What happened to the Jenna who hardly talked and never asked for anything? When did you turn into this assertive—some might say *pushy*—woman?"

I leaned back and propped my feet on the chair opposite me. "Get used to her. This Jenna is here to stay."

That night, when Linc called after Becca and Oliver had gone to sleep, I didn't waste any time before telling him about running into Trent. I knew someone in town probably saw me go into the bakery and Trent emerge a bit later, and there was bound to be talk. And I didn't want any secrets between us, not anymore.

"Do you feel better?" Linc's voice was low and intimate. I knew he was probably talking to me from his bed.

"I think so. I feel good that I didn't fall apart when I saw him. I was glad that we're both able to move beyond something that happened over two years ago."

"Was it hard? To see him again, I mean—after how you felt about him. What he meant to you."

"Not one bit." I was in bed, too, and I tugged the sheet up a little higher. My landlady was apparently still dealing with hot flashes and my room was like an icebox. "One thing I realized early on in my therapy was that I never loved Trent. I believed I did, but it was only infatuation, and that ran its course pretty fast after everything that happened. I didn't try to end my life because Trent broke my heart."

"I'm happy to hear that. Because I'd hate to have to break this jerk's face after all, if he wanted you."

I giggled. "He doesn't want me any more than I want him. Matter of fact, if you really want to know, there's only one man I want. He's super cute, he treats me like gold, and he makes me hot and bothered. Oh, and I kind of love him."

"Now this guy sounds like a keeper." Linc chuckled. "And this guy is also walking around with a hard dick all the time, because he can't get any time with his only girl. We got to do something about that, sugar."

"Well, I'm free all week and all weekend." I kept the phone against my ear as I snuggled down into the pillow. "Oh, except Saturday night. I have a family dinner at my mom and dad's house. Big fun."

"You need to talk to them, babe. Level with your mom

and dad, and work it all out."

"Hmmm." I was noncommittal. Avoidance was cowardly, but it was a hell of a lot safer than getting real with my parents.

"Jenna." Linc had that tone in his voice, the one that said he was about to bring up something he sensed I might not like. "I want to talk to the kids. Tell them about us. And then I want to see your parents and do the same. I'm tired of sneaking around like we're doing something we're ashamed of. I love you, and I want to have you with me, however that's going to look. I want to go to bed with you every night, and not just for sex. I want to eat breakfast across the table from you, and I want to hold your hand when we're out together with the kids. I'm ready to go public."

I'd have been lying if I'd claimed to be surprised by Linc's request. I'd known for a while that he wanted us to move forward, together, and we couldn't do that before we talked to Becca and Oliver, and to my mom and dad.

It wasn't that I didn't feel the same way. I wanted us to start our life together, too. But I was terrified that Becca would hate the idea of me dating her dad. She and I had come so far and had become real friends. I was afraid she'd feel betrayed when she found out that I was in love with her father. I was pretty sure Oliver would accept us; he was an easy-going, affable kid, generous with his affection. He liked me.

And then there was my family. I was sure they'd be quick to assume I was making another mistake, getting involved with a man who was over a decade older than me. I didn't look forward to arguing with them yet again.

But we couldn't live like this forever. And sooner or later, we were going to be found out, and that would be even worse. It would be far better to do this on our own terms.

"Okay," I whispered. "Let's do it. But what about work? What're we going to tell your crew?"

"I don't think we need to have a sit-down with my guys, share our feelings and sing Kumbaya, babe. They'll figure it out, and when they do, they'll also figure out that the two of us being together doesn't change a damn thing on this project. Right?"

"I guess so." Linc knew his men, so I trusted him to make sure it would be all right. "So when do you want to do this?"

He answered me swiftly. "Tomorrow night. You come for dinner, and we'll talk to the kids. And then how about we tackle your family on Saturday, at the dinner?"

"Wow. You're brave. You want to face all the Suttons at once?"

"Aw, baby, they'll love me. They already do, actually, but now they'll love me as someone who's part of the family. Trust me, you'll see."

"Uh huh." I sucked in a deep breath and let it out. "Well, I guess we'll both see."

Chapter Thirteen

Lincoln

"SWEET! SANDWICHES FROM FRANCO'S. DID Jenna bring them?" Oliver grabbed a foil paper-wrapped package off the counter and began to open it.

"Hey, kiddo, hold up there. That one might not be yours. Check to see which one has your name on it."

"And just why did you assume I brought them?" Jenna came over to the kitchen table with a pitcher of sweet tea. "It's not like I always bring you food."

"Yeah, but when you do, it's always awesome." Ollie grinned at her, his cheeks dimpling.

Jenna laughed, pinched one of those cheeks and poured him a glass of tea. And I thought, *yeah, she's got him.* Ollie wasn't going to object when we broke the news tonight. Matter of fact, I thought, he might want to celebrate.

I watched Jenna pull out a chair, sit down and began to

read the names from the sandwich wrappers, distributing them around the table. Despite her joking with Ollie, her lips were pressed together, and I could practically feel her nerves thrumming from over here. I wanted to go around the table and wrap her in my arms, just to reassure her, but that would've been a giveaway before we were quite ready. So instead, I made my way over to the bottom of the stairs.

"Bec! Dinner!" I bellowed, waiting to make sure she'd heard me. The tell-tale squeak of her door opening was followed by footsteps, and then she appeared at the top of the stairs, phone in her hand and the wire from her earbuds trailing around her neck. I repressed a sigh; since she'd started school this fall, I'd noticed a few changes, including the constant presence of those damn earbuds. I didn't mind her listening to music, sure, but sometimes it felt like she was using it to distance herself from the rest of us. When I laid down the law and told her no earphones at the table, she'd rolled her eyes and given me one of those long-suffering sighs that were also new this fall.

Now she jogged down the steps, pausing to give me a vague smile as she passed. I followed her into the kitchen in time to see her greet Jenna.

"Hey, Jenna. I didn't know you were coming tonight." She sounded pleased, so that was something. "Oh, cool, Franco's. Did you get me a cheesesteak?"

"Of course." Jenna pushed the still-wrapped sandwich across the table. "No onions, just sautéed peppers. On a wheat roll."

"Perfect." Becca scraped out her chair and dug in. Jenna glanced at me, biting the side of her lip, and I noticed

220

she hadn't even touched her own sandwich yet. Knowing my girl, she wouldn't be able to eat until we'd gotten this out of the way. Me, I could go either way, but I didn't want to see her sit there suffering. I decided we needed to rip this bandage right off.

"So, this is a special treat, having Jenna here on a school night," I began. "Pretty cool, right?"

"Uh huh." Ollie wasn't really paying attention to me. He was focused solely on the sandwich he was currently stuffing into his mouth.

Becca glanced up at me, though, her eyes suddenly cautious. "Yeah. I thought you said we had to eat, like, regular food during the weekdays. No Franco's 'til Friday, remember?" Next to her, Ollie smirked.

"Yeah, that's what we said. But tonight is kind of a special occasion." I cleared my throat. "Jenna and I wanted to talk to you both."

Oliver shoved another huge bite into his mouth, but Becca laid her sandwich down, her gaze shifting between Jenna and me, waiting and watchful. I thought with a pang how far my daughter had come since we'd moved to Burton. She wasn't the timid little girl anymore, almost afraid of her own shadow and worried about anything that could possibly go wrong or be dangerous. Whether she knew it or not, at least some of the credit for that change had to go to Jenna, who'd subtly guided her along a path she herself was walking at the same time.

"What's going on?" Becca's voice was filled with the same trepidation I saw on her face. A tic jumped in Jenna's cheek.

"Well, the thing is . . ." I hadn't actually planned the words I was going to say, and now I was regretting that. In the pressure of the moment, I was liable to blurt out something inappropriate, like *Jenna and I are having hot and wild sex as often as we can, fucking like bunnies whenever you guys are away from the house, and now we want you kids to know and be okay with that so we can do it more frequently.* I wasn't parent of the year by any means, but even I knew that wasn't the way to go about this.

As if she'd sensed my stall, Jenna picked up the baton and ran with it. "We wanted to talk to you both about something important. But first, your dad wants you to know and remember that you guys, the two of you, are his highest priority. You come first in everything, in every decision he makes and in every plan he has."

Two pairs of eyes swung to me, and being the articulate guy I was, I nodded, smiling as my head bobbed up and down.

"And we didn't necessarily plan for this to happen. Your father and I started out as work friends, and then friends beyond work, too. All of you were so great to me this summer, and we had fun, right? Hanging out and getting to know each other."

Becca didn't answer, but Ollie swallowed his last bite and grinned again. "Yup. And cookies, too. Don't forget the cookies."

"I never could, Ol." Jenna winked at my son. "Well, anyway, your dad kind of became my best friend. I had a tough time a few years ago, and your father cared about me enough to help me get over that. I'm a better person now, thanks to him." She met my eyes, and the love that shone there took my breath away. I wondered how the kids didn't see it and guess right away.

"Are you going somewhere?" Oliver lost his grin, suddenly looking worried. "Are you moving, Jenna?"

"No, honey, I'm not." Jenna glanced at me. "Kind of the opposite. Your dad and I are, um, we're a couple. We've been dating for a little while."

I suddenly found my voice again. "Yeah, we are. We weren't hiding it from you, but we didn't want to say anything until we were more, uh, sure about everything."

"*What*?" Becca hissed out the word. "Seriously? Is this some kind of joke? You're dating? What's that supposed to mean? Like, you're going to the movies together? Or . . ." An expression of utter distaste filled her eyes. "Are you sleeping together? You're having sex?"

Jenna's face went first red and then white as I hurried to respond, even I really had no idea what to say to that. "Becca, that's a private question, and it's really none of your business. What Jenna and I want you to understand is . . ." I took a deep breath. "We're in love. This isn't something casual or temporary. I want Jenna to be part of our lives, and not just here for dinner now and then or over to watch a movie with us. We're making this permanent, and we wanted to talk to you two so you understand."

"Well, I *don't* understand." Becca stood up and shoved her chair into the table, where most of her sandwich lay, uneaten. "I thought Jenna was being our friend because she liked us and wanted to—I don't know, just be like a big sister to me. That's what you said." She swung accusatory eyes my way, and guilt nibbled at me.

Shit. I had said that, way back right after the Fourth of July.

"I understand that, Bec, but like Jenna said, we didn't set out for this to happen. Jenna and I did start out as friends, and we're still friends. But now we're friends who love each other, too, in a romantic way, and we want to be together."

"So are you getting married?" Oliver sat back in his chair, seemingly unaffected. "Are you going to have a wedding? My friend Stuart back in Canton, his sister got married, and he had to wear this fancy suit and be in the wedding. If you have a wedding, I just want to wear my jeans and my boots."

"Shut up, Oliver." Becca shot her brother a furious look. "That's not even important. They're not getting married." She swung on us. "Are you?"

I shrugged. "We haven't made a definite plan yet, but if you want me to be honest . . . yeah, I hope Jenna and I will get married, eventually. Sooner rather than later, if I have my way." I reached across the table to take Jenna's hand in mind. Hers was clammy and shaking a little, and I was suddenly and hugely annoyed with Becca for her hostility. I was trying to be understanding, but couldn't she see that she was breaking Jenna's heart?

My daughter stared at our joined hands, and her bottom lip trembled. "This is disgusting. It's wrong. And you're never going to be my mother." She threw the hateful words at Jenna, who flinched. "I had a mother, and I remember her. You're not going to make me forget."

Ah. The truth began to sink into my feeble male brain.

Here I'd been worried that Becca would see Jenna as competition for my attention and affection, when in reality, she was afraid Jenna was going to try to replace her mom.

"Bec, that's not even a worry—" I began, but Jenna interrupted me.

"I'd never think I could take your mother's place, Becca. I'm not a mom. And I didn't know your mother, of course, but I've heard about her, and I know you and Ollie—and you're both so amazing, I can't help thinking of how incredible she must have been. I don't expect you to call me Mom or treat me that way. Nothing has to change between you and me. We can still be friends, the way we have been."

"If you were my *friend*, you wouldn't be sleeping with my father." Becca's tone went even harder. "I'm going upstairs. I don't want to talk to you, and I don't want to see anyone else tonight." She paused in the doorway to the hall, glancing over her shoulder at me, venom in her eyes. "If you're going to do this, then I'm moving back to Texas with Gramma and Grampy. I'm not staying here if *she's* going to be around all the time."

With that parting shot, she stomped up the steps. A few seconds later, we all jumped when her door slammed.

Around the table, silence stretched. Jenna dropped her head into hands, her shoulders slumped. I didn't know what to say to make this better. I'd expected that Becca might a little surprised, but I hadn't thought that she'd be so upset and—shit, downright mean. Cruel. It troubled me that my daughter could treat anyone this way.

"Hey, if Becca's not going to finish her sandwich, can I eat it?" Ollie picked up the food, glancing hopefully between Jenna and me.

It was just what we needed. Jenna glanced at me with a watery smile, wrapped one arm around my son and squeezed him to her. "Oh, Oliver, you're priceless. Never change, bud. I love you."

"Yeah, I love you, too." Ollie took a bite of his sister's sandwich as Jenna looked at me over his head. I was pretty sure we were both thinking the same thing.

One down, one to go.

I just hoped the second performance went better than the first had.

If there was one thing I knew for sure that my daughter had inherited from me, it was stubbornness. That trait had served me well in recovery, once I'd determined that I wasn't going to let booze beat me, and it had kept me going in the years since Sylvia's death. But just now, when I would have cheerfully wrung her slender neck, I didn't so much appreciate the child's tenacity.

She'd stayed in her bedroom, as she'd promised, for the rest of the evening. Jenna had gone upstairs before she went home, knocking on the door to tell Becca good night, but my daughter had remained silent. When I woke up Friday morning, she'd already eaten breakfast and retreated back into her room, where she remained until the very minute we had to leave for school.

The ride to school was filled only with Oliver's chatter. The kid was a morning person, which I didn't always appreciate, but on this day, I was grateful for his cheeriness. It seemed like the more he talked, the darker his sister's mood grew.

When I pulled up in front of the building, Oliver gave me my regular fist bump, but Becca jumped out and slammed the door without so much as a backward glance. I sat there for a few moments, watching her go, back stiff and movements jerky. She wasn't going to give in any time soon, at least not without some kind of intervention. I thought about Bridget Evans, who'd become Becca's best friend over the summer. She and her parents, along with her baby sister, were still out on the Reynolds' farm as Ali helped with the autumn harvest and the last burst of busy days at the farm stand, but since Bridget was homeschooled, Becca hadn't seen her as much since school had begun. I knew that the Evans family would soon be moving back to New York for the winter, but I wondered if maybe some time with Bridget might be good for my daughter.

I headed out to Oak Grove and got to work. Since when it rains, it pours, we'd run into a few snafus this week; there were some issues with a leak in the new piping, and some of the wallpaper that we'd ordered was suddenly out of stock indefinitely. It wasn't anything that I hadn't dealt with before, but I was busy all that morning, working with the plumber and texting with Jenna about a replacement pattern for the wallpaper.

She'd called me earlier, saying she wasn't coming over to the plantation until later, since she'd had a staff meeting that morning at the historical society. Her voice had been subdued and worried, no matter how much I tried to jolly her out of it. I hated that she sounded so sad, knowing that Becca's reaction only made Jenna more anxious about what was going to happen tomorrow, when we talked to her family.

I had just finished getting a report from the plumber when my phone rang again. Glancing at the screen, I frowned when I saw the readout there; it was Doris calling. My gut clenched; if Becca had made good on her threat and telephoned her grandmother last night, this had the makings of a very unpleasant conversation.

I stepped outside, walking toward my truck, as I answered. I didn't need my ever-curious crew to overhear me talking.

"Hey, Doris. How's everything in the Lone Star State?" I answered with a casual cheerfulness I wasn't feeling and braced myself for her response.

But my former mother-in-law sounded downright chipper as she answered me. "Hey, there, honey! Well, everything is just fine here. Hank and I are fixing to head into Dallas tomorrow to see that *Hamilton* show, the traveling performance of the play, you know? I can't wait."

I chuckled. "And how does Hank feel about that? He never was a big fan of anything where he had to sit still for more than a few minutes."

Doris laughed, too. "Oh, you know Hank. He's complaining like it's going to kill him, but just the other day, I drove his truck to the food store and dang if he didn't have the music from the show on his CD player in there. I told him he was *busted*, like the kids say!" Peals of merriment came over the phone lines. "You know, Linc, I do love that man. He makes me crazy half the time, but he's mine, and I'm blessed to have him. This summer, we've been getting used to having an empty nest again. There for a while, I thought it might break my heart, all that quiet, but Hank has kept me busy and entertained, and now, I'm actually enjoying it. Oh, don't get me wrong, you know I love my grandbabies, but I like having my peaceful mornings and the house all neat and tidy, too. Life has a rhythm, and it's meant to flow that way. When we have little ones, we're busy caring for them, but that's a season, not a lifetime. There comes a time when we have to look to our own happiness, not just to our children's, and them understanding that is part of growing up. They have to know that their feelings aren't the only ones that matter."

It dawned on me as she spoke that Doris wasn't just making small talk. She was telling me something, and if I were reading her right . . . hmmm. "I take it you had a phone call from Becca."

She sighed. "Yes, she called last night, all full of teenage angst and drama. Lord, she isn't even twelve yet. What're we going to do when she really *is* a teenager? Anyway, she went on and on about how you and Jenna were, uh, involved, and how wrong it was, and how much she hated it." Doris paused. "She started to say how much she hated both of *you*, but I put an end to that fast. You know I don't hold with people hating each other, and I told her I'd march all the way to Georgia to wash her mouth out if she used that word about any human being. Anyway, she told me that if Jenna moves in with you all, she wants to move back to Texas."

I tensed, waiting for the other shoe to drop. "And what did you say?"

Doris spoke crisply. "I told her to stop being ridiculous.

I said she belonged with her daddy and her brother, and if she were lucky enough to have someone like Jenna in her life, too, then she should be thanking the good Lord instead of making all this silly fuss."

"Really? You did?" Shock wasn't an adequate word for what I felt.

"Of course I did. Lincoln, honey, I might be an old lady now, but my vision is still twenty-twenty. When Hank and I were out there to see y'all, I could tell you were sweet on that little gal. I told Hank, if Lincoln lets her get away on account of worrying over his kids, that'll be a darn shame. Why, all the time Becca and Ollie were with us, it was *Jenna* this and *Jenna* that. Any fool could see that she's good for all of you." There was silence on the other end of the phone for a few seconds. "Lincoln, I miss my Sylvia every day. It's not natural for a child to go before her parents, and I'm never going to get over losing her. I think of her all the time, and six years later, I still pick up the phone to call her now and then. But I understand that life goes on. You're a young man still, and I hope you have years ahead of you. It would be a tragedy if you spent them alone. You're a good daddy, and you deserve some happiness, too."

A lump rose in my throat. "Doris, you never fail to amaze me." I swallowed hard. "You know . . . I don't know if I ever said how grateful I am for what you did for the kids and me. You raised them when I couldn't. You stepped in when I walked away. I'll never forget that."

"That's what family does, Lincoln." Affection filled her voice. "We do for each other, and there's no thank you necessary. As long as I live, you're part of my family, and I hope no matter what happens, even after you marry Jenna, I'll still be your mother-in-law." I could practically hear her smirk. "It isn't every man who gets to have two mothers-in-law at once. You ought to count yourself lucky."

"Believe me, I do," I said with feeling. "Speaking of which, tomorrow we're telling Jenna's family that we're together. Any words of advice?"

"Oh, Lord, honey, not one. Just be honest and tell them how much you love her, and they'll come around. Why wouldn't they? You're a catch, Lincoln Turner. You remember that." She paused. "And try not to worry about Becca. Leave her be, and she'll get glad soon enough."

Soon enough, apparently, was not that day after school, or that evening during our regular pizza date with Jenna, or the next morning when I made my special Saturday morning pancakes. Becca stayed silent, a sullen expression on her face, even as we all talked and laughed around her.

Jenna had stayed for a while on Friday night after Oliver went to bed—Becca had already been upstairs for a few hours at that point. We snuggled on the sofa, and I told her about my conversation with Doris earlier that day.

"So if my parents disown me tomorrow night, will Doris and Hank adopt me?" She was joking, but I heard the tension and worry beneath the humor.

"Sure. But that's not going to happen. Doris says they'll come around, because I'm a catch." I grinned and kissed her forehead. "Try not to stress about this, babe. This time tomorrow night, everything will be out in the open. I promise, it's going to be fine."

"I hope you're right," Jenna sighed. "I wish I had your confidence."

Actually, I wished I had my confidence, too. I talked a good game, but if I were honest with myself, I was nervous about facing all the Suttons and telling them that I was in love with their daughter, their baby sister. I wasn't sure Jenna understood my position as the guy who was eleven years older than the woman he loved. I couldn't imagine either of her parents being happy that their little girl wanted to choose a man who'd been married and widowed, a man who had two children.

Which was why I spent much of Saturday morning brooding over what might happen that evening. Since school had begun, I only went into work on Saturdays if Jenna was available to hang out with the kids. Given everything that was going on right now, we'd decided it would be a better idea for me to stick close to home.

So Ollie and I worked outside, mowing the lawn, clipping hedges and cleaning the garage. The physical work kept my mind from dwelling on Becca, still sulking inside, and on the Suttons, who were probably blissful just now in their ignorance of what was coming tonight.

We went inside for a late lunch of leftover pizza, eating it while sitting in front of the TV watching the Georgia game together.

"Hey, Dad?" Oliver wiped his mouth with the back of hand. "Is Jenna going to move in with us?"

I hid a smile. For my son, this whole situation was fairly simple. Jenna was part of our life, and it was a matter of what we were going to do next. I loved this kid.

"I don't know for sure, Ollie. I'd like it. I think it'd be fun for all of us to have her around." *Lots of fun for me, for sure.* "Why do you ask?"

He shrugged. "She likes to watch football, too, and it would be fun if we could hang out like this every weekend and eat pizza and maybe wings, just watching the games."

"That's very true, bud. Let's bring that up to her when we see her later." I hadn't told the kids that we were all going out to the Suttons' house tonight, but maybe now was the time. "Uh, tonight we're all going to eat dinner at Jenna's parents' house. That sound okay to you? You remember Miss Millie and Mr. Boomer."

"Yep. What're we having to eat?"

I laughed. "Not sure, son. It'll be good, whatever it is, I'm sure."

There was a knock on the front door, and Ollie jumped up to answer it, yelling, "I'll get it!" at the top of his lungs. Usually he was racing with his sister to open the door, but I was sure Becca wasn't in competition today.

"Look, Dad, Jenna's here." Oliver loped into the living room, with Jenna following. I stood up to greet her, but one look at her face stopped me.

"Ollie, can you go outside and finish putting all those tools away? The ones we were organizing?"

Oliver glanced from me to Jenna, and he seemed to realize what I was asking. "Sure. Be right back."

Once the garage door had slammed behind him, I drew Jenna into my arms. "Babe, what's wrong?" I traced the line of her cheekbone. "You've been crying."

"I was up all night, Linc, worrying about Becca. Worrying about my family. I love you, you know I do, but we're making so many people unhappy. I don't want to be responsible for you and Becca not talking. She looks at me like her enemy now, and it about kills me. Maybe . . ." She looked up at me, her teeth sinking down into her bottom lip. "I couldn't stand to sit at home alone anymore, so I came over here. I just hope we're not making the wrong decision."

"That's ridiculous." I blurted out the words, mostly because Jenna was echoing the fears that had been nagging at me all morning. "Jenna, don't do this to yourself. It'll all blow over."

"But what if it doesn't? Becca's at an age where she needs you. And my parents . . . I've made their lives difficult enough in the past few years. I can't put them through more worry. They're not going to understand." She sank down onto the sofa, buried her face in her hands and wept, breaking my heart into a thousand shattered bits.

I sat next to her and wrapped one arm around her shoulders. "Jenna. Shhh. Babe, it's going to be okay. You're just tired and worried, but it's going to be okay."

"You don't know that, Linc. You can't know that."

"Daddy?"

Jenna and I both jerked our heads up, over to where the living room led into the kitchen. Becca stood there, one hand on the arched doorway, her forehead drawn together and tears in her eyes.

"Why is Jenna crying?"

I exhaled heavily. "Why do you think she's crying, Bec? Maybe because you've been rude and nasty to her since

Thursday night. Maybe because she loves you, and she's afraid that by loving me, too, she's hurting you. Maybe because she's been nothing but kind and generous to you for months, and you've just thrown all that back in her face." I flipped my free hand, the one that wasn't holding onto Jenna. "Take your pick."

Becca's face crumpled. "Jenna, please don't cry. I'm sorry. I really am." She sucked in her lower lip as her eyes darted between us. "I just—I was scared, again. I was afraid that everything was going to change, again. And I thought maybe Daddy might want us to go back to Gramma, if he was going to have you, Jenna. And . . . and I don't want to forget my mom, but I'm starting to not be able to remember everything." She took a few tentative steps into the room. "But Jenna, I don't want you to be scared. You told me that we didn't have to be afraid, remember? Please don't cry. And don't—I'm sorry for how I acted. Gramma says I was being a little brat. I'll be better, though. I promise. But don't give up on me, okay? Please. I can be better."

Jenna sat very still at first, as though she was afraid that any movement might break the spell. When Becca finished speaking, her voice rising on a sob, Jenna stood up and gathered my daughter close.

"You don't have to be sorry, sweet girl. You don't have to be sorry for anything." She held her away for a minute, gazing down into her tear-streaked face. "We're all entitled to behave like little brats now and then, right? I know I've had my share of doing that."

Becca giggled through her hitched breath.

"I told you before, Bec, and I'll tell you now. I don't

want to replace your mom. I don't want to change what you and I have at all. We're friends, sweetie. And that is entirely separate from what your dad and I feel for each other. Okay? I don't want you to call me Mom or feel like you have to treat me any differently."

"Are you going to move in with us?" Becca glanced over Jenna's shoulder at me. "Because I guess I'd be all right with that, as long as I don't have to share a room with Ollie."

I laughed, relief making me weak. "Honey, if and when Jenna moves in, I promise she won't be kicking you out of your room. It'll be me who's going to have to share." I winked at Jenna, and Becca rolled her eyes. "And actually, I'm all right with that."

"Gross. Is there going to be icky lovey stuff around here all the time now?"

Jenna raised one eyebrow at me but spoke to Becca. "Is that going to be a problem?"

Becca hesitated and then shrugged. "I guess not, as long as you don't mortify me in front of my friends. I mean, Bridget's parents are always *all* over each other, touching and kissing and, like, saying things." She smiled. "Bridget acts like she hates it, but it's really kind of awesome."

"I think we can give Ali and Flynn Evans a run for their money when it comes to the, uh, what did you call it? The kinky lovey stuff?"

"Daddy!" Becca shrieked. "I said *icky*, not kinky, and ewwww!"

I laughed and gathered my two best girls to me, one arm around each. "So sorry, my bad. You know, they say hearing's the first thing to go." I squeezed them both in a massive group hug, until they both squealed. "Now that we're a united front on the Turner side, are we ready to face the Suttons and break the news there?"

Jenna groaned. "Don't remind me, please. You know I don't drink much, but I think I could use a stiff one before we go over there."

Becca shook her head. "Don't worry, Jenna. Your mom and dad are going to be fine with it. I mean, who wouldn't love us?"

I grabbed my daughter and kissed the top of her head. "Isn't that what I've been saying all along? That's my girl. We got this, right?" I snaked my free arm around Jenna's waist and pulled her close for a smacking kiss square on her lips. "We got this."

In the end, we were all right. All of us except Jenna, that is. And I was okay with that, too.

Family dinner at the Sutton home was crazy and loud, just as family dinners should be. Jenna had led us into the large kitchen, where we were quickly recruited into helping with cutting vegetables and then moving dishes piled high with food onto the long table. There wasn't a chance for anyone to say anything serious until the whole family was seated and ready to eat.

Boomer stood up to give the blessing, but before he could begin, Jenna rose. "Daddy, could I say something before you pray?"

There was a rumble of exasperation among her sisters, and Carla groaned. "We're hungry! Let him bless the dang food so we can eat."

Jenna glared at her sister. "It's only going to take a minute. And it's important." She took a deep breath and then reached for my hand. "I wanted to tell you all, while we were here in one place . . . Linc and I are, uh, together. We're dating. We're a couple." She paused, glancing over at her parents. "I know this is a surprise, and maybe I should have told you before, but—"

"Wait. *This* is your big announcement? That you're with Linc?" Jenna's sister Courtney shook her head. "Since when is this news? We all knew, right?" She looked around the table, which was now filled with bobbing heads.

"Jenna, honey, I've known how you felt about this boy since the Fourth of July." Millie smiled. "Which is why I felt so terrible, assuming he was a married man and asking him about his wife, God rest her soul." There was a murmur of sympathy among the family. Millie hesitated before adding, "And I felt even worse about what I said to you that day, sweetie. I didn't mean it. I hope you know how proud of you Daddy and I are, of everything you've accomplished and how strong you are. If we've made you feel otherwise, then we're sorry."

Jenna blinked, and her fingers tightened around mine. "No, actually. I didn't know. I thought you saw me as . . . weak. A screw-up. Someone who would always make the wrong choice."

Boomer cleared his throat. "Now that there's just wrong, Jenna. Your mom and I have always had your back. We love you, darlin', and there's never been nothing we wouldn't do for you. If we haven't made that clear, well . . ." He coughed, and I thought I saw a gleam of moisture in his eyes. "Well, that's a damn shame, and we all ought to do a better job of communicating, I guess."

"We're happy that you and Linc found each other, too." Millie beamed down the table at the kids and then at me. "I think you're all darn lucky to have each other. He's a good man, and he's raised lovely children. We couldn't be more pleased that they're going to be part of our family."

"All right, are we done with the touchy-feely stuff? And with telling news that we all knew, anyway? Because if we are, can you let Daddy bless the food so we can eat before it all gets cold and we starve to death?" Christy, sitting across from us, stuck out her tongue. "God, Jenna, always such a drama queen."

And so the family was laughing as Jenna sat down again, her fingers laced through mine. Boomer intoned a fast and fervent prayer, and as the noise swelled again, Becca leaned around her brother to grin at Jenna and me.

"See? I told you so. We're irresistible."

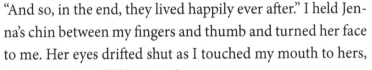

"And so, in the end, they lived happily ever after." I held Jenna's chin between my fingers and thumb and turned her face to me. Her eyes drifted shut as I touched my mouth to hers, nibbling on her full bottom lip.

"Did they?" She snuggled closer to me, her sweet ass rubbing over my already-stiff cock. We were on my sofa, sitting in the dim light of the television, making out like teenagers. After dinner, we'd stayed at the Suttons' house for a while, visiting and talking. Jenna had hung out with her sisters, who'd cast several assessing glances my way, along with grins that made me wonder what they were talking about.

When we'd finally left, Boomer had pulled me aside, rubbing his jaw and shifting his weight from foot to foot before he spoke. "Listen, son. I know you're not a kid. You're a grown man with kids of your own. I see how you look at my Jenna, and I see how she looks right back. It's good. I'm not going to bust your balls about that. I been through this, you know? Four daughters. This ain't my first rodeo."

"No, sir." I stood tall and kept my answers short and respectful.

"But Jenna, she's my baby girl, you know? She's the one who always had time to hug her old dad. She used to come into the shop with me when she was really little, and she'd pick up each tool and make me tell her what it was for. I still hear that little voice some times." He sniffed, once. "Anyway, point is, I like you, and I think you can make my Jenna happy. You're doing okay so far. But if that changes, and if I ever find out that you've done anything to make her cry or break her heart, boy, I will come for you. There won't be a place for you to hide. So you just keep that in mind, all right?" He slapped me on the shoulder as Jenna took my hand to draw me outside. "Y'all have a good night, hear?"

"Yes, sir. You, too." I'd half-stumbled after Jenna, a little stunned. But then as we drove home, I thought how I might feel when some bozo came around saying he was in love with Becca. Yeah, when I considered it that way, Boomer had actually gone easy on me.

Which brought us back to me, sitting on the sofa, necking with the girl who lit my fire like no one else and whose smile I wanted to see to my dying day.

"Yeah. Happily ever after. Why? You have doubts?" I threaded my fingers through her hair.

"Not doubts, no. But what does that mean, happily ever after? Does it mean nothing ever goes wrong again? Because I don't think that's realistic."

"Of course it isn't. But it means we're going to navigate those bumps in the road together."

"Hmm." Jenna traced my jawline. "Did you . . . back then, did you think you were going to live happily ever after with Sylvia?"

I blinked. "Sure I did. And we did have it. We had eight wonderful years together, made two perfect children. We laughed a lot, we loved whenever we could, and we held it together." I thought about my first wife, seeing in my mind's eye her smiling face, the way she'd look at me first thing in the morning. I remembered Sylvia at seventeen, my light-hearted, laughing first love. "Sylvia was my happily-ever-after then. But who I am now is someone Syl never knew. She might not even recognize parts of me. This is the me who's crazy in love with you, who's cocky enough to want another happily-ever-after, with the woman who is my future now." I kissed her nose. "That's you, by the way."

"I'm glad to hear that, because I'm not planning to let you go. Not ever." She leaned back her head against my arm and steered my lips to hers again. When we came up for air, she murmured against my mouth. "I thought I was too broken to be good for anyone again, but you proved me wrong. I'm ready to take a chance, as long as it's with you."

I stroked my tongue against hers, fanning the flames

that were building between us and then tickled her upper lip, teasing. "So what were you and your sisters giggling about tonight? I saw the looks they were giving me. Should I be scared?"

"Terrified," Jenna giggled. "They were asking me if we were getting married or just planned on shacking up."

"And what did you tell them?" I slid my hand down to just below her breast, my thumb rubbing the lower slope.

"Hmmm. I told them that we were taking it all slow."

"Did you?" My fingers crept closer to her nipple, and she moved a little, trying to get me to touch her where she needed me. "Does taking it slow include you giving your landlady notice and moving in here next month?"

"Next month?" She quirked an eyebrow at me. "That's not slow."

"Hey, I didn't say tomorrow. Next month sounds like a fucking eternity away."

"Linc, do you ever notice that you drop the F-bomb a lot more when you're getting aroused?" She slid a hand between us, her fingers curling around the hard ridge of my cock. "Exhibit A."

"Maybe I feel like if I say it more, I have a better chance of doing it." I waggled my eyebrows at her. "And stop trying to change the subject. You might as well accept it, babe. You're going to move in here sooner or later. And be ready, because I'm going to propose to you one of these days, too. I want you to be my wife. More than that, I'm fucking dying to be your husband."

"Annnnnd there it is again." She sighed, moving her palm languidly against me, getting me hotter with every caress.

"Maybe if I do this . . ." I closed my fingers around her nipple, pinching lightly through her clothes. "You'll start saying it, too. What do you think?"

Jenna hummed, arching her back, thrusting her boob into my hand. "I think you might be onto something. Matter of fact, if you keep that up, I can promise you one thing."

"What's that?" I nuzzled her neck, breathing in the sweet scent that was pure Jenna.

"We're definitely going to live happily ever after."

The End

EPILOGUE

A SOFT SPRING BREEZE BLEW ACROSS the manicured lawn in front of the Oak Grove Plantation House Historic Site. On the wide front porch, now painted pristine white, Cora Wellburn stood behind a podium, beaming at the crowd before her. It seemed the whole town of Burton had turned out today to celebrate the official grand opening of the plantation.

Behind Cora, I stood with Linc, our hands not quite touching as we listened to my boss outline the process we'd all gone through to bring the plantation from ruin to restoration.

"Hey, do you think she's going to mention me?" Alex Nelson nudged me and winked. On his other side, his new husband, Cal Rhodes, shot him a quelling glance. Cal was here in his capacity as Baker Foundation board member, and Alex, as he'd cheerfully told us all, was just along for the ride. The two were full of chatter about the baby they were expecting at the end of the summer.

I scanned the crowd, picking out all the important

people in my world who were here today to support us. My parents were front and center, beaming with pride, with my sisters scattered around them. Carla was hugely pregnant, and I watched Todd rub her back, trying to give her some comfort. A twinge of wistful envy struck me. Linc and I had talked about having children; I loved Becca and Oliver, and the more time I spent with them, the more I wanted to add to the family we were making. Linc was onboard with the idea, but neither of us was in a rush.

We had time.

Speaking of babies . . . Meghan and Sam Reynolds were on the other side of the lawn. If I thought my sister was large, Meghan was absolutely enormous. But she carried gracefully, and the accompanying glow outshone any discomfort she might be feeling. That, combined with the perpetual grin of triumph on her husband's face, was a joy to behold. Next to them, Ali and Flynn Evans stood with Bridget and Colleen as well as Becca and Oliver. The Evans family had made it back to town just in time for the dedication, and Becca was overjoyed to have her friend back.

Ryland and Abby Kent wanted to be here, but since their son Connor had been born just three weeks before, traveling had been out of the question. I'd met them several times over the past months, first when they came to visit us and check out the plantation, and then when Linc and I had taken a romantic weekend down to the Cove, to stay in the lovely Riverside Hotel. I was looking forward to seeing them again soon and meeting their sweet new baby.

My cousin Rilla and Mason were toward the back, Mason towering over everyone else. He'd donated all the food and beverages for today's festivities. Piper and Noah were restless, I could see, bored with the speeches. I couldn't blame them.

I spotted a few others who met my eye with smiles. Will and Sydney Garth had gotten married last month. Kiki had embraced her role as mother of the bride with finesse only she could manage. She and Troy stood near the Garths now. Maureen and Smith Harrington, whose veterinarian clinic had also sponsors the events today, were with Cory Evans.

This was my town. These were my people. We'd had our ups and downs, and I didn't wear rose-colored glasses when it came to the reality of living in Burton . . . but there was no place else I'd want to live, to love and to raise my family.

Out of the corner of my eye, I spied a huge butterfly fluttering above the branch of the dogwood tree we'd planted a few yards from the porch. Linc had come up with the idea of dedicating that tree to Lydia Bennett, the daughter who had taken her own life after her fiancé was killed.

"It doesn't seem right that she's forgotten," he'd told me gruffly. "This was her home, too."

A small brass plaque at the base of the tree bore Lydia's name and the dates of her life. I'd looked at those numbers more than once, thinking of the brief and painful life they represented, and I was filled with gratitude . . . for my father, who'd come home and saved me that fateful day when I'd tried to end the pain with pills, for my mother, who'd never given up on me, and most of all, for Linc, who'd believed in me and lured me back to life. I hoped that somewhere, Lydia knew how often I thought of her. Just last week, Cal and I had gotten a lead on a painting that had belonged to the family. Apparently, the picture was of a young girl who fit Lydia's age and description. I hoped it turned out to be her; Cal had promised that if it was, the Baker Foundation would buy it, and we'd hang it in the house, where it belonged.

My attention was jerked back to Cora as a swell of applause rose. She turned, holding out an absurdly enormous pair of scissors to Linc, Cal and me. Everyone else stood aside as together, we cut the wide blue ribbon that stretched over the doorway.

Oak Grove Plantation was officially back.

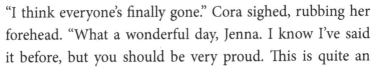

"I think everyone's finally gone." Cora sighed, rubbing her forehead. "What a wonderful day, Jenna. I know I've said it before, but you should be very proud. This is quite an accomplishment. The Bryan County Historical Society is lucky to have you."

"Thank you." Impulsively, I leaned forward and kissed her cheek. "And thank you for trusting me to do this. It's been . . ." I let out a deep breath. "Life changing."

"Oh, and it's not over yet." Cora's eyes twinkled. "Jenna, I'm going to leave you to lock up. Linc's in the parlor, waiting for you. I'll see you on Monday, dear."

I watched, puzzled, as Cora walked to her car. Come to think of it, I hadn't seen Linc in a while. Going back into the house, I made my way to the parlor. And then I gasped.

The room was filled with candles glowing from every surface. The part of me who was aware of the fire hazards in an old house was relieved to note that all the candles were in glass holders, making them safer. The romantic part of me only saw the man who stood in the middle of all the candle-light, holding out his hand to me.

"What's this?" I whispered, moving toward Linc.

"This is me, making my next move." He held my hand in his, threading our fingers together. "Jenna Sutton, you and I met on the front porch of this beautiful old house. We became friends within its walls. We had our very first kiss in the kitchen. Together, and with a lot of help, we brought it back to life." He lifted my hand to his lips, kissing my knuckles. "I couldn't imagine a more perfect place to ask you to step with me into the future. Into our future."

Reaching into his pocket, he drew out a small black velvet box and opened it, revealing the most beautiful ring I'd ever seen. It was antique, I could tell; the setting reminded me of something from a hundred and fifty years ago, at least. As I admired the ring, Linc dropped to one knee.

"Jenna, I love you. You are my life. You are what makes me want to get out of bed every morning, and you are who makes me even more eager to get back into bed every night." He paused to wag his eyebrows at me. "If I can live the rest of my life with you at my side, in my arms, as my wife, I won't need anything else.

"Marry me, Jenna. Make a new family with Becca, Oliver and me, and with any other souls who happen to find their way to us. Make me the happiest man in the world, and let me live to make you happy and whole, every single day of the rest of your life."

I was trembling, breathless, and tears rolled down my cheeks. A year ago, I could hardly have pictured how incredible my life could become. This man, who knelt before me, had hauled me back to a place where I could find out who I was, who I wanted to be. He'd made me want to be brave again.

I'd already given him my heart and my body. Now, as he slid the cool silver over my finger, I gave him the answer he wanted.

"Yes."

If you enjoyed reading Jenna and Linc's story, please help others enjoy it, too.

You can recommend it to your friends, book clubs and fellow readers.

You can review it. Please share with others about why you liked this book by reviewing it at your favorite vendor or Goodreads.

If you do write a review, please let me know by linking it on social media (tag me!). Or visit me at

www.tawdrakandle.com .

If you enjoyed the Always Love Trilogy, don't miss The One Trilogy and the Crystal Cove Romances. Some of your favorite characters just might show up there, too.

THE POSSE

prologue

"To Daniel."

"To Daniel." Five glasses clinked together, but instead of the raucous laughter and jives that would normally have followed such a toast, there was only silence. The men around the bar looked at the floor, the wall or into their glasses—any place but at each other, where someone might have to acknowledge the deep sadness sunk into each face.

Eric Fleming sniffed once, long and loud. "Can't believe it's been a year."

"Hell of a year for Jude, too," put in Matt Spencer.

"The real hell for her was the year before." Logan Holt reached beneath the bar and pulled out another bottle of beer. "Taking care of Daniel, watching him disappear right in front of her."

They all nodded, wagging their heads in unison. No one in this crowd would ever dispute the way Jude Hawthorne had nursed her husband during his fight with cancer.

"Dammit, did you see her face today? When we let go his ashes? I'm telling you, I've never seen anything sadder. But she held it together, man. Like she always did. Like she always does." Cooper Davis rubbed a hand over his eyes.

"Hell of a woman," Matt said.

"To Jude." Mark held out his beer. "My baby sister. She and Daniel . . ." His voice trailed, and he coughed. "They were amazing together."

"What's she going to do now?" Cooper dropped his empty into a nearby barrel and popped another top. "I mean, she's holding onto the Tide, right? She's not going to sell?"

Mark shook his head. "Nah, why should she? It's hers. It's our family's."

"I think the Tide and the kids are what kept her going this last year." Logan traced the path of a drop of condensation down the side of his glass. "She won't give that up."

"The kids are going back to school, right?" said Eric.

"Yeah, Meggie's heading back to Savannah this weekend, and Joseph is driving up to Gainesville with some friends next week." Mark stood and stretched. "I gotta head home. Back to school tomorrow."

"You can't go now. I've still got a bottle of Jack and three six-packs." Logan glanced around the room. "Plus we're not ready yet. To end this."

Mark sat down again without argument. Going home would mean more than the end of just the evening. Even though they had left the last of Daniel's ashes in the rolling waves of the Atlantic that afternoon, as long as they remained here in Logan's house, talking about their friend, he wasn't really gone. Once they left, it would be over.

The posse would be finished.

"What if Jude doesn't stay?" Eric spoke up from his perch in the corner. "What if she meets someone?"

"Who's she going to meet here in Crystal Cove?" Mark shrugged. "And I don't think she's even interested in that kind of thing."

"Not now. But she's not exactly a washed up old lady, you know? And people come to the Cove. Tourists. Someone could stop at the Tide for breakfast, sweep her off her feet—"

Cooper laughed. "You been hitting the romance stack at the library again, Eric? Sweep her off her feet, huh?"

Matt took a long pull of his beer. "Could happen. Stranger things, you know."

Mark shook his head. "Jude won't leave. Her life is here."

"Daniel was her life," Logan said. "And he's gone."

"She can't. If Jude leaves, the posse is done for real." Eric's mouth twisted into a worried frown.

They were silent again, each considering. If any of them were tempted to point out that with Daniel's death, over thirty years of unbroken friendship was gone anyway, no one did. Jude had always been an unofficial member. She stood for Daniel now; there wasn't any need to voice that.

"What can we do?" Mark slumped back into his chair, covering his eyes. "Free world. We can't *make* her stay. If she meets someone else, falls in love—or whatever, what are we going to do? Tell her no? As her big brother, I can promise you that doesn't fly."

"It could be us. One of us could be the one to sweep her off her feet." Matt's words were measured, careful. "I mean, why not? We've all known each other forever. If I was married and then I was—well, wasn't here anymore, I'd want one of you guys to take care of my wife."

"Daniel asked us to look after her." Cooper poured another glass of whiskey. "I guess that's true."

"Seriously?" Logan shook his head. "What is this, the Middle Ages? Our friend dies, so one of has to jump into his spot. Since when do we buy into arranged marriages?"

"Who said anything about marriage?" Matt asked. "But a relationship between two consenting adults—old friends, who know everything about each other—why not? Why wouldn't it work?"

They all thought about it. It was crazy, but they'd done worse. And when they thought about Daniel, about Jude . . . there wasn't anything any one of them wouldn't do.

"So who goes for it?" Cooper was the first one to speak. "How do we figure that out? Draw straws? Pissing contest?"

"Well, Eric and I are both out. Wives might raise a fuss, plus—" Mark hooked two thumbs to his chest. "Brother. It's between the rest of you."

"Why don't we let Jude choose?" Logan flickered bright eyes between Cooper and Matt.

"Are you crazy? Jude will never agree to that." Matt rolled his eyes.

"I don't mean we tell her. I mean, we all . . . you know . . . like, date her. What do all the girls say? Court her. And whoever clicks, that's the one." Logan flipped up a hand.

"You, me and Cooper?" Matt nodded. "Okay. Hey, I got nothing to lose. It's not like women are beating down the door."

"If Jude gets wind of this, she'll blow a gasket." Mark crumbled his napkin, aimed for the trash can and missed.

"I think we can keep it quiet. Nice shot, by the way." Cooper punched his friend in the shoulder.

"Basketball's not my game. But listen, I'm serious. How are you going to keep this from her? Take turns?"

"No." Logan spoke definitively. "We act natural. We do what we would anyway—check in with her, take her to dinner, whatever. And then we see what happens."

"And no hard feelings, right? No matter who she chooses. We say it right up front now, Jude is the final word. Agreed?" Cooper laid a hand on the oak bar, a gesture that was old as their friendship. Matt slapped his own hand down on top, followed by Eric and Mark. Logan was last, unfurling a fist on the pile.

"Deal," he said. "Now let's break out the good stuff."

ALWAYS OUR LOVE
PLAY LIST

I Can't Make You Love Me – Bonnie Raitt
Die A Happy Man Thomas – Rhett
Cowboy Take Me Away – Dixie Chicks
Come On Get Higher – Sugarland
This One's For the Girls – Martina McBride
For My Broken Heart – Reba McEntire
No Place That Far – Sara Evans
Summer Cassadee – Pope
Long Hot Summer – Keith Urban
Different for Girls – Dierks Bentley, Elle King
The Boys and Me – Sawyer Brown
You and Forever and Me – Little Texas
Song of the South – Alabama
Something to Talk About – Bonnie Raitt

Acknowledgements

Jenna Sutton's story was a long time coming, in many ways, as she was introduced back in *The First One*. In real-life time, that was only last year, but in the Burton/Crystal Cove world, it was quite a while ago. Jenna and Linc are two broken people who find a way to be whole together. Walking with them through that wasn't always easy, but it was immensely gratifying.

Their story also marks the end of another Burton trilogy. I think there are still some more stories in this town—at least, I hope there are. I'm not ready to say good-bye yet.

So who will we see in future books? Lucie, Jenna's best friend from high school, needs to tell her story. And who doesn't want to get all the details about how Kiki and Troy hooked up? Beyond those characters, time will tell.

This book touches on a subject about which I am passionate. Suicide is a tragedy that has become all too common, and prevention is crucial. If you are struggling with depression or thoughts of suicide, there is help. To find a hotline and other resources, visit twloha.com. And remember, I'm always around. Message me on Facebook. Tweet me. I promise, I will answer you and listen. Hope is real. Help is real. Your story is important. Don't let it end before it's over.

A huge thanks to my dear friend and fellow Rocker Olivia Hardin, for every wonderful favor she does for me, for listening to me daily and for keeping me balanced. And to Mandie Stevens, for every bit of encouragement, cheerleading and kick in the pants—many thanks and much love.

Thank you to the talented Meg Murrey for the gorgeous Always Love Trilogy covers. Smoking hot! And speaking of Always Love . . . Stacey Blake of Champagne Formats makes me always love the interiors of my books! Her talent and patience are extraordinary, and I couldn't imagine having anyone else as my Florida family.

My beta team rocks my socks! Big hugs of thanks to Carla Edmonson, Christy Durbin, Dawn Line, Marla Wenger, Ann Sutphin, Kara Schilling, Yvonne Farmer and Krissy Smith. You make everything so much smoother and keep me from making embarrassing errors . . . and you know what I'm talking about.

This book is dedicated my Temptresses, and I am so grateful to each and every one of you. Being an author is fun . . . most of the time. For those times when road gets bumpy, it's good to have friends.

And of course, massive love to my family, who put up with my quirks, idiosyncrasies and eccentricities. I love you guys—you make me laugh daily, in the best way.

ABOUT THE AUTHOR

Photo by Heather Batchelder

Tawdra Kandle writes romance, in just about all its forms. She loves unlikely pairings, strong women, sexy guys, hot love scenes and just enough conflict to make it interesting. Her books run from YA paranormal romance through NA paranormal and contemporary romance to adult contemporary and paramystery romance. She lives in central Florida with a husband, kids, sweet pup and too many cats. And yeah, she rocks purple hair.

Follow Tawdra on Facebook, Twitter, Instagram, Pinterest and sign up for her newsletter so you never miss a trick.

If you love Tawdra's books, become a Naughty Temptress! Join the group for sneak peeks, advanced reader copies of future books, and other fun.

Printed in the United States
by Baker & Taylor Publisher Services